A DEATH at Neptune COVE

BOOKS BY EMMA JAMESON

Jemima Jago Mystery Series

A Death at Seascape House

A Death at Candlewick Castle

A Death at Silversmith Bay

Dr. Benjamin Bones Mystery Series

Bones in the Blackout

Bones at the Manor House

Bones Takes a Holiday

Bones Buried Deep

Lord and Lady Hetheridge Mystery Series

Ice Blue

Blue Murder

Something Blue

Black and Blue

Blue Blooded

Blue Christmas

Untrue Blue

A DEATH at Neptune COVE

EMMA JAMESON

bookouture

Published by Bookouture in 2022

An imprint of Storyfire Ltd.
Carmelite House
50 Victoria Embankment
London EC4Y 0DZ

www.bookouture.com

ISBN: 978-1-80314-727-7
eBook ISBN: 978-1-80314-726-0

For everyone who's ever bought, read, borrowed, lent, reviewed, or recommended one of my books—thank you from the bottom of my heart.

1

BOUDICCA, BUTTERCREAM, AND A BODY

"Calling Boudicca. Target in position," came the man's voice over the Marine VHF radio. "Repeat, target in position at Neptune Cove. Boudicca, give me your ETA. Over."

Inside the darkened cabin of *Bellatrix*, Jemima Jago's little boat, those forceful words made her and her passenger, Pauley Gwyn, jump. Tightening her grip on her binoculars, Jem kept her gaze trained ahead, counting blinks from what she hoped was the all-important beacon that marked the entrance to Anneka's Quay. Earlier, she'd bumped a ledge because some pleasure boaters in a big yacht had carelessly flashed a super-bright torch her way as they passed, spoiling her night vision at the crucial moment. The glancing collision was no big deal—there would only be cosmetic damage, and *Bellatrix* was no trophy yacht—but it rankled nevertheless. Jem hated making pilotage errors more than almost anything. What if it boded ill for the whole operation?

"Boudicca, please respond with your ETA. Over," the man repeated.

"Who is Bart trying to reach?" Pauley hissed from behind Jem. *Bellatrix*'s bare-necessities cabin contained no seats, not even for the skipper, so Pauley perched on the closed chemical toilet. It wasn't a great place to rest one's bum; certain unkind people had dismissed it as a bucket with a lid. But Pauley needed to sit somewhere because her current role was holding on to the mission payload: a white cardboard box, eight inches by eight inches by five inches, unmarked by word or design.

"He's hailing us, I think," Jem said, still watchful. They were traveling through an archipelago called the Isles of Scilly, where jagged rocks appeared and disappeared according to the tides. In daylight, this lane between St. Morwenna and Bryher was a simple jaunt for an experienced skipper. But the sun had been down for an hour. The water was choppier than expected, and rocks and ledges, both above and below water, were often invisible right up to the moment they weren't—when it was too late to evade them.

"Why Boudicca? Is it supposed to be a code name?"

"Apparently. I didn't pick it," Jem said, deciding she *had* seen three green flashes from that critical beacon, which meant it was almost go time. "Okay, we're on our final approach to the quay. Text him that we'll drop anchor and disembark in ten minutes or less, will you?"

"Boudicca," Bart called, even louder. "Reply with your ETA. O—"

"Boudicca here," Jem snapped, snatching up her radio mic. "Use this channel for emergencies only. For updates, consult your mobile, *as we discussed.*"

As Bart digested that order, the open channel whined and crackled. Then he said, "Aye-aye, Admiral. Excuse the hell out of me."

Rolling her eyes, Jem restrained herself from responding in kind. Bart the Ferryman was up for anything, including strange operations like this, but he also tended to get out of hand. So much work had gone into this mission: lies, secret messages, and intensive coordination between various personalities, some of them hostile. Their target was slippery and streetwise, with one ear forever to the ground. If the target—or a confederate—was listening in to this Marine VHF channel, as they were known to do, someone might cotton on to the operation, alerting Jem's prey before the trap was sprung.

"Where are you dropping anchor?" Pauley asked.

"Next to the jetty."

"Are you sure you can get away with that?"

"Watch me," Jem said, refraining to add that since the IoS Police were involved in the operation, they were unlikely to caution her for blocking the jetty. Although it was a Saturday night, it was also mid-October—very much the off-season as far as Scillonian tourism went—and Bryher was lightly populated, without much local boat traffic. Of course, the jetty was meant for everyone's use, and to make it her own personal berth any other time would have been the height of Bad Boating Behavior, but tonight Jem expected it to go completely unnoticed.

"Put down the box for a sec, will you? Just long enough to drop anchor?" she asked.

"Box, yes. Anchor, no. I'm getting my kit on."

Jem turned to find the all-important box on the cabin floor and steadied by Pauley's foot as she pulled something out from her voluminous bag. A perky goth whose favorite colors were black, magenta, and purple, she'd boarded *Bellatrix* dressed head to toe in black—a black long-sleeved shirt, black yoga pants, black tights, and black ballet flats. The result was a ninja —well, a perky ninja. When combined with the cabin's profound darkness, it rendered Pauley almost invisible. Jem couldn't guess what she was doing. Probably layering on more black.

Squeezing past Pauley onto the deck, Jem was met by a brisk autumn wind and a twinkling expanse of stars. However you thought of them—loose diamonds strewn across midnight blue velvet, or pinpricks of light glimpsed through charcoal paper, or even as balls of hydrogen and helium in a still-expanding universe—the sight never failed to take her breath away. Tonight, of course, that moment of wonder had to be quick, but she enjoyed it all the same.

The anchor, five pounds of amorphous, galvanized steel, was located inside the boat's storage bin and she tossed it over the side. It made a satisfying splash, but that was all right. When Bart said the target was in position, he'd meant Jem's quarry was in Neptune Cove—almost a quarter of a mile away and tucked neatly out of sight by an outcrop of granite.

"Ready," Pauley sang out, emerging on deck. There was something bulky around her waist, hanging around her neck, and even wrapped around her head. The enhanced silhouette vaguely reminded Jem of a Royal Marine.

"What's all that? It's not some kind of cosplay, is it? You know how she hates it when—"

"I know everything she hates and how much," Pauley cut in. "You'll find out soon enough. But why did you wear those stupid trainers? White with reflective swooshes!"

"They're good on deck and on shingle. Besides, the only black shoes I have are dressy." Jem would've borrowed some of Pauley's, except they were too different in size and stature to share anything but jewelry. Pauley was short, busty, and chubby—or, as she cheerfully put it, fat, since that particular F-word bothered her not at all—with dainty little feet. Jem had the classic swimmer's build: tall and flat-chested, with broad shoulders, narrow hips, and big feet. Werewolf feet, as someone in gym class had once remarked. Whether they were genuinely lycanthropic or just overlarge, shoving them into Pauley's ballet flats would be like stuffing her great toes into Barbie shoes.

"Where's the box?" Jem asked.

Pauley made a sort of *eep* and darted back into the cabin. In a moment she returned with her arms protectively wrapped around the mission payload. Before she climbed down onto the jetty, Jem shouldered on her backpack, which was stuffed to bursting with party accoutrements. Bin liners, zip ties, stakes, a mallet, a tarp, and strips of cloth for blindfolds. Paper plates, plastic forks, and a cake knife, too. The other half of the operation—Sergeant I. "Hack" Hackman and his fellow officers aboard the Isles of Scilly Police Department's rigid inflatable boat, or RIB—carried the more hazardous items: fire starters and torch fuel.

The walk along Bryher's east coast to Neptune Cove was short and easy. This side of the island was mostly sheltered from the worst the Atlantic Ocean had to offer—gale-force winds, squalls, and storm surges. The other side of the island was scarred and rugged, but Neptune Cove was serene.

Faint sounds of music carried on the breeze, growing clearer as they approached. Somebody was playing "It's My Party and I'll Cry If I Want To" by Leslie Gore on a portable Bluetooth speaker.

"Oh, for heaven's sake," Pauley muttered. "She's spiraling over the news. I blame Lissa."

"You could blame Rhys," Jem countered, though that seemed a trifle disloyal. Her boyfriend—wait, could she really call him that yet? Her *new flame*—that sounded better—had made a command decision. He'd decided to explain Kenzie's parentage to her. Now everyone, including him, had to deal with the fallout.

"No, thank you, I'm absolutely committed to blaming Lissa. She's the one who announced the day Kenzie was born that she could never know the truth about her father. Lissa's the one who insisted we put it off and put it off. Rhys was the one catching hell about it."

Jem made a half-hearted sound of agreement. All that was true. Poor Kenzie had long believed Rhys was her father, a case of mistaken identity he'd found excruciating. Of course, he'd wanted to clear the air. But the timing!

Tonight was supposed to be our night at the Egyptian House, she thought. *And now—*

Her mobile vibrated with an incoming text from Hack, typed out for once and full of errors. No wonder he preferred voice messaging.

> *Were in position. can See your approaching. You shoes I mean. Flash you torch at bakery when ready*

Jem passed her mobile to Pauley, who snickered. "Bakery? Poor Hack. You know he's meant to wear varifocals or something. Too vain to accept them. I reckon 'bakery' means bay."

"Yeah. Are you quite ready?"

"No," Pauley said lightly, passing over the white box. "Just need a few finishing touches to my kit..."

As she began pulling and snapping things around her neck, waist, and head, neon colors sprang to life: hot pink, fluorescent green, and sizzling blue.

Glow sticks! Enough to kit out a rave, Jem thought. Wishing she'd thought of them, she set about helping Pauley activate them. In a minute flat, Pauley was lit up like a booze cruise at Christmas.

Jem's mobile buzzed again. This time Hack had sent an emoticon: the big thumbs up. With Pauley transformed into a fluorescent rainbow, there was no longer any need to flash the bay. The lighthouse keeper on Bishop's Rock could probably see Pauley through his binocs. Super-attenuated green people on Planet Asparagus, too.

"Let's go," Jem urged Pauley.

"Sorry, am I too slow for you?" She broke into a run, a pink, green, and blue streak heading toward the music.

Jem followed her lead, but awkwardly. Usually she was the fastest by far, but with the cardboard box clutched to her chest and her overladen backpack, she was at a considerable disadvantage. Ahead of them, a pinpoint of green light—that Bluetooth speaker—winked into existence, as Leslie Gore's bleating grew louder.

Somebody in a white T-shirt and trainers as bright as Jem's scrambled up from the sand. It was Kenzie DeYoung, now fourteen years old and burdened with the sure and certain knowledge that she was unappreciated in her own time.

"Who are you?" She cut off the music. "What do you want?" she demanded, sounding startled by the glow stick apparition barreling her way.

"Happy birthday, Kenzie!" Pauley cried.

"Hap—" Jem chimed in. And then disaster struck.

Something unseen, probably a clump of seagrass, snagged her toe. Running headlong and weighed down, she pitched forward, the momentum impossible to resist. Instinctively, she clutched the precious box to her chest, proving yet again something she already knew—instincts can be dead wrong.

She hit the beach without a sound. Winded and slightly dazed, she watched as Pauley now a Day-Glo goth, seized Kenzie in a bear hug. From Jem's vantage point, the girl's white T-shirt seemed to disappear as her reflective trainers shot up, rotating jerkily. It took Jem a moment to realize that Pauley, who'd been in the habit of picking up Kenzie since she'd first arrived—weighing only three kilograms—was swinging the girl around in a circle.

"You followed me! You followed me!" Kenzie squealed in delight, but Jem was too shell-shocked to fully enjoy the moment. Nothing hurt—her knees had been cushioned by cool sand and her upper body had been cushioned, too. Unfortunately, that cushion was the mission payload. Now the cardboard box was compressed to roughly half its height, and something gooey had squirted out, decorating her chest and neck.

"Jem! Jemmie!" Pauley bellowed after releasing Kenzie. "Where'd you go?"

"Down here." Groaning, Jem rolled off the box. Some of the dark goo on her T-shirt picked up sand. It looked disgusting and smelled delicious.

"What are you doing down there?" Kenzie asked.

"Oh my God, did you trip?" Pauley gasped. "Did you *drop it?*"

From the water, *Merry Maid*'s lights snapped on. Over the boat's PA system, which Bart had rigged to transmit music with good clarity, came the toot of a pitch pipe, followed by him singing "Happy Birthday" in his pleasant light baritone.

Pauley's mobile torch switched on as she demanded, "Where is it?"

"Just there." Climbing to her feet, Jem pointed at the half-flattened box. "I, erm... fell on top of it."

Pauley shrieked.

"What? Was it my present? Did you fall on my present?" With the naked greed of the newly fourteen, Kenzie dropped to her knees beside the box to assure herself any material offering was unharmed. "Oh! It's the cake." Wiping away some goo, she popped her fingers into her mouth.

"None of that!" Pauley cried.

"But it's chocolate buttercream," Kenzie said, the words slightly garbled. "Good stuff. Bit sandy, but good."

"I said back off! Away with you," cried Pauley, who like any good cook was a stickler for presentation. "Kenzie, turn your back. I mean it! Let me look and see if I can salvage it." Seeming to visibly steel herself, like a paramedic preparing for the sight of an especially gruesome injury, Pauley aimed her torch at the box. Bravely she told Jem, "All right. Open it up."

Out in the bay, Bart's song ended. On a prearranged cue—a cue Jem had completely forgotten—Hack gunned the RIB's engine. The sexy *Fast and Furious*-style roar made Kenzie cheer. Jem and Pauley almost jumped out of their skins. The RIB's floodlights snapped on, sweeping the beach as the agile police boat zoomed around *Merry Maid*, zigzagging its way to the jetty.

"Yeah! Hack and Bart!" Kenzie clapped her hands. "Who else is coming?"

"Your mum, of course," Jem said. "And Rhys. And Randy Andy. Who I should probably try to call Mike, at least for tonight," she added. Michael Anderson, the Isles of Scilly's ex-police chief and one of her least favorite people in the world, had been dating Kenzie's mother, Lissa, for some time. He expected Kenzie to call him "Uncle Mike," something the girl refused to do—possibly because even the other grown-ups in his life had trouble calling him anything but Randy Andy, the nickname his womanizing had earned him.

Kenzie made a pouty noise. "Oh, this is so uncool. *Deeply* uncool. I thought you two did some detective work to find me because you actually understood..."

"No detective work required," Pauley said briskly. "We knew you'd come to Neptune Cove to sulk. We asked Bart to hang around the quay so he'd be the first to offer you a ride. Then he went dark and lurked around the bay to make sure you didn't catch a ride home with someone else."

"But why couldn't it just be the three of us?" Kenzie whinged.

"Because your mum is your mum. It's not rocket science," Pauley said. "And Randy Andy—sorry, *Mike*—goes with her."

"As for Rhys, he deserves to be here," Jem put in. "After you canceled your party and threw everything up in the air, he gave up a lot to help make tonight happen."

"I'm still cross with him," Kenzie huffed. She sounded almost as bratty as she'd sounded on Wednesday, her actual birthday, when she'd texted all the guests to inform them there would be no party, and if anyone tried to drag her out of her bedroom, she'd call BBC1, BBC2, and MI5.

"Kenz," Pauley began in a warning voice.

"I'm grateful," the girl insisted, waving her skinny arms. "And I'm not so very cross with him, I reckon, now that I think of it. At least *he* told me the truth, finally. But Mum—why'd she go round letting everybody and their ferret think Rhys was my dad? I thought about it, and if anyone has a right to the truth, it's me!"

"No argument there," Jem said. "But look, kiddo, it's your birthday. You'll only turn fourteen once. We all understand why you flipped out and canceled the party. But we all want to help you celebrate, your mum included. Can't you meet her halfway?"

"I guess." Kenzie heaved a long-suffering sigh, then suddenly perked up. "Does this mean my friends are coming?"

"Nope. You're the one who disinvited them," Pauley said. "Some of their folks are upset. Besides, sneaking a pack of kids all this way would've been a nightmare. You're stuck with the old folks. But we'll still have fun. We brought along the kit to play volleyball, blind man's bluff, limbo—"

"Limbo! Prepare to be destroyed." Kenzie, never one to maintain a mood for long, had already bounced back to happy anticipation. "Oh, Jem, you've never played limbo with me. Fair warning—I always win. And Rhys always humiliates himself because he's so tall. This one time—" She broke off, something occurring to her. "Wait, wasn't he meant to be in Penzance tonight? Weren't both of you?" she asked Jem.

"All a smokescreen," Jem said. Though untrue, the little white lie was necessary to keep the girl from feeling guilty. Besides, Kenzie DeYoung wasn't entirely to blame for the postponement. Ever since Jem had arrived in the Isles of Scilly, the universe had been tossing spanners into her love life. The interruptions and distractions took many forms—anything from a ringing phone at exactly the wrong moment to a murder weapon in her bathtub.

Twice now, Jem and Rhys had planned to spend a romantic Saturday night in Penzance's Egyptian House Hotel. Weather had canceled one date; a hotel booking mishap had canceled the other. Rhys had probably never imagined that telling Kenzie the truth about their blood relationship—that he was her much older half brother, not her father—would muck up the booking yet a third time. But the revelation had triggered two monumental tantrums—Kenzie's and her childish mum Lissa's—postponing the night indefinitely.

The big night, Jem reminded herself with a mental eye-roll. She was a grown woman, not a lovesick teenager. But that was the problem with her and Rhys—he was her first love and she was his, yet they'd never sealed the deal. Worse, they'd had twenty years of separation to achieve near-mythic status in each other's minds. Somehow they'd hit upon the idea of a Penzance getaway, and now that had been delayed so often, Jem felt as though the reality couldn't possibly live up to the hype. It was an awful feeling, mostly fears about herself rather than Rhys, but there it was.

Nope. Nope. Noping out of those thoughts right now, she told herself. *Tonight is going to be one hundred percent fun.*

"All right, birthday girl," Pauley said briskly. "I need you to hightail it over to the jetty and welcome your guests. But first, put on this glow necklace. And this hot pink halo," she added, crowning Kenzie with a fluorescent disk. "While you're doing that, Jemmie and I will deal with the cake."

"Don't you dare bin it. I don't care what it looks like," Kenzie said.

"I care," Pauley snapped. "Off you go."

As Kenzie trotted toward the jetty, Jem took a deep breath and opened the box. It was hard to peel back the lid flap, since most of the cake's lovingly piped decorations, as well as the top layer of chocolate buttercream frosting, was now stuck to it. What remained was a somewhat compressed and ragged mass of checkerboard vanilla and chocolate cake.

"Oh, Pauley. I'm so sorry." Jem sounded as horrified as she felt.

"I've seen worse. Don't you dare cry. What's wrong with you?"

Jem gulped, snapped back to normalcy by her friend's no-nonsense tone.

"Sorry. Only—you worked so hard on it! The only reason we even bothered coming separately on *Bellatrix* was because we didn't trust Hack or Bart to transport the cake without ruining it. And then I had to go and fall on the ruddy thing!"

"This is why you'll never make a good baker." Pauley wagged a finger. "Baking is nothing but a string of disasters, punctuated by the odd disappointment. Yes, this is bloody bad luck and I'm not best pleased, but it was an accident."

Jem's shoulders sagged with relief. Pauley continued, "Having said that, I'll admit I can't think of a worse place to have a cake emergency than the blinking coast of Bryher! Good thing the wind's mild tonight. Otherwise it probably would've blown the box out of your hands and into the sea."

"The cake knife's in my backpack," Jem reminded her, searching for a way to be helpful. "And paper plates and napkins."

"I know. But what I really need is a countertop, running water, and an overhead light."

That sounded like a tall order in a place called Neptune Cove. Still, as secluded as the stretch of beach appeared, it wasn't completely cut off from humanity. Not far to the east, a cottage overlooked the bay. And the lights were on, all the sea-facing windows uncovered. Those cheery golden rectangles gave Jem hope. Clearly, Neptune Cottage was still let. It was unusual for holidaymakers to extend their Scillonian stay into mid-October, but not unheard of. Bryher's isolation was perfect for artistic types. Writers in particular tended to hole up in out-of-the-way cottages in hopes of finishing that thorny manuscript.

"Someone's home," she said, pointing. "Maybe they'll let us borrow their kitchen."

The well-trod path provided an easy climb from the beach to the cottage, which sat upon a little shelf of rocky heather. Jem expected a face to peer out of a window as they approached, since there was no way the inhabitant was unaware of people on his or her beach. From the RIB's floodlights to Pauley's glow sticks, not to mention Lesley Gore and the vocal stylings of Bart the Ferryman, the holidaymaker might well be annoyed. But as they drew closer, the front door didn't open, and no one looked out.

"Maybe they're in the loo?" Pauley suggested when they reached the front door.

"Maybe." Jem looked through the front window. Neptune Cottage's living room was furnished in what Jem supposed was the universal season rental palette: white walls, royal-blue carpet, and blonde wood furniture. Over the sofa hung a huge oil seascape that probably bore Rhys Tremayne's slashed RT in the lower right corner. But no one sat on the sofa, and the telly was dark. The pool of light *did* allow her to see the chocolate buttercream frosting smeared all over her front.

No wonder I smell delicious. She reminded herself it was generally bad form to lick a T-shirt, even your own.

Pauley tried the door handle. Not surprisingly, it was unlocked, like most doors in the Isles of Scilly. "Opens on the kitchen," she said, stepping aside so Jem could look through the door's inset window.

She saw more white walls and blonde wood cabinets. Holiday cottages deliberately cultivated an anonymous, picture-yourself-here vibe, with plain crockery and few knickknacks, but this kitchen was slightly untidy. Bits of paper were stuck to the fridge with magnets; various items were spread across the counter. Jem spied a wooden cutting board, four brown eggs, a stick of butter still in its wrapper, a loaf of white bread, and a serrated bread knife.

Something about the sight of the large knife lying on the counter struck Jem as ominous. A prickle started at the nape of her neck.

"Cover me. I'm going in," Pauley told her. Opening the door wide, she called in her friendliest voice, "Hello, the house! So sorry to be a bother, but we're in the midst of a great British baking dis—" She cut off, stopping dead in her tracks.

"Hey!" Swerving to keep from plowing into her friend, Jem saw what had brought Pauley up short. A man lay on the kitchen floor, arms spread wide, one cheek pressed to the tiles. He wore red-and-navy striped satin pajamas, but his feet were bare. They were bone-white, and for some reason Jem found herself zeroing in on their pallor. They looked inhuman—the molded plastic appendages of a mannequin, not a person.

Pauley looked at Jem, eyes wide, mouth trying and failing to form words.

"Yeah," Jem said, answering the unspoken question. "He's dead."

2

BAKING HINTS FROM A SLIGHTLY DERANGED MARY BERRY

Even as Jem said the words and knew them to be true—the poor bloke's hands and face were as pale as his feet and he lay utterly still, without a flutter of respiration—her librarian's love of certitude prodded her to confirm it.

"The cake will be safe here," she told Pauley idiotically, depositing the box on the counter. Could anything worse befall it at this point? A direct blast from a fire hose, maybe.

Pauley didn't acknowledge the words, just kept staring at the dead man. She'd seen corpses before, both in everyday life and while sleuthing with Jem, but something about this one seemed to transfix her.

Approaching the man, Jem started by nudging his ribs with the toe of her shoe. Then she squatted beside him, pressing two fingers against the side of his throat. She wasn't sure she was even doing it right—his head was at an awkward angle—but it wasn't like she really expected to find anything. His skin was cool to the touch. No one could feel that cold and live.

Grasping the man by the shoulders, Jem gave him a half-hearted shake. It was more than a little horrible doing that to something that had recently been a person.

"Rigor mortis has set in," Jem muttered. This was her third —make that fourth—dead body, and she could sound calm about it, even as her heart pounded in her ears. Glancing over her shoulder at Pauley, she said, "Ring Hack, will you?"

"Okay."

Jem went back to surveying the dead man. Those red-and-navy pjs were a striking color combination—she hadn't even realized men still wore pajamas—and beautifully tailored. They looked like something out of an old black-and-white movie, the kind with peroxide blonde-women and champagne served in coupes. He'd been tall, fit, and probably quite handsome, with a high forehead and a strong jaw. Thirty-five or forty years old, if she were any judge. That made a natural death unlikely. There was no pool of blood, no gaping wounds, no knife in the back. Just a patch of blood on the crown of his head, amid his dark blond hair.

Pauley wasn't speaking into her phone, so Jem glanced up again, wondering if her friend's call had failed to go through. But it seemed her friend hadn't tried to ring Hack yet. She just stood there looking at the dead man, eyes wide, arms hanging loosely at her sides.

"Pauls. Ring Hack, please."

"Okay," Pauley mumbled again. "But, Jemmie. My mobile. Where is it?"

"In your hand, love. Just there. You're holding it."

Pauley lifted her hand, staring at the device as if someone had performed an especially baffling magic trick. "Oh. Sorry." Her eyes returned to the dead man. "What's that on his head? Baking chocolate?"

"Um, no. It's dried blood."

"Of course." Pauley managed a slight smile. "*Not* recommended for baking."

"Erm, yeah. True." Rising, Jem glanced around the kitchen for a discarded weapon—a blunt object, perhaps, like a cricket bat or a length of pipe. Nothing on the countertop met that description. As for the floor, it was shiny-spotless except for one thing: a huge loaf of dark bread lying in a puddle of water.

Pauley still wasn't talking into her phone. Biting back a sigh, Jem said, "Pauley, love, I really need you to ring Hack."

"Sorry. Only—do you know his number?"

"Right. I'll do it. Now where's my phone?"

"In your hand," Pauley said.

Jem looked down and saw that it was true. *Well. Maybe I'm a wee bit shell-shocked, too.*

"Aren't we a pair? Never mind." Patting Pauley reassuringly on the shoulder, she steered her to a step stool and helped her sit down. "You just collect yourself while I give him a bell."

"I don't mean to be such a dozy donkey." Pauley looked imploringly into Jem's face. "Only I know him."

"What? Really?"

Pauley nodded.

"I haven't seen him around."

"Well, you wouldn't," Pauley said patiently. "On St. Morwenna, you're a weekender. And just since last June. He's been in the islands since April. He's called Arthur Ajax." Taking a deep breath, Pauley added in a slightly wavering voice, "I've had a crush on him since the first moment I saw him."

Jem was slightly taken aback. Pauley had never been one to turn wobbly over a man. Book boyfriends like Edward Cullen and Mr. Fitzwilliam Darcy, sure. But actual flesh-and-blood blokes? She'd always kept a good head on her shoulders.

"Wow. All right. I'm surprised you never said."

"I wasn't ready to," Pauley said after another deep breath. "He just seemed so perfect I didn't want to spoil the opportunity by talking about it. Good-looking. Charming. Came from high finance—only forty-two, but he'd already made his mark and taken early retirement. He came to the islands to unwind for a bit, then figure out his life's second act. At first, he planned to leave in September, but by August he said he'd fallen in love with the Scillies and was going native."

"Seems like you were getting close to him," Jem said.

"We were friends. I mean, friendly. With a lot of potential," Pauley said, voice going quavery again. "That's why I was taking it slow. I kept dreaming up these scenarios, trying to get it just right. Checking out coffee shops I could ask him to, looking over the dance clubs to see which one had the best atmosphere. It was so much fun—a secret project, almost a secret mission. Every Monday I'd think, this is it. This is the week I put the plan into action. But I left it too long."

"Oh, Pauls." Jem patted her shoulder again. Later they'd crack open a pint of Moomaid of Zennor ice cream and talk about Arthur for as long as Pauley wanted. At Lyonesse House there was always a carton of Shipwreck flavor—caramel and honeycomb—tucked behind the frozen peas for emergencies. But right now they needed to get the authorities involved.

Jem said, "Let me ring Hack and get the wheels in motion. Then we'll talk about it, all right?"

Hack picked up on the second ring. "Hiya, Stargazer. You up at the cottage? The birthday lass said there was an accident with the cake and you two ran off to fix it."

"Believe me, that ruddy cake's the least of our problems. Do you have me on speaker?"

"Nope! Can't hear you," Rhys Tremayne called from the background. His smooth baritone, just a little deeper than you expected to go with his big frame and broad chest, sent a tiny shiver up her spine. Even in the presence of a corpse, he triggered that reaction, and she wasn't sure if it said more about him or about her.

"We can all hear you. Is the cake kaput?" demanded Lissa DeYoung, Kenzie's mother.

"No cake is ever really kaput," Pauley murmured, back to her vague tone. "Worst case, you can crumble it up, sear the crumbs in the oven, and use them as garnish on ice cream or pudding."

Ignoring that, Jem decided to ignore Lissa, too. The woman had done almost nothing to contribute to her daughter's replacement party. Instead, she'd been too busy brooding over what she viewed as Rhys's betrayal and generally acting as if *she* were the one who should throw a tantrum and get cosseted with a surprise party. But that was typical Lissa—slow to pitch in, quick to bitchin'.

"Who cares? *God*, Mum," Kenzie huffed. "Concentrate on fun! This is meant to be fun!"

"And it will be," Rhys cut in, sounding like a man with two kid sisters instead of one. Jem smiled, happy to hear Kenzie dismiss the cake mishap as no big deal. She was a good kid, despite the inevitable blow-ups and meltdowns of youth, ready to party no matter what.

But a dead man in Neptune Cottage is a bridge too far, Jem realized suddenly. *What possessed us to open that door? Once the police start swarming the beach, it's game over.*

Maybe those thoughts were rather cold-blooded toward poor Arthur Ajax, dead on the floor of his holiday cottage. But the fact was, she didn't know Arthur and had no special loyalty to him. She knew and loved Kenzie, who deserved a fourteenth birthday party that didn't revolve around a corpse.

"Aaaand now we're speaking privately," Hack said smoothly, like a DJ back from the break. "Fire away."

"If you're standing close to Kenzie and the rest, move away so they can't overhear."

"Done. Now tell me." His tone indicated a shift from affable off-duty Hack into Sergeant I. Hackman, the ever-vigilant and suspicious copper. Jem wasn't surprised. Hack had spent half his career working with the Devon & Cornwall Police's murder squad. Although he'd now been exiled to the Isles of Scilly after trying to blow the whistle on a powerful enemy, Hack's instincts for serious crime were still sharp. He yearned to get back in the game, especially since his work life now mostly consisted of warning unlicensed fishermen, telling off unruly teenagers, and giving directions to confused emmets—a Cornish term for tourists.

"We found a dead man inside Neptune Cottage. If you're facing away from the water, you can probably see the lighted windows."

"I do," Hack said. "I take it no one answered the door, so you just barged in?"

"In the islands, it's not barging in. You hello the house, and if no once answers, you come on in to check and see if their hands are full. Especially when the place is lit up like Christmas and all you want is permission to fix up a cake."

"If you lived in Exeter—"

"I lived in London, thanks very much," Jem said briskly. "Yes, it's different here. Thank goodness. Anyway, we entered the kitchen and found a corpse on the floor. Pauley says he's called Arthur Ajax."

"Natural death?"

"I don't see how. Pauley says he was only forty-two. Even now he looks, healthy, apart from being dead. He's lying face down. There's a wound on the crown of his head. It looks like he was hit with a blunt object, hard enough to split the scalp."

"Any sign of the murder weapon?"

"Nope. Maybe the killer took it with him."

"Or her," Pauley said reflexively. Whenever Jem brought up a hypothetical murderer, she tended to use the masculine pronoun, prompting Pauley to remind her not to be sexist. Little girls could grow up to be heinous murderers, too.

"All right. Sit tight and please assure me you two won't scamper about, leaving fingerprints and DNA all over my crime scene."

"Sergeant Hackman," Jem said primly, putting on her

librarian voice. "I'll have you know this kitchen is precisely as we found it. We've touched nothing but the corpse, and that was only to make sure he *was* a corpse. Of course, there's a bit of food spread out on the counter, as if he were making breakfast when the killer struck, and there's a loaf of bread that's lying on the floor. It's in a puddle of water, which is strange, but it's not my fault."

"Never defrost your bread on the kitchen floor," Pauley said in a blandly cheerful tone.

"What's that?" Hack asked.

"Baking hints from a slightly deranged Mary Berry," Jem replied. "Maybe he dropped a frozen loaf when he was attacked because I'm quite sure the poor bugger didn't set out to defrost his loaf on the—" She stopped, blinking at Pauley, who was still off with the faeries. "Wow."

"What?"

"Hang on." Jem squatted down for a closer look at the loaf as Pauley added, "Clarence won't be best pleased."

The soggy bread *did* resemble one of Clarence Latham's hearty pumpernickel loaves. Ever since the weather turned, Clarence, part-owner of the Pirates' Hideaway B&B and amateur baker, had been turning out trays of autumnal goodies: pumpkin scones, gingersnaps, and pumpernickel bread. The baked goods came wrapped in tissue with a list of serving suggestions, including a recommendation to freeze anything you didn't plan to enjoy right away. Jem's own allotment of scones and gingersnaps were long gone, but her loaf of Clarence's dense, heavy pumpernickel remained in her freezer back in Penzance. Pauley had one tucked in her deep freeze. Neither of them were pumpernickel people.

"Hack, get this," Jem said, rising. "I think the loaf used to be frozen solid. That means this soggy bread could be the murder weapon."

"Of course it is. Everything you touch gets weirder and

weirder. No, I'm not criticizing you. Just stating a fact." Hack blew out his breath. "All right. Give me two shakes while I ring the mainland and set things in motion. Better gird your loins. The rockslide that walks like a man will want to be in on this case," he added, meaning Detective Sergeant Conrad of the Devon & Cornwall Police.

"Gird my loins?" Jem repeated.

"Yeah. You know. Be ready."

"How are my loins involved?"

"I don't know."

"What do you mean, 'gird?'"

"I couldn't say. I reckon it's a manly thing. Our loins are extra sensitive, you know. Got to guard them."

Jem grinned. During her adventures in Library World, she'd come across the true meaning of the phrase. It harkened back to antiquity, when warriors had to hitch robes into their belts to permit free movement during battle. She was tempted to keep pressing him—Hack in his lawman persona was fun to tease—but visions of Detective Sergeant Conrad intruded.

I embarrassed him pretty badly on that last case, she thought. *Lord knows he had it coming, and it was nice to see PC Kellow get the compliments while he sat back and stewed. But he's not the kind of person to take his lumps and move on. What he did to Hack's career proves that.*

With his stony unwavering gaze and low, rumbling voice, DS Conrad really did put her in mind of an avalanche. And like an avalanche, it was best not to take chances with him. Jem wasn't afraid of confronting him, but this wasn't the night for it.

"Hack, don't think I've lost the plot, but this is still Kenzie's birthday party. I don't suppose there's any hope of us carrying on as planned?"

"Not a chance. Murder ruins things. You know that." As if dismayed by his own knee-jerk callousness, Hack sighed. "Sorry. Only if there's a way to salvage the night, I can't see it.

The cove is about to become a staging area. Karaoke, volleyball, a bonfire... none of that will fly."

"I know. How about this?" Jem asked, thinking fast. "Suppose Pauley and I hand the scene over to you? Then we could just beat it and take the whole party with us. Move it over to St. Morwenna. It'll put us behind about half an hour, but that way Kenzie still gets her party on the beach."

"You want me to lie for you to Conrad and the team? Say I'm the one who went into the cottage and found the body?"

"Please?" Jem asked plaintively, crossing her fingers.

There was a long pause. Then Hack said, "You had me at lying to Conrad. My pleasure. But I'll need a few minutes to scramble the team. Wait quietly in the kitchen. Do *not* mess about with the crime scene and make me regret this."

"Thanks, Hack! You're the best."

He didn't reply, just muttered something about his ungirded loins and rang off.

"Did you hear all that, Pauls?" Jem asked Pauley, who half-jumped at the sound of her own name.

"Hear what?"

"Hack will be coming soon to take over. First he's got to inform all the authorities. But he's going to tell them he found the body, so you and I don't have to spend all night being interrogated."

Pauley nodded—the bobbing, oh-I-get-it nod of someone who hadn't caught one word in ten.

"So you and I will be free to move Kenzie's party to a different beach," Jem added with a touch of exasperation. Only as she said it aloud did it hit her—maybe the sight of Arthur Ajax's corpse had left Pauley in something less than a partying mood.

"Oh, crap, listen to me," she said quickly. "I'm sorry. This has hit you really hard."

Again, Pauley looked startled, coming out of cloud cuckoo

land with a rapid blink. "What do you mean? I'm fine. It was just a crush." Hopping off the step stool, Pauley forced a big, brave, completely insincere smile. "And here we are, alone in the crime scene for what? Five minutes? Ten?"

"Maybe a little longer," Jem said. "I promised Hack we wouldn't muck about. But it's already eating at me. Do you have any idea who would want to kill Arthur?"

3

PAULEY GWYN, JUNIOR DETECTIVE

Pauley Gwyn's knee-jerk reaction was to say no one wanted to kill Arthur Ajax. Everyone adored him, he was beloved by all. But was that true? Or just a symptom of her long-simmering infatuation?

Arthur had the distinction of being the handsomest man she'd ever seen around the Isles of Scilly. All right, the handsomest was actually Rhys, but he was like a brother to her and therefore didn't count. And Arthur was definitely the best dressed. Even the pajamas he'd died in were stylish.

He'd been rich, too, and not shy about casually alluding to his success in the worlds of hedge funds and cryptocurrency. In the islands, locals worked hard for their little slice of paradise, many holding down more than one job or juggling various side hustles to make ends meet. Part of Arthur's charm had been his casual confidence, his willingness to be seen enjoying the finer things. Was it possible not everyone had found that charming?

"Envy," she said. "I mean, assuming of course that someone wanted him dead. That this wasn't a theft gone wrong, or an argument that got out of hand."

Jem nodded. "I suppose it could be theft. It's not impossible that somebody dropped anchor in the cove, broke into the first place he saw, hit Arthur over the head and made off with some cash. A sunrise break-in seems odd, though."

"Why predawn? Oh," Pauley said, feeling foolish, as if her intellect wasn't firing on all thrusters. "He's in pjs. There's butter and eggs on the counter, and all the lights are on. The bread makes it weird, though."

"Why? I mean, I wouldn't fancy pumpernickel toast for breakfast, but..." Jem tailed off with a shrug.

"If he'd wanted it for brekkie, he would've thawed it in the fridge for at least twenty-four hours first," Pauley said, pleased to point something out to Jem for once. "And look at what's laid out on the counter. Eggs, butter, a bread knife, and a loaf of white. To me, it looks like Arthur was standing at the counter, about to make eggs and toast, when someone behind him opened the freezer, pulled out the loaf, and hit him from behind."

The words came out with surprising ease, even as the image made Pauley cringe. She could envision Arthur whistling to himself as he set out the eggs, intending to crack them over a sizzling pan, only to turn in bemusement as the intruder—

"No. That's not quite right," she said.

"What's not right?" Jem was roaming around the kitchen like a cat up to no good, eyeballing everything and almost visibly restraining herself from peeking in cabinets and pulling out drawers.

"The intruder scenario. Even if I make it complicated—if I imagine the killer slipped in, then hid somehow as Arthur entered the kitchen and got ready to cook—it doesn't make sense that he or she would know about the frozen loaf in the freezer." Pauley crossed her arms, hating the realization even as she said it. "The killer knew about the pumpernickel and was able to slip up behind Arthur—to open the freezer without alarming him. And it was first thing in the morning."

"I know. That was my first thought," Jem said. "I reckon Arthur had—you know. An adult sleepover. One that ended in murder. Which makes him kind of a rat, if he was stringing you along while seeing someone else. I know how you feel about cheating and two-timing."

Pauley shrugged. Those feelings came mostly from observation, from books, and from her own ironclad rules about fairness. If you wanted out of a relationship, you pulled up your big girl knickers and said sayonara. You didn't creep about, lining up potential escape hatches and auditioning them on the sly. Cheating just meant you were too much of a coward to face things properly.

How could Arthur have cheated on you when you barely knew him? asked a voice in the back of her head. Pauley hated that voice. It had a nasty, sing-song quality, like Vampire Willow from the "Doppelgängland" universe. And surely just as sadistic as that twisted version of Buffy's bestie.

"He wasn't two-timing me," Pauley said. "It was just a crush. I thought he liked me—he was always turning up on St. Morwenna, in the Co-op and at the Duke's Head, and he even walked to Lyonesse House and asked for a tour. But he never asked me out, and I never asked him out."

"Any idea who might have stayed the night?"

"No. I mean, lots of women commented on him. Even Bettie Quick sat up and took notice when he walked by. But I never saw him single out one for special attention, other than me."

"Well, we'd better take a look around the cottage while we can," Jem said. "Hack thinks DS Conrad will want to handle the case personally, and—"

"And he hates you," Pauley finished, nodding. "He's a godawful detective, too. Rhys would probably still be locked away if it wasn't for you. The second he hears that Clarence baked that loaf of bread, he'll clap him in leg irons."

"Oh! I didn't think of that." Jem frowned down at the soggy loaf. "Is it weird that Arthur had one of Clarence's loaves in the freezer?"

"Half the population does," Pauley said. Not long after becoming Clarence's business partner she'd quickly come to adore him, but on the subject of baking, there'd always been a certain amount of expert disagreement. Pauley believed in giving the people what they wanted; Kenzie's cake was a perfect example.

Pauley's idea of a birthday showstopper was a toffee apple cake with plenty of spices, a vanilla cream center, and mini toffee apples on top. Kenzie liked vanilla sponge, chocolate sponge, and traditional buttercream frosting, full stop. A toffee apple cake would've tested Pauley's skills and felt like a fitting tribute to the girl she loved, but Kenzie wouldn't have liked it nearly so much. So Pauley had baked something she knew the birthday girl would enjoy.

Clarence was more of a challenging baker, fond of tweaking recipes in unexpected ways. He also liked to whip up creations with *very* intense flavors and got sniffy if people didn't like it. As far as Pauley was concerned, his dark, molasses-heavy pumpernickel loaf wasn't his best work. It also contained walnuts, sultanas, and more than a smidge of instant coffee, which made her shudder to think about. Because of her affection for Clarence, Pauley kept those opinions to herself. The last time he'd popped into Lyonesse House, she'd rearranged her deep freeze to hide the still-frozen loaf, in case he happened to look inside. According to gossip in the Square—St. Morwenna's nerve center—he'd nearly had a row with an islander when he peeked in her freezer and found a loaf buried under the chicken wings.

"It's hard to imagine anyone seriously trying to pin a murder on Clarence," Jem said. "Then again, he's a Latham. Micki says the police view them all as incorrigibles."

Pauley shrugged. "Who knows what DS Conrad will stoop to? I just hope he doesn't get Clarence's back up." Her business partner was flamboyant, opinionated, and slightly acerbic in manner. He didn't suffer fools gladly and was likely to clap back hard if insulted. As far as Pauley knew, he'd led a blameless life —many of the wild and woolly Latham clan might have strayed on the criminal path, but not him. While he had no history of violence, he wasn't afraid of a fight. Once, when she and Jem's lives were on the line, Clarence had turned up with a long gun, ready to use it. At least he'd seemed ready to use it, for which she'd been profoundly grateful.

"All right, let's have a quick look around before Hack gets here." Jem rubbed her hands together, that gleam in her light-brown eyes. "Remember not to touch anything. Use a handful of tissue if you absolutely have to turn a knob or flip a light switch. First, we'll tackle the front room, then—" She broke off, her face changing. "Oh, love, I'm sorry. I'm about as sensitive as a sea urchin. Why don't you wait outside? Away from Arthur?"

The note of concern was the very worst thing for Pauley, who felt her throat tighten and her eyes sting. "Nope," she said stoutly, a bit too loud but without a wobble. "Like you said. Front room first."

Jem gave a low whistle as they entered the front room. "This place is immaculate. How long did you say he's been staying here?"

"Since April." Pauley looked around, stealing herself for some evidence of the other woman. A vague scenario was taking shape in her mind; the usual jealous if-I-can't-have-you-no-one-will scenario that sometimes led to murder. Either Arthur had embarked on the world's deadliest one-night stand, or he'd been embroiled in some kind of self-destructive romance.

To her relief, there was nothing feminine in sight. No handbag draped over the arm of a chair, no strappy sandals in a corner, no tube of Pouty Pink lipstick on the coffee table. On second look, Pauley realized there was nothing very masculine in sight, either. The place was a showroom. Not a speck of dust showed on the coffee table; the floorboards were sand-free.

"No mean feat when you live a few steps from the beach," she muttered.

"What? You mean this never-lived-in look? I know," Jem said, inspecting a bookcase that was seventy percent empty. Two of the objects it displayed were old coffee table books about the sea. The rest consisted of some artificial flowers, a pair of brass cranes, and a big conch shell. "Was Arthur a homebody? The strictly indoor type?"

"Nope. He was a bundle of energy. Always on the move." Turning in a slow circle, Pauley realized she'd taken in almost everything the anonymous room had to offer. All that remained was a small wooden cabinet by the sofa. A lamp and a box of tissues sat on top. The door had a brass pull, but no lock.

"If he was in and out, he must've vacuumed three times a day," Jem said.

"Or else he didn't spend much time here. It's possible he had a yacht," Pauley said. "He never said, and I hinted about it, but never asked him straight out. Some guys in the Square said they'd seen him sailing around the islands. Not in a cheap runabout like Rhys rents out or a little Cuddy cabin job. A proper thirty-foot Sunseeker."

"But, of course, nothing was berthed at the cove." Jem tapped a finger against her lips, the way she did when she was intrigued. "You said it's possible. But is it likely?"

"Looking around this place, I'd say, yes," Pauley said. "If only I'd asked him straight out! I just didn't want to sound materialistic. Like I was trying to gauge his net worth. I suppose stealing a yacht is a good motive for murder."

"Except it could've been done without entering the cottage. Much less killing the owner. Unless Arthur was the rare sailor who didn't leave his keys in the engine. Maybe he was careful about that, unlike the rest of us."

Pauley sighed. She didn't really believe Arthur had been killed for cash, or his yacht, or anything else that amounted to simple theft. Even if he had owned a yacht, and the killer had escaped aboard it, the basic scenario seemed blindingly clear: he'd been struck from behind by someone he'd trusted. Someone he'd quite likely intended to cook breakfast for.

Her throated tightened again. Instantly the sadistic Dark Pauley voice piped up, asking, *What are you on about? He was a daydream. A diversion. If you liked him so much, why did you never tell him?*

"Are you going to open that?" Jem asked, practically in Pauley's ear and making her jump.

"Oh! Good Lord. Right." Taking a handful of tissues, she used them to gently open the cabinet without adding her fingerprints to any the killer might have left behind. There was a wicker hamper inside.

"Pull it out," Jem said from over her shoulder, like the proverbial devil. Pauley half-expected Hack to appear on the opposite side, wearing a halo and reminding her it was unlawful to tamper with evidence.

Again using tissues, Pauley pulled out the oblong hamper. Over a foot long and about a foot tall, its lid was secured by a leather strap looped over a peg. Throwing it back, she found a haphazard pile of letters inside.

"Whoa. There must be a hundred," Jem said.

"Closer to two hundred, I reckon." Lightly, Pauley rifled through the top layer of post. "They're all sealed."

"And all addressed to John R. Derry," Jem said. "Who's that?"

"No clue." Pauley delved deeper into the pile. On some, the directions were handwritten, and the return address was a gummed label. On others, the directions were typed, and the return address appeared rather official. "This one's from HMRC," she told Jem, who flinched reflexively.

"*Unopened?*"

"Yeah. Whoever John R. Derry is, he's braver than me," Pauley said. There was only one thing worse than opening a notice from Her Majesty's Revenue & Customs to say if you don't soon pay up, bailiffs shall be dispatched to seize your things and sell them—*not* opening such a notice and waking up to find said bailiffs at your door.

"John R. Derry of 71 Grenoble Lane, Putney," Jem said thoughtfully. "No junk mail. Just personal letters and official notices. What's the cancellation date on the stamps?"

"Let's see. April of this year. April, April..." Pauley dug to the bottom, pulling out one at random. The handwriting on that particular envelope was sprawling and shaky, as if done by a child. "It's all from April. This mountain is one month's mail."

"And most of it personal in the age of email. Popular bloke, our John. Ruddy celebrity. All right, Pauls, close up the basket and put it back," Jem said. "We need to go over the bedroom before Hack arrives."

Accustomed to a certain bossiness from Jem, Pauley nodded. The best thing about old friendships was the familiarity of the rhythms. While in sleuth mode, Jem set the agenda, issued marching orders, and decided what was what. But she was very good about stepping back and letting Pauley call the tune for all things domestic and recreational, so she put the wicker hamper full of letters back in the cabinet and rose to her feet.

"We should check the bathroom, too," she told Jem. If traces of the other woman were to be found anywhere, it would surely be there.

The bathroom door was already open, and the overhead light was switched on, so they could visually inspect the room without touching anything. Pauley steeled herself for a pink can of Superdrug Extra Firm hairspray or an overnight bag, but the bathroom was beyond clean. It positively gleamed.

Oh, Lord. This proves it. He was the perfect man.

Jem seemed similarly impressed. Her low whistle echoed slightly off the white-tiled walls. "Why can't Rhys keep his place like this?"

Pauley bit back a snort. Jem had no idea how slovenly Rhys had let his living situation become, especially in the days before his drinking hit rock bottom. His shower curtain had been gray with mildew, his sink had been a beard-stubbled horror, and his loo hadn't been scrubbed since the Blair administration. The current state of his cottage, which Jem apparently found subpar, had been achieved only with a lot of behind-the-scenes help from Pauley. Rhys was many things, but neat and tidy weren't among them.

They took a quick peek inside the cabinet, finding nothing but the minimum manly accoutrements: razor, shaving cream, soap, mouthwash, floss, and cologne. Bleu de Chanel, his signature scent. Pauley was tempted to snatch the bottle as a keepsake, though of course she did no such thing. But in addition to being the handsomest man—bar Rhys—in the islands, Arthur had also been the best smelling. Just a whiff of Bleu de Chanel in the Co-op had made her smile, knowing she'd soon turn a corner and find him buying oranges or contemplating a bottle of wine.

"And here's another perfect room," Jem announced, leading the way into Arthur's bedroom. "Military corners, no less. Was he in the army?"

"I don't think so," Pauley said, looking over the precisely made-up bed. "He said he went into finance right out of uni." A wristwatch sat on the bedside table, next to some coins in a small brass tray.

"I really don't think the killer was interested in theft," Pauley told Jem. "That's a Patek Philippe worth a quarter mil just lying there, ignored. Yes, I got a bit stalky with my Google searches. So what? I—oh my God!"

The words came out in a hysterical screech, prompting Jem to whirl about like a superhero caught out of costume. She even did the karate hands, which was completely hilarious, though Pauley couldn't focus on that at the moment. She was too stunned by what she saw wedged in the corner.

"What?" Jem demanded, looking around for someone or something threatening for her to karate-chop. "Why did you scream?"

Pauley pointed a trembling finger at the device in the corner. It sat on a small wooden table facing a ladder-backed chair, so surreal she could hardly take in the reality of it: incontrovertible proof that Arthur Ajax had been the perfect man.

"All right," Jem muttered, coming closer. She no longer looked prepared to visit some half-arsed martial arts on whoever or whatever Pauley had found. "It's... a sewing machine?"

"Not just *any* sewing machine," Pauley said, reminding herself that Jem didn't know a running stitch from a standard forward/backward. "This is a Janome Atelier 6. A fully computerized sewing machine."

"Oh. Is that... good?"

"It has two hundred preprogrammed stitches," Pauley cried, screeching again. "An automatic thread cutter. An automatic needle threader. *And* it does about a thousand stitches a minute. This is the starship of stitchery."

"You sound like an advert. A very niche advert. So, I take it this means Arthur liked to sew?"

"Yes, and I can't believe he never said. Mind you, I never asked. It never even crossed my mind that we might have that in common. This is amazing."

"Could it have come with the cottage? Like the cooker and fridge?"

"Oh, sure. All the most sought-after amenities for your

holiday let," Pauley retorted. "Mod-con kitchen, Blu-ray player, Jacuzzi tub, and naturally we'll throw in a Janome Atelier 6 sewing machine. Just in case you're an advanced tailor who whips up ballgowns and brigadier's uniforms in your spare time."

Jem still looked unconvinced, but she examined the sewing machine a second time, as though forcing herself to give the device its due.

"What's that blue bit under the whotsit?"

"What? Oh. You mean the footplate," Pauley said, examining the ragged bit of fabric she'd overlooked while rhapsodizing over the machine in general. "Looks like cobalt-blue silk. Wow. Talk about a motive for murder."

"Seriously?"

Pauley goggled at her friend. "Come on, Jem, you may not sew, but you've watched me do it a thousand times. Have you ever seen torn fabric left on my machine after I'm done?"

Jem shook her head.

"That's because it shouldn't happen. Probably the only way it *could* happen is if someone ripped your project right off the machine while it was going. And silk! That's ruddy tough to repair, even for expert restorers."

Finally looking genuinely interested, Jem withdrew her mobile and snapped several pictures of the Janome Atelier 6, including several close-ups of the ragged blue fabric under the footplate. Pauley was about to suggest they return to the front room and photograph some of John R. Derry's voluminous unread correspondence when a man bellowed, "Well. If it isn't the Scilly Snoop and Pauley Gwyn, Junior Detective. Didn't I tell you two numpties to sit tight and touch nothing?"

4

"THEY SAY COMEDY IS TRAGEDY PLUS TIME"

"First of all," Jem said, refusing to look or sound abashed, "*Bright Star* named me the Scilly Sleuth, not the Scilly Snoop. Second of all, we've *touched* nothing." She waggled her mobile at him, and Pauley waved her tissues. "Third of all, what are you doing in uniform? You wore your full copper kit and nitrile gloves to a child's birthday party?"

"I'm in uniform because I ferried Lissa, Mike, and Rhys over in the RIB," Hack said, surprising Jem by using Rhys's name. For a long time, he'd never called Rhys anything but "Tremayne," or "your big blond ex." Maybe now that Jem and Rhys were getting serious after their twenty-year hiatus, Hack meant to stop singling Rhys out in minor but noticeable ways?

"It's against regulation for anyone but an officer on duty to pilot the RIB. As for the gloves, we carry a box of two hundred onboard. But enough about me." He folded his arms across his chest. "Let's hear it."

"Hear what?"

"You know what."

Jem swapped glances with Pauley. "An apology? Not bloody likely."

For a moment he just glared at her, one hundred percent disapproving copper. Having lost his signature hot-rod red spectacles in a Celtic Sea mishap, he'd replaced them with arguably less appropriate eyewear: DITA aviators with smoky-blue lenses. Combined with Hack's precise goatee and pointed black sideburns, he looked like a loose-cannon copper—the sort who caught the bad guys by breaking all the rules, Monday nights at nine on ITV.

Hack held his expression for another moment. Then the stone face cracked, and he grinned at her. "No apology. I want to hear what you've found. Everything. And make it quick—five minutes max. Then you lot will be off this island like you were shot out of a gun."

Jem explained about the cache of unopened letters directed to John R. Derry of Putney and the starship of sewing machines with a bit of cobalt-blue silk under the footplate. She tried not to take it personally when Hack interrupted to ask what she'd touched and whether she was *sure* there was no evidence concealed on her person. She was becoming an old hand at this, and part of the ritual was being accused of contaminating the crime scene. Which she'd only done once. Well, twice, if you counted the time she'd accidentally concealed evidence. Or three times, if you counted that time she'd scooped up a clue and helpfully returned it to the prime suspect. But that had been an accident! And beyond those minor hiccups, she had a sterling record of helping the police with their inquiries, whether they fancied her assistance or not.

After hearing everything Jem and Pauley had to offer, including Pauley's suspicion that Arthur Ajax might have owned or had use of a yacht, Hack gave the corpse a cursory once-over.

"He's probably been dead about twelve hours. But I'll let the white-coverall brigade make the final determination on exactly how long and due to what," he said. "They get ultra-sniffy if you do more than feel for a pulse. Where's the alleged murder weapon?"

"There," Jem said, pointing at the big soggy loaf.

"Looks like an Alsatian popped in and did a poo. This used to be some frozen pumpernickel, eh? That rings a bell," Hack said thoughtfully. "Jem, didn't you say something about Clarence not being best pleased?"

She nodded. "He baked goodies for virtually everyone in the islands. The biscuits and scones were to die for. The pumpernickel got mixed reviews. If he didn't give you some, count yourself lucky."

"Oh, he tried," Hack said. "I took the sweet stuff and handed back the pumpernickel. Talk about ultra-sniffy. He was so offended I thought he might take back the scones. You don't reckon..." He trailed off, watching Pauley.

"What? No. Never," Pauley said quickly. "Come on, Hack, you *know* Clarence."

"I make no accusations. Just a question. Now. Pumpernickel. Under normal circumstances, what does a loaf like that weigh?"

"Close to two kilograms. Or about four pounds," Pauley said.

He whistled.

"The big delicatessen loaves are twice that," she said. "Clarence learned to cook in his gran's bake shop. He can't recalibrate himself to small batches."

"Murder and pumpernickel," Hack murmured, as if that bell was still ringing. Then his face lit up. "Scotland Yard," he cried. "That's it. Back in the nineteen eighties. Some poor bugger crossed off with a loaf of bread. The inspector said, and I quote, 'Worst case of pumpernickeling I've ever seen.'"

Pauley clapped her hand over her mouth. Jem gave a kind of strangled, against-her-better-judgment laugh. "Hack. Come on. Jokes in the presence of the dead?"

"Sorry. Bad habit—comes with the job. But you'll think of it later and laugh. They say comedy is tragedy plus time."

Jem risked a look at Pauley, trying to gauge whether or not she should tell Hack about her friend's romantic interest in the dead man. Pauley's eyes spoke as clearly as telepathy. She didn't want Hack or anyone else to know.

"You two leave something out?" Hack asked shrewdly.

"Nope," Pauley said too quickly.

"Not a thing," Jem said firmly.

"Right." He sighed. "Anyway, all joking aside, it appears that Mr. Ajax was murdered, and I promise to take the crime seriously, even if I have a bit of fun over the modus operandi. What's more, when my time comes, I give everyone permission to laugh themselves silly over the manner of my passing."

"I don't believe you," Pauley said.

"Why not? I'll be dead. I won't have the foggiest." Touching the radio on his shoulder, he said, "Right. It's been five minutes. Time you ladies were out of here and off the island. I assume you'll set off for St. Morwenna?"

"Where else?" Retrieving the box with the semi-squashed birthday cake, Jem handed it off to Pauley. "Thanks, Hack. We owe you big time."

"I know," he said lightly, his gaze lingering on Jem's face. That faint jolt of electricity went through her, infuriating because it was so unwelcome. She'd made her choice. Hack was the road not taken, and while a touch of speculative curiosity was acceptable, this tug of regret was not. Knowing he was still interested made it worse—not only was she letting Rhys down, if only in the inner recesses of her heart, she risked leading Hack on. His powers of perception certainly weren't limited to homicide.

Unable to think of anything appropriate to say, she gave him a nod, leading Pauley out of Neptune Cottage and out into the breezy night. It was a short walk back to the party, where the revelry was well underway. It felt like they'd been away for hours, but when Jem checked her mobile, she was shocked to realize it was less than forty-five minutes—time Kenzie and the others had used to throw things into high gear.

Thumping dance music blared and a bonfire big enough for Guy Fawkes blazed on the sand, fed by chunks of driftwood tossed in by Bart the Ferryman. Everyone was decked out in glow stick jewelry. Three lime-green hoops glowed around Lissa DeYoung's neck, while Randy Andy wore a sizzling pink crown. Rhys, who had a circle wrapped around each ankle, was dancing with Kenzie, who was more glow stick than girl. Despite her neon headdress, bracelets, and anklets, she matched Rhys step for step. Jem stopped short halfway down the beach path, amazed.

"Pauls, are they swing dancing?"

"Yep. It's called the Lindy Hop. Rhys learned it ages ago," Pauley said. "He was seeing a girl in Mousehole who belonged to a dance group. When they competed, she wore the full vintage kit—poodle skirt, crinolines, and saddle shoes. Rhys bought his very first suit so he could dance with her on the circuit. It was mental. But fun to watch. And they won a couple of ribbons."

"Sounds like they were serious," Jem said. There was a long stretch of Rhys's life between age sixteen and now that she knew little about, except that some of it had been quite dark. "What split them up?"

"The same thing that ended all his relationships. She wasn't you," Pauley said lightly. At Jem's glance, she added, "Oh, give over, don't pretend you didn't know. He spent twenty years looking for another you. Back when I wasn't sure which way you'd go—between Rhys and Hack, I mean—I pretended I was Switzerland. But now I can say whatever I want. And let's just say Rhys went out with a lot of tall, long-haired, exasperating women, because he's meant to be with you."

Jem kept her eyes on the dancing pair, marveling in their shared grace. When Rhys picked up Kenzie and swung her around, the birthday girl whooped. Jem did, too, delighted. The maneuver came easily for Rhys; Kenzie was whip-slim while he was a big man, six-foot-four, with wide shoulders and a tapered waist. By age thirty-five, plenty of men started to soften, but for Rhys, the lithe surfer physique of his younger days had hardened into solid muscle. She knew he went running every morning—barefoot on soft sand, no less, to force maximum effort—and pumped iron three days a week, but his motivation wasn't virtue, or even vanity. Now in his tenth month of sobriety, he'd turned to exercise to address the emptiness that alcohol once filled. Or tried to fill.

Jem couldn't personally relate to his specific struggle. She'd never been much of a drinker, mainly because she hated feeling out of control. But she was no stranger to that gnawing, bottomless inner gap. In her case, she tried to fill it with control, books, control, overwork, and a little more control. Not to mention friends, now that she'd ditched the self-isolation of Planet Jem, as her younger sister, Tori, called it, and rejoined Planet Earth.

Books, work, friends, and the obligatory pop-up corpse, Jem thought wryly, envisioning Arthur Ajax on the kitchen floor. Even though it wasn't her problem, a section of her brain was already beavering away on the possibilities. Why was he in possession of another man's unopened post? Had he stolen it? Was it his, meaning he had another identity? And what did the presence of the Janome Atelier 6 sewing machine mean? Her gut instinct was to focus on the letters, but Pauley seemed to think the torn blue silk was proof of an altercation. One that might push the person operating the machine to pick up a frozen loaf of pumpernickel and win the argument with one final, irrevocable point...

Focus, she told herself. *My job is to move this party to St. Morwenna without letting news of the murder ruin it for Kenzie.*

Pauley's thoughts must have bent in the same direction, because she pointed at Bart, who was shambling along the foreshore with another massive driftwood branch in one hand and a big square bottle in the other. "He's about to throw more wood on the fire. And that's got to be booze he's carrying. Did you invite him to stay for a child's birthday party?"

"Of course not. But you know Bart. Never one to take a hint. Pauls, run and make him stop feeding the fire, will you? Then douse it with seawater."

That was beach safety 101. Emmets, who loved to build fires bigger than necessary and traipse off after merely kicking a bit of sand over coals, were often unaware that the sand might actually insulate the coals, allowing them to smolder for hours, unseen. Sometimes hidden fires generated a lot of heat—enough to transform sand into shards of glass. After the fire finally burned out, the shards would lie hidden within the sand, ready to cut open some unlucky beachcomber's foot.

As Pauley headed off to deal with Bart, the Lindy Hop ended with an acrobatic flourish—Rhys lifting the birthday girl over his head. Jem took that opportunity to pounce on the speaker and kill the music.

"Oi! Donut! Don't tamper with my tunes!" Kenzie bellowed. Clearly, she was in an exultant mood since she was back on her London slang, most of which she'd picked up on telly.

"Don't call people 'donut,'" Rhys said. "What does that even mean? Is it like muppet?"

"Waste man," Kenzie cried, throwing her arms up.

"Well, that can't be good."

"It isn't! It means you're old and useless!"

"Kenz," Jem objected.

"But I love you," she added, throwing herself into Rhys's arms. "Big bruv!"

"That's what I like to see," Lissa said. She was clearly making an effort, but Kenzie rounded on her anyway.

"You never wanted me to know!"

"I did. Just not so soon."

"Were you going to wait till I was eighty?"

It only escalated from there. Exasperated, Jem stuck two fingers in her mouth and emitted a piercing whistle. Everyone froze, even Randy Andy, who was drinking quietly near the bonfire, and Bart and Pauley, who were down by the surf, probably arguing over how to extinguish the fire. Rhys let go of Kenzie, both gaping at Jem.

"Listen to me," Jem bellowed, pinning each of them with a look. "The man living there"—she pointed at Neptune Cottage—"is very poorly. We found him ill in bed. He needs help, not a pop-up rave on his doorstep."

"So that's where Hack ran off to," Kenzie said. She was meant to call the IoS PDs top cop "Sergeant Hackman," but refused to observe such niceties. Should the Duke of Cornwall, also known as His Royal Highness Charles Philip Arthur George Prince of Wales, Duke of Cornwall and Rothesay, Earl of Chester and Carrick, Baron of Renfrew, Lord of the Isles and Great Steward of Scotland, ever turn up on St. Morwenna for a look-see, Kenzie would no doubt greet him with, "How's it hanging, Chuck?"

"Fire & Rescue will arrive any minute," Jem continued, no longer at quite the same volume, since to continue in that vein seemed to contradict her own argument. "If we stay, we'll just be underfoot. Therefore, we're moving the whole shebang to St. Morwenna."

Lissa tossed back a swig from that opaque, insulated travel cup she carried with her absolutely everywhere. The beverage within was concealed, but Jem assumed the contents to be at least one hundred percent proof. And unless Jem missed her guess, Lissa had been enjoying it, or its predecessors, since at least mid-afternoon.

"I don't care how poorly he is, he doesn't own Bryher," she announced. "Bloody emmet should keep his beak in his own nest."

Randy Andy, a man who could never resist putting his beak in, harrumphed disapprovingly. "Sorry, love, but Neptune Cove is a private beach. The let includes the tenant having exclusive use of the parcel, including the foreshore. The law isn't much enforced, especially in the off-season, but he's within his rights to order us off."

"We won't go," Lissa declared, following it up with some language salty enough to earn her a BBFC 15 film certificate warning.

Kenzie cringed. She liked being the young teen in the family, with all the privileges of flightiness, disrespect, and immaturity that role entailed. But she didn't like seeing her thirty-six-year-old mum try it, Jem thought. No more than anyone else did—including Randy Andy. If Kenzie cringed, he wanted the earth to swallow him up.

After retiring from the Isles of Scilly police, the man who'd earned his nickname by cheating on his first wife all over the archipelago—plus the mainland—had appeared ready to turn the page and settle down with Lissa. He was past fifty, no longer much to look at, and so creakily patriarchal, his preferred sort of female—under twenty-five, blonde, and easily impressed—saw him as granddad, full stop. Perhaps he viewed Lissa as the closest thing available to him. She could still rock a bikini, she was still blonde, and while she had to fake the easily impressed part, she gave Randy Andy all the worshipful attention he wanted. Except when she'd had a few too many, like tonight. He was so annoyed with her, he turned to *Jem*, of all people.

"I assume Hack will stick by the poor blighter till Fire &

Rescue arrives?" he asked politely. "In that case, I'll pilot the RIB back to St. Morwenna."

"But my party! We only just started!" Kenzie cried, looking stricken.

"If you'd been listening, you'd know we were moving the party, not ending it," Jem said, motioning for everyone to step aside as Pauley and Bart approached carrying buckets of saltwater. The steel pails, surely from the RIB's kit, held a good bit of liquid. Just two of them half-quenched Bart's blaze, sending clouds of smoke billowing up. Lissa, the only person to ignore Jem's hint to move, shrieked and coughed, stumbling after them.

"Can we go to Snoggy Cove?" Kenzie asked, referring St. Morwenna's most secluded beach.

"Kenz, you know it's not safe to take a boat there in the dark," Jem said. "I'm thinking Crescent Beach."

"But everyone parties on Crescent Beach. It isn't special. Neptune Cove is my place."

"Don't whinge," Randy Andy snapped.

"But, babe, it's her plaaaaace." Lissa tried to embrace him, looking shocked when he pulled sharply away. "Don't be like that. Take our side. It's my little girl's plaaaace..."

"God, Mum, you sound like Stacey on *EastEnders*." Kenzie folded her arms across her flat chest, suddenly all grown up. "You're right, Jem. Crescent Beach makes sense. We'll have fun there."

Good kid, Jem thought fondly.

More smoke gusted from the fire as Bart and Pauley dumped two more buckets on it, snuffing the yellow-orange flames. Suddenly the beach went pitch dark, apart from surreal Day-glow halos and a double handful of stars.

"I'll let you sit in the RIB's prow on the way over," Rhys told Kenzie.

"No," Jem announced, an idea coming to her in a flash. "Kenzie's coming with me. It's high time she learned to handle a boat like *Bellatrix*. Doing it at night will be that much more of a challenge, which will make it even more fun."

Kenzie let out a whoop of joy, throwing her arms around Jem and squeezing her tight. "Oh my God, I can't believe it! I'll make you proud, I promise. I know I'm not very good about reading a compass, and I get muddled about markers and buoys. But I know all the rules of the water by heart," she insisted fervently, as if convincing herself. "When crossing, the boat to port always has the right of way. I mean, starboard. Wait. Give me a sec, it'll come to me. Now I won't have to create waypoints, will I? Once I tried and made a mistake and my mate's dad who was skipper got *so* cross with me..."

Rhys, whose eyes had apparently adjusted to the sudden darkness quicker than Jem's, startled her by whispering in her ear.

"This will either be good for a laugh or good for a cry."

"They say comedy is tragedy plus time."

"Oh, *that* makes me feel better." He brushed his lips against her earlobe, and she shivered with pleasure. "Stay safe, Stargazer."

"See you back on St. M."

Mindful that Fire & Rescue's helicopter would soon arrive, followed by Cornwall & Devon investigators either by air or sea, Jem led Kenzie and Pauley toward *Bellatrix*'s berth. As they climbed aboard, she saw a small yellow light, like an old-fashioned hand-held lantern, bobbing inland away from Windswept Cove. Before she could point it out to the others, the light winked out completely, as if it had never been.

5

RHYS TREMAYNE, PI (PILLOCK INSTIGATOR)

The ride from Bryher to St. Morwenna was an uncomfortable affair, but Rhys Tremayne was not bothered. Or as Kenzie might say, *not bovvered.* Assuming, of course, that quoting Lauren from *The Catherine Tate Show* was still current London slang and not simple proof of his general decrepitude.

"Are you listening to me?" Lissa screeched. "I swear, sometimes I hate you as much as I hate him," she added, throwing a glare at Randy Andy, piloting the RIB with a stoic concentration that was somewhere between grinding fury and beatific peace.

Rhys smiled at her. Indicating his expression by circling a finger, he asked, "Do I seem bothered?"

"You're the reason my life sucks!"

"Sorry about that."

"You had no business telling Kenzie about Harold."

"He was my dad. And her dad. That made it my business."

"But I'm her mum, and I had a plan to tell her when the time was right. You interfered with that plan and now I... I have a resentment against you," Lissa declared in sudden triumph. "I have a resentment, and that means you owe me an amends."

He rolled his eyes. Lissa had dipped her toe in the local recovery community just enough to (1) decide she didn't have a problem and (2) to pick up a few key words and phrases, all of which she misused. It was no good telling her people worked through their own resentments, or that she couldn't checkmate him by announcing he owed her amends.

"Whatever, Lis. Good luck with that."

"You have to make it up to me or you can't stay sober!"

He pointedly looked to Randy Andy for help, but he was still in some kind of autohypnosis. Rhys wondered if the man were fool enough to actually marry Lissa, as she believed was imminent.

I asked her to marry me, once upon a time, he reminded himself. *Luckiest day of my life was when she said no.*

Well—not anymore. Jem's return to the islands was his luckiest day. Unless and until that event was dethroned by something even better.

"Coming up on the shore," Randy Andy announced, cutting the RIB's engine. "Rhys, help me bring her in, will you?"

"Gladly." That meant getting wet at least up to the middle of his cargo shorts, and the water was a little brisk for that, but he couldn't let the ex-chief do all the work. He really did owe the man endless amends for years of bad behavior: fights, minor vandalism, trespass, disregard for proper authority, and, of course, public drunkenness, without which all the rest would not have happened. Randy Andy wasn't the sort to accept an apology, even grudgingly, but that was all right; actions often made for more effective amends, anyway.

"That's it. Run away from me. I ought to toss this in your face." Lissa brandished her travel cup. "Give you a taste of Jack and see if it don't make you fun ag— Hey!"

Easily snatching the lidded cup away, Rhys hopped out of the boat and into the surf. Steadying himself by gripping one of the RIB's side-mounted rope holds, he wound up and hurled the cup toward Crescent Beach. Shooting like a missile over the sand, it landed somewhere in the dark grasses beyond.

"Well done you!" Randy Andy shot Rhys the first truly friendly grin he'd given him since... well, ever. "Good arm. You'd make a strong bowler. Though I'd have chucked it that way," he added, nodding toward the sea.

"Arrest him!" Lissa cried.

"Throwing it in the drink was my first thought. But ten to one she would've flung herself in after it. And she's never been a strong swimmer," Rhys said.

"True, true."

"He stole my property and destroyed it!" Lissa tried to stamp her feet in the RIB as Rhys and Randy Andy hauled it onto the wet sand, but only succeeded in falling on her face.

"You all right?" Rhys asked. He didn't care, mostly, but a tiny part of him still concerned itself with Lissa's well-being for precisely one reason: she was Kenzie's mum.

"She's fine. It'll take more than a pratfall to silence that one." Randy Andy cupped a hand to one ear, leaning toward the RIB. Sure enough, Lissa seemed to be weeping down on the cabin sole. The sound was too tremulous and pitiful to be real. Kenzie had also been prone to such fake crying, but she'd outgrown it. Around age six.

"Well, *Merry Maid*'s already put to anchor so that must be *Bellatrix*," Rhys said, pointing at lights on the water. "I'm off to find Jem and set up a new campsite."

"You do that. I expect we'll be along." Randy Andy heaved a sigh, his heavy features settling back into their habitual scowl as the moment of levity passed. He looked Rhys up and down critically, and Rhys expected to be sent on his way with a mild insult, or at least a reference to the bad old days. The ex-chief generally couldn't be in Rhys's presence for ten consecutive minutes without bringing up some past arrest or indiscretion.

"Sorry about that," he said at last.

"What?"

"You must've caught a wave just right. Looks like you've peed yourself."

Rhys checked his cargo shorts and saw it was true. He shrugged. "I can pull it off," he said, and loped down the beach toward *Merry Maid* and *Bellatrix*. Only when he'd covered half the distance did it occur to him that his former arresting officer had let him go with an apology instead of the standard parting insult.

And people say there are no more miracles.

Putting himself in the shadow cast by Bart's ferry, Rhys watched as Jem allowed Kenzie to drop anchor, took the girl through the final safety check, and then followed her—along with Pauley—down the ladder and onto shore. Pauley carefully handed down the boxed cake to Jem before disembarking, Rhys noted with amusement. They were still handling the ruddy thing like the American nuclear football, even though it had already blown up. Pauley looked stressed. Surely that couldn't be due to the cake situation. She hadn't fretted over a charred crumpet or a mangled macaron since she was thirteen years old. As for Jem, her eyes were wide and her normally lovely lips had compressed into a squiggly line. He knew that look. It was the one before she turned shouty.

Maybe finding the sick bloke in the cottage gave her a turn. Like, she mistook him for dead and thought she'd stumbled across another *corpse...*

But no, it couldn't be that. Jem lived for that sort of thing, and when she was caught up in a mystery, she sort of glowed. Was that what he meant? Maybe shone was a better word? He shook his head. He could envision it, and probably paint it, though he'd never been one for portraiture. Jem Jago unraveling a mystery probably couldn't be captured in a portrait, anyway. It would have to be abstract, with slashes of darkness to fully reveal the fiery light.

"Stargazer," he said, stepping out of *Merry Maid*'s shadow as she passed.

"Oh my God," she snapped, almost jumping out of her shoes. When truly startled, Jem always popped up like toast out of the toaster.

He regarded her innocently. "Sorry. How'd the piloting lesson go?"

Kenzie's grin answered even before her lips started moving —and move they did, spinning a fantastical tale of quick reflexes and natural seamanship that would've made Magellan envious. Pauley still looked distracted, which was unlike her—she was always tickled by Kenzie, especially when the girl went off on an ego tangent. He'd have to pull her aside and find out what was eating her. As for Jem, the squiggly line was back, and at a couple of Kenzie's statements, her eyes almost bulged out of her head.

The girl finished by asking, "Where's Mum and the muppet? Did they do me a solid by heading home?"

"No, I'd say they're having a chat by the RIB," Rhys said. That chat involved planted feet and crossed arms from Randy Andy and wild gesticulations from Lissa.

Pauley huffed. "They should be setting up the party again. The second wave of guests will be here any minute."

Kenzie broke into her Snoopy dance, which was always annoying, but especially so when it heralded the arrival of her schoolmates. Rhys called them the Drama Llamas. They were bad influences in many ways, not the least of which was their collective ability to go dark and emo at the drop of a hat.

"Pauls, would you mind corralling everyone? Getting them

back on track with the party set-up?" Jem asked. "I need to talk to Rhys."

"*Ooooh*," Kenzie emitted the universal lovey-dovey mockery tone. "Jemmie and Rhysie!"

"Hop to it," Pauley snapped, and Kenzie obeyed as if swatted across the backside. More and more, she met Lissa's efforts to reel her in with disdain, but when Pauley told her to move, she moved. Rhys smiled as he watched them go. Then he turned to find Jem walking in the opposite direction, toward the rocks that marked the end of Crescent Beach. She had a long stride, forcing him to jog a bit to catch up.

"I guess I should be glad you're walking toward Hobson's Farm and not into the ocean. Piloting lessons went that bad, huh?"

"You know I'm a teensy bit of a control freak."

Rhys choked back a laugh. "A bit."

"I was frightened out of my mind the whole time. For *Bellatrix*. For our lives. For my freedom, since I came close to strangling her."

"That could get you five to seven years. But probably in one of those open prisons where you get to work, and visit the shops, and have a quick one down the pub before lights out."

"Yeah. I mean, I did everything, really. I plotted the course, I read signals from the buoys and beacons, I insisted she keep it under ten miles per hour, and I stuck to her like glue in case I had to take the helm."

"And did you?"

"No. We arrived in triumph. At least in Kenz's mind. I couldn't have given her a better birthday present."

"But you're shaky and stressed out."

She nodded.

"Did it rub off on Pauley?"

"What? No. She knew the poor man in the cottage. Had a bit of a thing for him, as it turns out. Though she never said."

Rhys digested this. Putting a hand on Jem's shoulder to still her—she seemed intent on climbing over the sharp and slippery rock piles like a mountain goat—he gently turned her to face him. "You found another dead body?"

"What? Oh. Yeah. I should've led with that." She rubbed her face. "That plus pilot training made me loopy. Otherwise, you never would've startled me that way. I should've known you were there."

"How?"

"By catching a whiff."

He snuck his nose under one arm. It was fine—better than usual, if he were being honest. "Liar."

"Not that. Your hair. Ever since you cut it, it smells of Nivea Men. Which is good, since you look like you ought to smell of a latrine."

He shrugged off the wet shorts, which were halfway dry already. "I realize it's getting routine for you, but I wouldn't mind hearing a little more about the corpse."

A sudden swell of electronic dance music surged, followed by happy laughter from Kenzie and Lissa. It seemed that mum and daughter were back on track, at least for the moment. Turning back to Jem, Rhys said, "This one had to be a natural death, surely?"

"Surely not. Murder. Conked over the head."

"No wonder you hustled us off the beach so quickly. Hack stayed behind to wait for the mainland murder squad, I take it? But you say Pauley had a thing for him?" He didn't believe it. He knew her better than he knew anyone, except maybe Kenzie, and Pauley wasn't in the market for romance. Not in the islands, anyway, where the available men were a known quantity and none of them measured up. "What was his name?"

"Arthur Ajax."

"What did he look like?"

"Maybe forty. Big bloke, nice-looking, blond..."

Rhys had a sudden vision of a smarmy git in the Duke's Head Inn. The man had been holding court over a pint, explaining blockchain and bitcoin to the old duffers who practically lived there. At least he'd claimed to be explaining those hot financial buzzwords. To Rhys it had all sounded like a lot of bragging stuck together with the occasional "As you see" and "I think you'll find." Then again, he was still new enough to complete sobriety to feel a stab of jealousy if forced to watch another fellow enjoy his lager.

"I think I know who you mean. Smarmy emmet, ultra-groomed, always going about like God's gift?"

"I don't know about all that," Jem said, raising an eyebrow. "And I'm dead certain Pauley fancied him, so don't snark about him around her. Finding him dead left her in a complete state of shock."

"But he was completely wrong for her. What would she want with an emmet?" Rhys asked, still convinced Jem had got it wrong.

"You *do* realize she's eventually going to settle down with someone, don't you? And she doesn't need your permission to do it?"

"Sure I do. But it better be a proper someone. Not an emmet who's all flash and cash."

"We're not at school anymore. Your guard dog routine wasn't cute then. It's total bollocks now."

"Of the two of us, who's been around for the last twenty years? She's an heiress. Last of the St. Morwenna Gwyns," he shot back. "You think the sharks haven't been circling? She might not have much ready money, but she has the house, the name, and some of her trust fund leftover. Plus she's gorg, obviously. I've had to beat the fortune hunters off with a stick."

"All for her own good?"

"Why else?"

Jem shook her head.

"Seriously, why else?" She wouldn't meet his eyes. "Jem, you don't think... you can't believe I'm trying to keep her for myself?"

Her bark of laughter came as a relief. "Of course not. But Pauley's no muppet. I wish you wouldn't treat her like one."

"Unfair."

"Then why are you balling your fists and shuffling your feet like you want to swim back to Bryher and kill Arthur all over again?"

"I don't," Rhys said, unclenching his jaw as well as his fists. "I only want to kick the body a few times, just to be sure. Seriously, Jemmie, he was a phony. It rolled off him in waves like—"

"Like the scent of Nivea Men?" She grinned at him.

He grinned back, struggling for a rejoinder. Suddenly a happy cry came from Kenzie, carrying over the sound of her electronic dance music. Looking over his shoulder, Rhys saw that Bart had built up a new bonfire and two familiar figures approached it. Long curls streamed behind the first, Micki Latham, as the wind off the sea picked up. Beside her was her cousin and housemate, Clarence Latham, a dark-skinned, big-bellied man of perhaps sixty.

"I'm glad you saved the party for Kenzie, corpse or no corpse," he said, watching Pauley crown Micki with a hot pink halo, then slip a hoop of fluorescent green around Clarence's neck. A fresh gust of wind made Bart's inferno flare, sending a shower of sparks up into the night. Then Kenzie seized Clarence's hands, pulling him into an impromptu Lindy Hop. Unsurprisingly, he was a natural. The man had a zest for good times, just like the irrepressible Micki.

"Look at him go," he told Jem.

"Yep. Did you know he used to have a crush on you?"

"Impossible. He hardly looks up when I say hello. Barely grunts at me."

"Some people are shy."

"Does that include you?" He slipped his arms around her and wasn't surprised to feel Jem stiffen, instinctively beginning to pull away before slowly relaxing back into his embrace. He knew she wanted him. He could feel it in her kisses, her tremulous fingers over his body, the dilated pupils and quick, hitching breaths. *After* he made the first move, *after* he all but held her fast, squeezing her into place until she silently overcame that obvious instinct to flee.

She never even said she was disappointed about having to cancel tonight, he thought, then immediately rejected it. The pull between them was real. It always had been, since the days when they'd been too wide-eyed and clueless to fully recognize their feelings. Whatever made Jem keep herself apart, the exit door propped open, the bolt-hole chosen, it had nothing to do with lack of desire. And he refused to believe it had anything to do with Hack. It couldn't—could it?

She chose not to answer his question about shyness, so he decided to tease her a bit. "I really think you owe me, Bart, and Hack an apology. After telling us we couldn't be trusted around your precious birthday cake, and insisting on taking it separately on *Bellatrix*, *you* destroyed it with a bellyflop. All because your head's so far up in the clouds, you can't walk three feet without falling over."

"I can walk," Jem shot back, wrestling free of his grip and striding with great confidence toward the bonfire. "My head is *not* in the clouds, and I can certainly—"

She broke off, tripping over something and pitching forward. She was heading for a face-plant, but Rhys caught her in time, hauling her up with only mild difficulty. In his time, he'd dated all sorts of women, some of them like Lissa, delicate and extra petite, but he preferred one of proper size: tall, long-limbed, and no featherweight. That made them a bit more unwieldy when it came to keeping them from going arse over teacup, though.

"Jemmie, you could trip over the pattern in a rug. Didn't you see the hole?"

"No. Because I was busy. Proving to you that I can walk," she muttered. Glaring at the divot that had caught her trainer, she added, "What's this doing here, anyway?"

"Okay, one, it's a beach. Kiddies dig in it. Two, there's Buck," he said, reminding her of his dog's existence. Buck, an inveterate digger of holes, lived for his daily romps on the beach. Rhys had only excluded him from the party because even brave little pups didn't care to embark on nighttime sea voyages. Now that the party had moved to St. Morwenna, Rhys was tempted to jog up to his cottage and get him. Excluding Buck always made him feel guilty.

"Do *not* go get that dog," Jem said, apparently reading his mind. "You've already spoiled him rotten. It won't hurt him to spend one quiet night at home while—"

"Something's in there."

"Where?"

"The hole," Rhys said, dropping to one knee for a better look. Fumbling for his mobile, he thumbed on the torchlight and was rewarded with a dull glint off something rectangular-shaped.

"Is it a pail?"

"I think maybe it's pirate's booty." Sticking his mobile into the sand so the light shone on the hole, which probably was one of Buck's—two feet wide and perhaps two feet deep—Rhys felt around inside. The damp sand provided some suction, but with a sharp tug, he pulled the item free. It was an ornately decorated, silver-tone box.

"There you have it. The first official discovery of Rhys Tremayne, PI."

"Pillock instigator," Jem retorted. But she looked interested, and maybe—just maybe—a bit impressed.

6

TREASURE, TASTY BITES, AND TETHER DOG

"Is it silver?" Jem asked. Absurd as that seemed, the box certainly looked as if it might be. Ten inches long and four inches deep, it seemed like a relic from Victorian times. Every millimeter of the lid and sides was embossed with scrolled designs, squares, or flourishes.

"No, it's too light. Probably tin. Looks like something your gran would've kept her bingo money in." Rhys passed it over.

"And you're relinquishing it to me because...?"

"You're the Scilly Sleuth. And because statistically speaking, your presence almost guarantees it contains either a murder weapon or a severed limb."

"Ha. Ha. Hilarious." She didn't open the thing right away because damn the man, he was probably right. Best to proceed with caution.

She weighed the box in her hands. Two or three pounds, perhaps. The box's hinged lid had a loop and hasp but looked too delicate to actually padlock, even with the smallest lock made. Besides, despite its regal decorations, the box was indeed tin. Even padlocked, it could be defeated with nothing more than determination and a pair of stout snips. She ran a finger over the lid's embossed words: HOLLAND TREASURE CHEST.

"I reckon some kid buried their contraband in it. Let's see." To her surprise, the lid lifted with some difficultly—the hinges were stiff with sand—and when she shone her torch inside, she half-expected à la carte eyeballs or a smoking gun. Instead, the brilliant flashes of deep color—royal blue, brilliant green, deepest red, and pure white—made her gasp.

"Whoa. Are those... real?" Rhys breathed.

Jem drew out a delicate tennis bracelet in a clear press-seal pouch. "It sparkles like diamonds. And every one of these stones is a carat. Maybe two," she said. Her relationship with fine jewelry had always been shaky. Special Collections Librarians never got rich at their trade. They also spent far too much money on books.

She dug deeper into the treasure chest. A quick estimate suggested there were two-dozen pieces, all in individual, clear sealed pouches.

"Dump it out," Rhys said.

"No way. Someone will come along to see what we're doing. Probably Bart. He perks up whenever anyone rattles a couple of pound coins."

A hulking figure seated near the bonfire stood up. "Oi!" he bellowed. "What are you two about over there in the dark?"

"Or mentions a couple of pound coins, apparently," Rhys muttered. "Let's head for my place, it's closest."

"Suppose the others get curious and decide to follow us?" Jem asked. She didn't know if the treasure chest's contents were real or paste, someone's legitimate stash—buried on the beach? —or some thief's cache of stolen goods. She certainly didn't know if it had anything to do with Arthur Ajax, dead in Neptune Cottage. But she was sure that if Kenzie and Lissa spied the gems, they'd insist on trying them on. Bart would probably produce a jeweler's loupe out of his armpit and start appraising pieces. As for Randy Andy, he'd turn suspicious copper, which wasn't nearly as sexy as when Hack did it, and probably find a way to accuse Jem of stealing them. Or at least imply that her recklessness had created a serious problem. He'd never gotten past her wayward youth.

"Of course," Rhys groaned.

"What?"

"The Drama Llamas. Here they come. Always at just the wrong moment."

A group of kids loped along the beach trail, laughing, pushing one another, and talking loudly. Now and again one of them would shout or screech for no apparent reason and the others would jeer or chuckle knowingly. Jem had expected them to all be about fourteen, like Kenzie, but there was a surprising range of ages. Some were short enough to be tweens, while a couple of the boys looked tall enough to be card-carrying adults, full stop.

"Which ones are bad news?" Jem asked.

"As if I can tell one pulsating lump of teen angst from another," Rhys scoffed. "I've told Kenz time and again that I don't like the big blokes and they're not welcome at the lighthouse. But I don't reckon I'd get away with running them off the beach."

"Big blokes are super sus," she agreed, falling into some of Kenzie's London slang. She'd never heard a real live person say "sus" for suspicious, but Kenzie and telly assured her it was the correct usage. "But what about all the rest?"

"Irresponsible. Disrespectful. Delusions of cleverness."

"So just like we used to be? Yikes. I mean, on the one hand, they may kick up enough ruckus to keep anyone from following us back to your place," Jem said. "Buy us enough time to really go through the treasure chest. But is it safe to leave them alone with only Pauley as supervision? I don't count Lissa. I mean, there's Bart, and he's fairly imposing..."

"Bart? He'd pass his bottle round for a quid a sip if he thought he could get away with it," Rhys shot back. "But don't forget about Randy Andy. He'll keep them in line. He hates the new generation twice as much as he hated us."

"Which is really saying something," Jem said lightly. Maybe hate had its uses.

She fired off a text to Pauley and Micki, letting them know she was retreating with Rhys to his cottage. Hopefully they'd read romance into the message and give them enough alone time to go through the treasure chest and decide what they were dealing with.

If I had any sense, I would *be slipping off with him. Why wait for a frou-frou night at the Egyptian House in Penzance when there's a cottage with a bed just steps away?*

Climbing the beach trail toward Tremayne Lighthouse, Jem tried to tell herself she was being responsible. First, she was a fairly accomplished amateur sleuth, and hours ago she'd discovered a murdered man. The case was bizarre on the face of it, and she hadn't even had time to dig into the crime scene's peculiarities. Second, Rhys had gotten into the act by discovering a cache of jewelry. Was it really just a coincidence—a dead man and such a curious find? Even without a murder, she would've found the sheer strangeness irresistible. Third, it was Kenzie's special night, and if Jem wasn't unraveling a serious crime, she was supposed to be there for the birthday girl.

Flawless logic, said a little voice in the back of her mind. *No one would ever suspect that you're as afraid of taking the plunge with Rhys as Pauley was afraid of Arthur Ajax. Maybe if you faff about long enough, you'll lose him, too, and the pair of you can form a support group. Scaredy Cat Singles? Chickenshit Chicks?*

Jem suppressed the idea. She wasn't scared of Rhys. She was cautious. She was approaching the relationship with all due caution. She was...

"Hey, slow up," Rhys said, jogging to reach her side. "I

stopped for a minute to make sure the DLs were passing around sodas, not ciders, and when I looked back, you were marching like a bat out of hell. Mind on the case, eh?"

"You know it," she said, grateful for the relative darkness and his assumption.

"Now about the house..." He cleared his throat. "There's a reason, besides setting the mood, that I wanted us to go away for —you know. Our first night together. I know I said I'd cleaned up, but I fell behind. So we should probably keep to the front room and the kitchen."

"You make it sound like a haunted house. If we split up, the monster gets us?"

"Perfect way to think of it. Especially with regards to the downstairs toilet."

"Arthur Ajax kept his living space immaculate," Jem said with calculated wistfulness.

"Bet his corpse spoiled it."

"Only a little." The paved island thoroughfare known as the Byway had led them to Tremayne land. The decommissioned lighthouse—short, squat, and painted an incandescent white—looked out to sea. On the right was Rhys's cottage, a two-story affair that was white stucco with a gray-tiled roof. On the left was the lovely old glasshouse with its mismatched panels. Some were clear, while others were semi-opaque with age or scarred by their previous lives as house windows or car windows. Atop the glasshouse sat the St. George and the Dragon weathervane, which—apart from the Gwyn family library—was Jem's favorite thing on St. Morwenna. When the breeze stirred them, the saint and his nemesis swung toward one another, always dancing, never closing.

Jem waited on the threshold while Rhys fumbled in his cargo shorts for his keys. Like most islanders, he was unaccustomed to locked doors. But since Jem had returned, developing a penchant for stumbling over dead bodies in the process, Rhys and Pauley had begun religiously locking their doors each time they stepped out, even if it was only to pop down the lane. Micki and Clarence were doing the same and encouraging their guests at the B&B to do so too. It was a little sad to see St. Morwenna losing its innocence. But it only took one instance of a killer surprising you from the inner recesses of your own house to transform a person from carefree to cautious.

Of course, a killer trying to hide in these inner recesses might mistake it for a madhouse and go away, Jem thought, looking around the front room in astonishment.

Rhys's old walnut-framed sofa with the garish orange and brown upholstery was gone—no, disassembled. A stack of cushions towered in the corner. The walnut frame had been dismembered with a handsaw—Jem was quite sure of that, as there was more than a trace of sawdust on the floor. That wood had been used to form a sort of abbreviated spiral in the center of the room.

What exactly am I looking at?

The carpets were gone, revealing floorboards scored by what seemed to be fresh scratches. His mum's old wall art was down, and by driving three-inch nails into the plaster, Rhys had strung up three clotheslines across the middle of the room. Only one was of the proper height to actually dry clothing. The second was too low; the third only a few inches off the floor.

Jem turned in a slow circle, trying to guess the point of it all. The side tables and lamps—hideous even when Rhys was a boy, and violently out of style today—were gone. The front room's only illumination came from two artists' tripod lamps. Even Rhys's thirty-inch flat-screen telly, his pride and joy, was missing.

A sharp bark came from the kitchen. Mumbling something that sounded like "Sorry"—doubtless meant for his pet, not her—Rhys hurried through and came back carrying a small white mutt with brown patches and the occasional black spot.

Wiggling in Rhys's arms, the bright-eyed little dog was trying to wag, sniff, and lick his master, all at the same time. In the midst of this orgy of pure canine affection, he caught sight of Jem and broke off, barking with fresh excitement.

"Come here, you," Jem said, taking the warm bundle of excitement from Rhys and giggling as that pink tongue and cold black nose went everywhere. "Please tell me what your dad thinks he's doing in here."

"Isn't it obvious?"

Jem widened her eyes and slowly moved her head from side to side.

"Buck's in training for the Doggone Olympics," Rhys said proudly. "This is an obstacle course. In here we work on agility and tracking. Outside we do frisbee. Maybe herding, too, if I can find a way to make it work with the cows from Hobson's Farm."

"The Doggone Olympics. Never heard of it. Is it strictly IoS?"

"No, the first annual event will probably be in Penzance. Bart hasn't finalized all the details yet—"

"Bart!" Jem cried. "You really have lost it, haven't you? Remember the Pirate Fest that got him banned from Tresco?"

Rhys waved that away. "That was a half-baked idea. This is genius. And Buck will be in it to win it. After we have a look through the treasure chest, I'll put him through his paces."

"You can't really mean to go on with your front room like this."

Frowning, he glanced around at the doggy nail-scarred floor, the makeshift obstacles, and the clothesline crossbars, as if perplexed by her statement. "Well, not forever. I mean, the whole cottage needs an update, starting here. Once training is finished, we'll... I'll renovate."

Jem nodded, pretending not to notice Rhys's slip-up. Now that she'd made her decision to be with him, he was moving so fast. They hadn't even had their big night, and he was already imagining her moving in with him, at least on weekends.

"Right. Buried treasure," she said firmly. "First let me pass the Buck..."

"Har de har." Rhys accepted the little dog, who barked again and performed a complex sort of oozing maneuver when Jem opened the tin chest. One moment she was looking at his tail, the next at his bright button eyes. He tried to lunge for the chest, squirming determinedly in his master's grip.

"Look at that. A pup with *very* expensive tastes." Jem led the way back into Rhys's kitchen, which she was relieved to find more or less intact. Except for a length of rock-climbing rope, terminating in a locking carabiner that was nailed to the wall. Apparently one long steel nail wasn't sufficient. Rhys had used three.

"That had better not be what I think it is."

"You try living with Hairy Houdini and see what lengths it drives you to," Rhys replied unapologetically. "I only attach it to his collar when I leave him behind. Otherwise, he gets out every time."

Jem tipped out the Holland Treasure Chest's contents onto the table. Along with the tennis bracelet, Jem saw what looked like a pair of sapphire chandelier earrings. Were they genuine? If so, it made her head spin to imagine what they were worth. Next came a triple strand of pearls with a golden clasp and several rings bearing precious stones. There were emeralds, canary diamonds, and a big red gem that was either a ruby or a finely cut garnet.

"They might be fakes," Rhys said.

"I suppose. But good fakes are still worth a bit of cash," Jem said.

"Stolen valuables are a motive for murder."

"True. Thanks for that." She shot him a look, half-amused,

half-admiring. Like Pauley, he really seemed to be getting into the amateur sleuthing game.

"Except you said Ajax's place was terminally tidy," Rhys said, working through the possibilities. "Still, I reckon a place doesn't have to be ransacked after a theft. Maybe there was a safe or a strong box and the killer knew the location."

"Hold on, you're making a lot of leaps," Jem broke in. "First... I don't think Arthur was dead more than twelve hours. When did you go running with Buck?"

He considered. "Around eleven o'clock."

"So you came across something that had already been buried. It doesn't —oi! Buck!"

"Come on. There's nothing in there for you," Rhys said, pulling the little dog's face out of the empty treasure chest. Buck clearly begged to differ, his pink tongue covered with crumbs. He tried going back for seconds, but Rhys tucked him under one arm.

"I guess someone kept food in this tin before they decided to bury it?" Jem asked.

Rhys sniffed the residue. "Yeah. It's Buck's favorite treat. Tasty Bites."

"You can really be sure with just a sniff?"

Shrugging, Rhys wet a fingertip, touched it to the residue, then tasted it. "Yep. Tasty Bites. Totally sure." Jem gaped at him. It was bizarre. Then again, the man had transformed his living room into a doggy obstacle course. So perhaps not totally surprising?

Buck barked in protest, trying to wriggle out of Rhys's grasp so he could dive in again.

"I'll make you a deal," he told the animal. "You go back to tether dog, and I'll give you some fresh Tasty Bites."

"Tether dog?" Jem stared as Rhys connected the heavy-duty locking carabiner, surely big enough to restrain a wolf—maybe a werewolf—to Buck's collar.

"Tether dog," Rhys repeated with satisfaction as Buck surged forward on his rock-climbing line about two feet, then stopped, held back by the nails. "It's that or the crate, and Buck can't abide the crate. He thinks it's false imprisonment."

Jem's mobile chimed. It was Hack. When she picked up, he said, "Securing the scene continues. You ready for some weird developments?"

"It can't be weirder than this. Shoot."

7

THE MAN WHO WASN'T THERE

"Where are you?" Hack asked. "I expected to hear dance music."

"Rhys and I took a break from the party and went back to his cottage. We found something on the beach and brought it here for a look. Probably nothing," she fudged, not wanting to distract him from any details about the murder he might be willing to relate. In the beginning, Hack had tried to keep their friendship completely separate from his copper duties, only ringing her on his official line, keeping mum on virtually every investigatory milestone, etc. Lately he'd begun to loosen up, either because her persistence had worn him down, or because her Scilly sleuthing often yielded results. Maybe a little of both.

"Anyway, I know you won't leave it alone if I don't give up a little info, so here goes. Preliminary cause of death is blunt force trauma to the parietal bone. Toxicology will take a few days and might yield some surprises, but the forensics team doesn't expect it."

"That's really all it takes to kill a man? One whack with a frozen loaf of bread? I suppose it is a weird development."

"Oh, that's not the weird part," Hack said. "I've seen a guy miss a step, hit his head on the curb, lose consciousness, and wake up unable to read. He still knew the alphabet and could break each word down, letter by letter, but he couldn't fathom even simple sentences. Don't underestimate what a right royal pumpernickeling can do. In this case, stroke or subdural hematoma probably did him in."

"All right. I don't suppose you have a line on a suspect?"

"Please. We're still trying to find out who the victim is."

Jem's breath caught. "So 'Arthur Ajax' is an alias?"

"Seems so. We got in touch with the cottage owner and went through his personal details. His next of kin has a phone number and address that isn't real. His home address in London is real enough, but other people live there, and they've never heard of anyone of his description. It will take a little while to confirm it, but we believe his driving license and passport are fakes. High quality fakes, which is interesting."

There may be a lot of that going around, Jem thought, eyeing the sumptuous-looking jewelry in their clear plastic bags and again wondering if they could possibly be genuine.

"So Arthur Ajax must be John R. Derry, right?" she asked.

"As in the letters you showed me? Much too soon to tell."

"Have you run that name through your fancy copper database? Scotland Yard calls theirs SHERLOCK, right?"

"HOLMES, actually. And, no, because I'm not running this case. I'm only allowed to nibble around the edges. On sufferance, as it were, because I'm in charge of the islands."

"Well, surely even a mutton-headed blowhard like DS Conrad can't ignore something so obvious."

Hack chuckled. "Not at all. He's being... reserved."

"Stone. Yes. Checks out," Jem said, recalling the block-headed copper's stolid manner and craggy features.

"Not just stone. He's not saying much. Going about like he's taken a vow of silence. Every so often I see him lean over and whisper in the ear of a subordinate. He doesn't want me to overhear. I don't think he even wants me to be able to follow his reasoning."

"Such as it is," Jem said. "You don't reckon he's turning over a new leaf?"

"No. I don't want to speculate too much, but I think it's possible that the meeting I had last month with the retired living legend might have shifted the balance of power. Everyone, including me, expected my complaint to be officially closed. Now that it's going into phase two, maybe Conrad is trying not to make waves."

"I'd like to see him sacked, and fined, and maybe sent down for abuse of power, but just keeping schtum is a start," Jem said. "Did he seem more interested in the cache of letters, or the bit of blue fabric, or how eerily clean the cottage was?"

"None of the above. And Jem... he didn't keep totally schtum. He gave me a message especially for you."

Jem emitted such a sound of frustration that Rhys, who appeared to be doing some rigorous googling on his mobile, glanced up in surprise. She waved him off, and he resumed whatever he was about.

"I'll just bet he had a message. Tosser. But what do you mean he wasn't interested in the letters or the fabric? Those are primo clues!"

Hack sighed. "Promise you won't fly off the handle?"

"Sure," Jem said, mentally crossing her fingers behind her back.

"Well. PC Robbins came to view the scene, and she recognized the pumpernickel. Said she had some in her freezer. Then I had to open my big gob and say I was offered some, and Clarence didn't take my refusal too well. Then the landlord turned up with Ajax's paperwork and he said Clarence gave lots of people pumpernickel and he's *very* sensitive about it. As in, if they're anything less than rapturous over it, he sulks. Or he rants. Or he threatens."

"Threatens?" Jem repeated. "Now hang on..."

"I know. I think the landlord was just nervous. Being questioned by Conrad is a bit intense for people who aren't accustomed to the police, as I'm sure you remember. But, of course, the minute he used the word 'threatens,' Conrad got that gleam in his eye. The one that means he's latched on to a clue and means to build a case around it."

"So he's made Clarence the prime suspect. Based on the loaf."

"Yeah. And probably based on his surname. After all... it was Eddie Latham who went free in Penzance because of you."

"Yeah. Poor Micki. She was tearing her hair out over Eddie. If it's Clarence's turn in the barrel, she's liable to march up to Conrad and shake a fist in his face."

"If it comes to that, she might as well punch him and make it ABH. If you're going to be charged, at least enjoy it, that's what I always say."

"Are you sure you're a police officer?"

"Do you want to hear Conrad's extra special message for you or not?"

"Bring it."

"Here goes. Section 89(2) of the Police Act, 1996."

"Is that it?" Jem scoffed. "He can't scare me off with that."

"He went so far as to say he's aware you won't let its mere existence deter you. So, while we waited for the landlord to arrive with Ajax's paperwork, Conrad rang up one Mr. Lancelot Atherton. Got the poor bugger out of bed at nine thirty at night."

Jem groaned. Mr. Atherton, her boss at the Courtney Library, was a fussy little man who lived in terror of offending the library's donors. During Jem's first case, when she'd briefly been the prime suspect, she'd been arrested under Section 89(2) of the Police Act, 1996, which in her case amounted to annoying a police officer. She'd been forced to ring Mr. Atherton in order to access the Courtney's legal counsel, an act that had created a ripple of disapproval through her little corner of Library World. Since then, Mr. Atherton had regarded her suspiciously, as if she would inevitably bring still greater shame upon the Courtney.

"I don't suppose you heard what Mr. Atherton said?"

"Of course. Conrad had it on speaker. He told your boss you have a history of obstructing police operations because you're an attention-seeker obsessed with personal notoriety. And that maybe he should consider sacking you or at least getting you transferred across the country, before the Courtney finds itself embarrassed in the media."

Midway through Hack's words, Jem grew so agitated she squeezed her mobile, accidentally engaging the speaker. Rhys's head came up as he heard the last bit about being sacked or transferred far away. His brows drew down in alarm.

"Hang on. I hit the button and Rhys heard half of that," she told Hack. To Rhys she said, "Don't look like that. It's just bullying. I refuse to be scared off."

"Conrad said that attitude was precisely why he'd decided to ring your boss. He told Mr. Atherton that if you broke the law again, he'd see to it you were charged."

"That clay-faced gargoyle!" She half-rose from the table, fists clenched.

"Jem," Rhys said urgently. "You're not dealing with Randy Andy anymore. Conrad has real power. And he probably feels like he owes us one. The last time we tangled with him, we sort of rubbed salt in his wounds, didn't we?"

"He had it coming," Hack said. "Still, he thinks you two made him a figure of fun around Exeter HQ. PC Kellow's on track for promotion thanks to you, Jem, and he's out for her blood, too. He means to make someone pay."

"If he thinks any of this will work with me, he's got another think coming," Jem snapped. "I helped Eddie Latham and he was virtually a stranger. Clarence is a friend. You'd better believe I'll go to the mat for him."

"But carefully, right? Legally?" Rhys asked.

"Listen to him," Hack said. "Accusing Clarence based on *bread* is a harebrained scheme, even for Conrad. You don't have to go nuclear just yet."

But I want to, Jem thought, still stung by the idea of nervous, reputation-obsessed Mr. Atherton being awakened by DS Conrad at his most menacing. She'd never been to his home, nor did she know anything about his personal life, but in her imagination, he slept in an antique four-poster bed under lace-edged sheets with a tasseled sleeping cap on his head. He was exquisitely vulnerable to threats in a way she was not. And Conrad, like all bullies, had a preternatural instinct of where to apply pressure.

"Quit looking at me like that," she told Rhys, who seemed to be waiting for her to promise she wouldn't get herself sacked or sent back to London.

He held up both hands like a bank clerk looking down the barrel. "Hey, I'm on your side, remember? I'm the one helping you sort through the stolen jewelry, aren't I?"

Jem looked at her mobile in horror, but it was too late to take it off speaker. There was a moment of silence, and then Hack asked, "Come again?"

"We found it on Crescent Beach," Rhys said, ignoring Jem's glare. "While Jem and I were walking, she managed to step into a two-foot doggie divot. I don't want to reveal the canine culprit, but let's just say he's known to me. We found an old tin buried in the sand. It was originally a biscuit tin, according to Google, but someone used to store Tasty Bites in it for a while. There were crumbs in the bottom, verified by forensics..."

"What forensics?" Hack broke in, puzzled.

"Buck tasted them. So did I. Anyway, now the chest is packed with pieces of jewelry in little plastic bags. I'm no expert, obviously, but it looks like white and yellow diamonds, sapphire, rubies—"

"Garnets," Jem cut in, unable to stop herself. The urge to be a know-it-all was powerful, even whilst fuming.

"Disputed rubies," Rhys continued without missing a beat. "And ever since last summer, after a completely mortifying triumph of bank account over brains, I for one don't want to be accused of keeping lost or stolen goods for myself. Even if certain people think it might be an important clue or even a motive for murder."

"Smart decision," Hack said. In his coldest copper voice, he added, "I have no doubt Jem was moments from reporting your discovery to me. Isn't that right, Jem?"

"Of course," she muttered.

"All right. Stick the box some place safe and tell no one about it. Tomorrow I'll come round to your place as soon as possible to take custody of the stolen gems."

"But you don't know they're stolen," Jem said.

"True. But how often does a real-life copper actually get to say those words? 'Take charge of the stolen gems,'" Hack repeated with satisfaction. "This is my third—no, fourth—murder, not counting that attempted one a few months back, and now there's a cache of *stolen gems* on my patch. The Isles of Scilly are getting better all the time."

"Goodbye, Hack," Jem said, and stabbed the END button before he could return the sentiment. Then she dropped back into her chair and glared at Rhys.

"I had to tell him."

"I know. Fine." She folded her arms across her chest. "So a Holland Treasure Chest is an old biscuit tin?"

"From the nineteen forties. That could mean whoever buried the jewelry is an older person."

"And a dog owner." Jem picked up the clear bag containing the sapphire chandelier earrings and studied them under the kitchen's strong ceiling light. "They certainly look real. You should google jewelry thefts. Words like 'heist,' 'smash-and-grab,' 'cat burglar'..."

He grinned at her, running a hand through his thick blond hair the way he always did when pleased with himself. He looked exactly like a movie star in that moment, which made her heart turn over, even while her brain still fumed. DS Conrad was already doing his level best to shut her out of this case, one that at least peripherally involved Pauley and Clarence, and after fate allowed her to trip over a possible advantage, Rhys had given it away. Still, he looked like sex on legs, and that was something.

"I take it you googled all that already," she said, trying not to smile. When he turned on the charm, it was difficult.

"I did. I didn't come up with anything recent. There's a lot on the Hatton Garden heist, but that was years ago. Other stories mention smash-and-grabs by region, but don't name the actual shop that was hit. It seems like jewelers don't want the theft publicized."

"But crimes always get publicized."

"I guess. But it seems like jewelry companies just get seen as a soft target after it happens. The Hatton Garden bank vault company went bankrupt even though the gang that robbed them went to prison."

She raised an eyebrow. "You must've been googling up a storm."

"No, I knew that already. There's a fellow who—" Rhys stopped, frowning. "Crikey. I can't tell you. What happens in AA meetings stays in AA meetings."

"Couldn't you just depersonalize it? I mean, if you think it's relevant."

"It could be. I go to two different meetings. In one, there's an old-timer—that means someone who's been sober a long time—who got banged up for theft. He did seven years inside and had to pay restitution for stealing loose diamonds out of a vault."

"You only get seven years pinching diamonds?" Jem asked.

"Yeah. Seems like that's the maximum sentence unless you threaten someone or pull a knife or whatever. He always talks like he was a suave cat burglar, not a violent thug."

"There's a book about someone like that," Jem said, feeling that familiar rattling in the back of her head. "*Noble Thief*? No—*Gentleman Thief*. By Peter Scott. The king of the cat burglars."

"Is he British?"

"Irish. And dead," she added, "so there's no chance you've broken anyone's anonymity. Do you think this old-timer is telling the truth about his past? I suppose in a closed AA meeting, no one has any reason to lie."

Rhys snickered. "There's as much lying in an AA meeting as anywhere else. People drop in to say they're sober and happy when you can smell the booze on their breath. They can say anything they want. This old guy might be having us on. Trying to wow us with his criminal past to make his recovery seem that much more impressive."

"Does he have a dog?" Jem asked.

Rhys put his head to one side. "How would I know that?"

"Because you talk to anyone and everyone about dogs," she said, glancing fondly at Buck, who had curled up for a nap after scarfing down his Tasty Bites. "That's probably how you introduce yourself at meetings. 'Hiya, my name is Rhys, and I'm an alcoholic with a dog named Buck.'"

"It just so happens that I've discussed dogs with certain members. Including this particular old-timer, who has a golden retriever named Muggins."

"Does he live on St. Morwenna?"

"Tresco."

"My goodness. Full-time?"

Rhys nodded.

"Maybe he did make his living as a jewel thief. Did the authorities let him keep it all?" Even as Jem asked the question, she mentally backtracked, realizing her mistake. "Oh! He only had to return what he stole from the specific case they convicted him on, right?"

"Right. One mistake in an otherwise brilliant career, apparently."

"Well, then, if you really want to play PI, that's your assignment for tomorrow," Jem announced. "Find out more about this fellow. Maybe he's up to his old tricks again. Or maybe he can give us some advice about how to proceed. If he really is an ex-jewel thief, he might still be in contact with folks who haven't gone straight."

She expected Rhys to protest that he couldn't go about pumping AA members for unrelated information, but his mouth quirked in a smile. Apparently, he'd been thinking something along the same lines.

"And what's your assignment tomorrow? Ringing your boss to do damage control?"

"Nope. I'll be spending every minute working on Arthur Ajax. Or whatever he's really called. The man who wasn't there."

Nodding, Rhys stood up. Scooping up the bags, he stuffed them back in the Holland Treasure Chest.

"What are you doing? I wasn't done looking at them." Nor had she completely talked herself out of trying on that sparkly tennis bracelet.

"I need to stash this until Hack picks it up tomorrow. And you and I need to get back to the beach. The Drama Llamas have been on the rampage for at least half an hour. I need to make sure they aren't skinny-dipping or stealing my runabouts off the beach."

"There could be a thief out there," Jem agreed, also rising. Her curiosity over the dead man and the treasure chest came with a pang of unease. *There could be a murderer at the birthday party, too.*

8

FLAN MAN

Just as Jem and Rhys started out of the cottage, her mobile chimed, signaling a text from Pauley. It read as a bit stressed.

> *Where are you? Come back this minute! And bring an ice cream scoop!*

Guess she gave up on the cake, Jem thought. Groaning, she darted back into Rhys's kitchen, dug through his utensil drawer, found the item looking distinctly dirty, washed it, and hurried out again. The sea breeze hit her like a harbinger of winter. Hairs on her arms rose, and she found herself wishing for a jacket. Rhys was already off the Byway and striding rapidly toward the kids partying around the bonfire. Something about the way he moved suggested he wasn't happy with what he saw.

Once she was off the path and onto the sand, she saw Rhys by his rental boats, which were chained and padlocked to a bit of wooden fencing. No kids were in evidence, but Rhys examined the boats carefully, one by one. When he tugged on the last one, the fence slat came away. Unable to defeat the chains and padlocks, someone had sabotaged the fence.

"Kenzie," he roared. "Come here!"

In the midst of the dancing, the birthday girl stopped gyrating. Cupping her hands around her mouth, she shouted, "I'm busy!"

The kids weren't so angsty and emo that they couldn't laugh. In fact, they laughed so much, Jem could practically see Rhys's heat signature rising from yellow to red.

"Kenzie! Get over here now!"

Shoulders sagging, the girl began trudging toward the boats. Certain it wasn't her place to insinuate herself in that particular big brother–kid sister confab, Jem hurried over to Pauley, whose heat signature was also trending red.

"Finally," Pauley cried, taking charge of the ice cream scoop. "I'll fill the plates. You pass them out."

Great idea, Jem thought, marveling at the simplicity of her friend's solution. Unable to repair the cosmetic damage, Pauley had stirred the cake and frosting into a sort of rustic parfait and was parceling it out in gooey, generous scoops. The Drama Llamas seemed to appreciate the horror of a ruined cake. Jem heard them muttering about how it was sure to be a bad omen for Kenzie's upcoming year, and those kids were obviously enamored with doom—make that Doom with a capital D. They also clearly found Pauley's cake scrumptious, judging by how fast those scoops disappeared.

Rhys came back with Kenzie in tow, neither of them looking especially happy. Jem gave them the last two plates of cake, which they ate in silence. Then Kenzie dashed back to dance with her friends while Rhys folded his arms across his chest and scowled at a lump of clothes in the sand.

Except that's not a lump, Jem realized, goggling at the sight of Lissa DeYoung, curled up on the beach and dead to the world. Not far away sat Randy Andy, staring out to sea with a face like a slapped arse. For him it seemed the night had gone from bad to worse.

"I can't believe she fell asleep," Jem said.

Rhys shook his head. "When you climb in bed and switch off the lamp, you fall asleep. When you assume the fetal position at your kid's birthday party, you've passed out."

"She's not the only one," Jem said, nodding toward Bart, who was also sitting in the sand, nodding over an uneaten scoop of cake. His big square bottle of liquor lay beside him, empty. Turning to survey the rest of the party, she had the distinct feeling it was time to rein things in.

There was a girl off by herself, sobbing. A boy, this one with a nose ring, was dejectedly scrolling on his phone. Pauley looked tired and frustrated, though to be fair, Micki and Clarence looked to be having a bang-up time. They were in the thick of the dancing, which had moved away from the Lindy Hop or anything approaching swing dance. As for Kenzie, she was doing a sort of full-body shimmy with a boy who looked old enough to vote.

"Oh, hell no," Rhys said, handing Jem his plate and starting toward them.

Jem felt a little sorry for the boy. Whip-slim with a goatee and hair that was long on one side and shaved on the other, he yelped as Rhys seized him by his leather vest.

"Stop that!" Kenzie cried.

Ignoring her, Rhys hauled him down toward the sea. Jem was certain he intended no more than a quiet word—menacing conversations were often quiet—but Kenzie seemed to think he was about to drown the boy. Someone cut off the music and the group fell silent, watching the action with wide eyes and parted lips.

"Rhys! I mean it," Kenzie shrieked. "Hands off my man!"

He released the leather-vested young man, who stumbled backward. Then the poor fool stumbled forward as Kenzie threw herself at him in what she probably meant to be a show of reckless passion. Maybe she wanted to shield him with her body or melt in his arms. What she actually did was knock him head-first into the surf. When he hit, he squeaked like a spooked rabbit.

"Listen up, mates," Rhys boomed, addressing the party at large. "Glad you could make it, now go home. The party's over. Thank you, drive through."

The Drama Llamas started muttering, glancing at one another uneasily as if those instructions were too esoteric to work out. Rhys heaved a sigh as he realized he'd have to be more specific.

"How many of you live on St. Morwenna?" He looked at the show of three hands. "Fine. Take the Byway home. Is anyone here from the mainland?" No hands went up. "Good. You locals are in luck. Kit Verran has a standing weekend offer to run stranded islanders back to their home island. Anytime between sundown and midnight, ten quid a head. Take the Byway to the Quay, give him a bell, and he'll take care of the rest."

These instructions roused Bart the Ferryman from his semi-slumber. Throwing down his plate and heedless of the cake scoop that hit the sand, he surged to his feet as if reinvigorated by outrage.

"Kit Verran! Are you mad? Kit Verran's a no good, dirty, sneak thief of a scoundrel," Bart proclaimed, swaying slightly. "He should be run out of the islands, not carrying you—*youves*," he finished.

"What was that?" someone whispered by Jem's ear, making her jump.

"Youths, I think," Jem said, turning to find Pauley, Micki, and Clarence beside her.

"I think the slurring adds conviction," Micki said.

"Passion, anyway," Clarence agreed. "Poor Bart. He hates Kit Verran."

"C'mon, Rhys," Bart said plaintively. "Kit's killing my business. Let me take these fine *youves*—er, kiddos on *Merry Maid*. I'll give them a special deal. Only—"

"Bart, you're in no shape to row a dinghy, much less pilot a boat," Rhys said.

"Ten quid a head?" one of the kids repeated. Muttering commenced among them, and Rhys looked about to throw up his hands, though Jem saw him control himself with effort.

"You," he said, pointing at the leather-vested boy, his hair now wet from falling in the surf. "What's your name?"

"M-Marv."

"Marv what?"

"Marv... in."

Beside Jem, Pauley erupted in silvery giggles. She stifled them with her hands.

"Surname," Rhys growled.

"Bennett. Marvin Bennett."

"Top marks. Marvin Bennett, your old dad lives in Hugh Town, doesn't he? Called Steve?"

The boy nodded slowly, looking horrified, as if Rhys were displaying some kind of clairvoyance.

"Stop badgering him!" Kenzie cried.

Rhys gave her a look that would've flattened a bullet, midair. Then he turned back to the boy.

"All right, Marvin, son of Steve—who I've known for thirty years, if you want to know. I'm putting you in charge. Lead your people to the Quay," he said, waving a hand at the disheveled group to specify them, as if they might not be readily identified as people. "When you get there, ring Kit's ferry, board it, and make sure you and every last one of your friends gets home. Don't fret about the fee. Tell Kit that Rhys Tremayne will pay it. Got it?"

"Yes, sir," Marvin said. Approaching his duties with evident solemnity, he gathered his people and led them up the beach path to the Byway, without so much as a word or glance at Kenzie.

"Forgotten by her man," Micki murmured. "I wouldn't be fourteen again for anything. Would you?" She nudged Clarence.

He made an affronted sound. "Don't bother me while I'm admiring Captain Kernow. So very *butch*. Jem, how do you stand it?"

She chuckled. What she'd mentioned to Rhys about Clarence's low-key crush on him was true. During his first weeks on St. Morwenna, Clarence had started calling Rhys Captain Kernow. "Captain" because of his resemblance to a patriotic blond superhero, and "Kernow" because it was Cornish for Cornwall. Throughout the infatuation, he'd never tried to meet Rhys, or even learned his real name, content to admire him from afar. While he clearly had a deep and abiding appreciation for the male of the species, especially those younger, prettier variations, Jem considered Clarence talk and no follow-through.

I just don't get it, she thought. Around Jem, Pauley, Micki, and indeed all the ladies of St. Morwenna, Clarence was a live wire—quick-witted, salty, and always up-to-the-minute on the latest goings-on around the islands. He wasn't half bad to look at, ran a business, and was a pure delight, as any woman or man he wasn't attracted to could vouch. But around a man he liked, Clarence became a completely different person. Which was to say, he could barely utter a peep. Even his recent foray into acting with Hugh Town's theater group, the Tidepool Players, hadn't cured him of his shyness. He could recite complicated dialogue before an audience full of paying customers—but when it came to chatting up a man he truly fancied, Clarence turned dead silent and all but invisible.

"Kenz, your friends are litter louts," Rhys said, beginning to pick up discarded paper plates. "Help me tidy up the beach. We can't leave it like this."

Kenzie, who'd been watching her friends troop off in mute fury, turned a look of pure betrayal on Rhys. Bursting into tears, she took off running up the beach path, either to rejoin the Drama Llamas, or to make her way to Lissa's place on the other side of the island.

"Kenzie, come back here," Randy Andy called half-heartedly.

"Some stepfather he'll be," Micki muttered.

"Give him a break. He hates kids. He knows he can't taser her or jail her, so he's out of ideas," Pauley said. "Besides, his days with Lissa are numbered. Mark my words."

Rhys tossed a handful of paper plates into their makeshift bin, then turned apologetically to Jem and Pauley. "Thanks for everything. Sorry about all this. It isn't that Kenz isn't grateful. It's just that—" He broke off, eyes sliding to Lissa, still curled up in the sand. Then he said carefully, "I haven't been the best role model. And I'm not the only one."

"Should we dump a bucket of sea water on her?" Randy Andy asked. "I can't carry her all the way home. Not without giving myself a hernia."

"I have a wheelbarrow in the glasshouse," Rhys said. "We'll load her up in it and take her to my place. She can sleep it off in my parents' old room."

Slipping off his trainers—he never wore socks—Rhys sprinted toward the beach path with a ferocious, ground-eating stride that would take him to the glasshouse.

"I'll say it again. So very butch," Clarence murmured.

"Cheating in your heart is still cheating," Micki said. "What about Flan Man?"

Clarence shushed her with a look toward Randy Andy and Bart the Ferryman, but neither man appeared to be listening.

"You're not really planning to pilot that heap of yours,"

Randy Andy told rather than asked Bart, sounding as if he were still chief of police.

"I live on *Merry Maid*," Bart wailed. "What else can I do?"

"C'mon. I reckon Rhys will let you sleep on his floor. He's not a bad sort."

Jem and Pauley exchanged glances. It was the first kind word they'd heard the ex-chief say about any of them since... well, ever. But neither of them had time to marvel over it, because they'd both twigged the implications of Micki's remark about cheating.

"Clare, have you been holding back on me?" Pauley asked. At the same time, Jem demanded, "Who's Flan Man when he's at home?"

Clarence tossed his head and tried to look mysterious. "My dear cousin is mental. Nothing she says can be taken seriously."

"Ha! He baked flan twice last week," Micki declared, pointing at him as if identifying him across a courtroom. "Yet no flan was served to anyone at Pirates' Hideaway," she continued, referring to Clarence and Pauley's B&B, where Micki was a permanent paying guest. "Those flans were baked and spirited away under cover of darkness."

"If I want to bake flan and distribute it, that's my business. I'm a single man. No boyfriend. And even if I did have a boyfriend, that wouldn't stop me from visually feasting on Captain Kernow, or anyone else."

"Flan Man. Reveal him," Micki snapped, getting in his face.

Pauley pushed her aside. "Clare, from a business standpoint, I'm the only one who really has to know," she said, deploying a tone of sweet reason. "As your partner I have to look out for your emotional well-being. Just whisper his name into my ear."

Jem tried to elbow Pauley aside. Finding it impossible—Pauley was solid, not to mention determined—she planted a fist on each hip and announced, "You might as well spill it. Otherwise, I'll make it my business to find out who eats flan in the islands. It can't be that many people."

Clarence pretended to be affronted by the three of them, but his eyes sparkled. He fanned himself as if overheated by their intensity. "*If* I choose to disclose the gentleman's name, I will require complete discretion," he said firmly. "This isn't a relationship, per se. More of a possibility. It's at a delicate juncture, so I don't want anyone accosting him or making insinuations." That last was directed at Micki.

"I never make insinuations!"

"No, she makes accusations. I'm the only choice," Pauley said. "Tell me and I'll help you decide if those two can be trusted."

"I will find out. I'm the Scilly Sleuth!" Jem cried.

"Oof," Micki said.

"Tragic." Pauley shook her head pityingly.

"Now, ladies. I believe it falls to us to finish tidying the beach," Clarence said, still obviously basking in the attention. "There are still plastic forks and globs of cake everywhere."

"Here's a cider bottle," Micki announced, plucking it out of the sand.

"Lovely. Underage drinking on our watch. How'd we miss that?" Pauley shook her head in disgust. "And one of those cheeky monkeys almost got one of Rhys's runabouts off the chain."

"I don't mean to criticize," Clarence began in an unambiguously critical tone. "I was glad to get the last-minute invite. But this reeks of plan B. How was the party actually supposed to go?"

Jem and Pauley swapped glances.

"It's a secret..." Pauley began.

"Maybe we could do swapsies?" Jem asked.

"Hey! That leaves me out in the cold." Micki shook her head. "Clare, here's what I know. Kenzie likes to hang out on a private beach on Bryher, so the party was supposed to be there. I reckon they got chased away. The landlord must've turned up. That, or Jem tripped over another dead body." She laughed, glancing from Jem to Pauley and expecting them to join in. When they didn't, her trademark laugh, a wheezy *heh-heh-heh*, died away. In a small voice, she asked, "Another one? Really?"

"Really," Jem said, binning the last of the plates. "Pauls and I made the mistake of going into the nearest cottage to try and repair the cake and there he was."

"Surely it was a pensioner this time," Clarence said.

"A hundred and two years old? Died in his sleep?" Micki asked.

"Nope. Youngish. Around forty. We found him face down on his kitchen floor." As Jem spoke, she realized something that would have occurred to her much sooner, if not for the night's myriad twists and turns. If she described the manner of death, she'd have to break the news that Clarence's own pumpernickel bread was the murder weapon.

From the look on his face, it was almost like he anticipated the news. "I'm sorry. Which island did you say this was?"

"Bryher."

He stared at her. "The private beach. It isn't—" His voice broke. "It isn't Neptune Cove."

Jem swapped glances with her friends, alarmed. Normally, Clarence's deep, resonant tones were authoritative and soothing. It was startling to hear his voice climb right up to the brink and crack, fractured by irrepressible emotion.

"I'm afraid so," Jem said carefully. "We found the dead man in the holiday let. Arthur Ajax."

Clarence cried out, then clapped a hand over his mouth in a vain attempt to silence himself. Holding Jem's gaze, he began shaking his head wildly, denying the truth of it over and over again, if only with his eyes. He looked unsteady on his feet.

Flan Man, she thought, rushing to catch him as he fell. *Arthur Ajax was Flan Man.*

9

A GNAWING SUSPICION

Pauley caught Clarence just before he hit his knees.

"Oi!" Micki cried, grabbing his arms and helping her steady him. With an assist from Jem, the three of them managed to get him back to his feet.

Hearing that her friend had been attracted to Arthur came as no surprise to Pauley—Arthur had been scrummy by anyone's standards. But Clarence's reaction seemed a bit over the top. Unless...

Did he say the relationship was at a delicate point? Does that mean he was seeing *Arthur the whole time I was mooning over him?*

"I'm all right," Clarence said, trying to shake them off. The moment Pauley and Jem let go, however, he stumbled again, causing them to each grab an arm.

"Right. You need a sit down and a moment to collect yourself," Jem said.

"Rhys's cottage is closest," Pauley said, and steered Clarence toward the beach path. He didn't speak as they climbed, just breathed raggedly, like a man fighting to get the air in and out of his lungs. Suddenly she saw the body on the floor again, face down in those almost absurdly stylish pajamas, gorgeous even in death. The loss of her delicious flirtation, her cherished daydreams, all the moon-spinning she'd done since meeting him, had hit her like a wrecking ball. But then she'd pulled herself together, helped move the party to Crescent Beach, and even enjoyed herself a little. Clarence had dropped like a puppet with cut strings.

Because they had an actual relationship of some kind? While what I had with Arthur was never real, she told herself brutally. A backlash of disappointment followed the words, and she flinched, forcing herself to acknowledge the emotion without pursuing it. *I can't go down that rabbit hole right now. Not when Clarence needs me.*

"What's happened?" Micki demanded of her cousin.

"He's had a shock," Pauley said. "We should get him off the beach so he can sit down. Maybe have a shot of whiskey."

"I thought we were going to Rhys's cottage. He won't have any booze," Jem reminded her.

"Just a chair would be fine," Clarence said, straightening his shoulders and lifting his chin determinedly. "Besides, I think if I tried to get anything down, it would come right back up."

Despite the quaver in his voice, he shook Pauley off, told Micki he wasn't an invalid, and led the way up the beach path with the three of them trailing behind. Once they were on the lighted portion of the Byway in sight of the cottage, Micki mouthed silently at Pauley, "What happened?"

She responded in kind with two words. "Flan Man."

"Buggered off?" Micki whispered in Pauley's ear.

She drew a finger across her throat. Micki looked appalled but not shocked. Sudden death was becoming a part of their lives whether they liked it or not.

Rhys's cottage was lit up brightly. At the door they were greeted by Buck, who was practically wagging his tail off with delight. Clarence didn't seem to see or hear the dog, so Pauley picked him up and accepted some happy face licks. As oblivious to the living room's bizarre doggy obstacle course as to the animal itself, Clarence headed for the only chairs in sight, arranged around the dining room table. Micki, however, glanced around in astonished consternation.

"Has Rhys suffered a breakdown?"

Pauley started to explain—she'd known him far too long to be shocked by any harebrained scheme he embarked upon—but Jem summed it up in one word:

"Kinda."

"I can hear you lot," Rhys shouted from inside the master bedroom.

Pauley, Jem, and Micki all chuckled weakly—more a knee-jerk social response than anything else—and Clarence surprised her by joining in, though quite faintly.

He's brave, she thought. But the very next idea her brain generated wasn't so admiring. *Or all this emotion is an act, and he already knew Arthur was dead. Because he had something to do with it.*

It wasn't a comfortable thought. She considered herself a loyal person, someone who had her friends' backs, not the suspicious type. Was it just the inevitable offshoot of what she'd already acknowledged—that sudden death was becoming part of their lives? Jem's earlier cases had revealed more about human nature than she'd ever truly wanted to know. Suppose a friend turned out to be a killer? Was the inevitable price of sticking your nose in secrets and lies a gnawing suspicion? The fear that everyone around you contained an inner trapdoor that could plunge them into rage? To fathomless violence?

The notion was disturbing. Dwelling on it, Pauley allowed Jem and Micki to accompany Clarence to the kitchen table while she diverted to the master bedroom to give Rhys a heads-up. If the conversation went one way, he might have a sobbing man in his kitchen, and Rhys wasn't great with big displays of emotion. When women cried, he fidgeted; when men wept, he practically left his body. And if the conversation went the other way—if Jem, being Jem, started asking questions that spiraled into something resembling an interrogation—it was always good to have a big, intimidating bloke on their side.

There I go again. Clarence isn't dangerous. He isn't!

Rhys's master bedroom, once the exclusive provenance of his parents, had never been updated or repurposed in the wake of their deaths. Pauley had often urged Rhys to clear it out—sell the well-worn furniture, give it a lick of paint or some fresh wallpaper, and send the old ghosts packing. The cottage had been his for over a decade, and he deserved to sleep in a proper adult bedroom. But he still slept upstairs in his childhood room, while the master's sagging double bed currently hosted Lissa, dead to the world atop the duvet. She'd maintained her curled-up fetal position despite being transported by wheelbarrow. Randy Andy was nowhere in sight.

"Is she on her own, then?" Pauley asked Rhys, who was rooting around the closet as if seeking backup linens.

"Yep. You-know-who went home to pack."

"He told you?"

"Of course. He's hoping I'll break the news to Lissa when she wakes. I won't," Rhys said with a shrug, coming out of the closet with a pillow in one hand and a folded patchwork quilt in the other. "It's none of my business."

"Zen Master Rhys," Pauley muttered. Even though she knew him better than anyone, she was still coming to terms with the version of Rhys that didn't constantly erupt in fits of temper. The minor showdown on the beach didn't count. His frustration with Kenzie had been perfectly reasonable, and the Drama Llamas could drive anyone nutty. Still, she couldn't help worrying that one day his short-lived serenity might disintegrate into a long-suppressed explosion.

"You know, it's okay for you to have an opinion," she ventured. "Not just on Kenzie's behavior but on— Oh!"

"Sorry, love," Bart the Ferryman rumbled from the floor, where he'd halted her next step by seizing her ankle. "Only I thought you were about to tread on my face."

He was lying in the space between the chest of drawers and the window, flat on his back and green of face. As Pauley retrieved her ankle with a jerk, backing away, Rhys handed Bart the old blue ticking-striped pillow—another artifact that Pauley thought should be burned—and placed the old quilt by his feet.

"You're a good one," Bart said humbly.

"You do realize he'll probably puke on them," Pauley said.

"He already spewed on the first set. I tossed them outside to deal with tomorrow," Rhys said, with the unruffled confidence of the man who lives alone. "Try to sleep it off, Bart. I'll see you and Lissa in the morning."

As they exited the master bedroom, Pauley heard Bart mutter from his dark corner of the floor, "Bloody Kit Verran. I wouldn't drink like this if not for him."

"Clarence is in a bad way," Pauley informed Rhys quietly. "Turns out he was seeing Arthur secretly. We told him about the murder and now he's in a state of shock."

Rhys's brows drew down. "He hasn't gone all... *emotional*, has he?"

"Two minutes ago, you'd found inner peace. Now you're scared of a little grief?"

"I am."

"Too bad. I'm going to do everything I can to help Jem crack this case. And you are, too." Having issued those orders, she grabbed his hand and yanked him forward into the kitchen.

"Oh, hon, I'm so sorry," Micki was saying. She held one of her cousin's hands; he swiped at his eyes with the other. "Poor Flan Man. I hope it turns out to be an accident."

"It won't," Jem said. At Micki's sharp look, she said, "Look, if you want to shout at me, go ahead. I can take it. I know the last thing anyone wants to deal with is a murder in the islands. But the person who hit Arthur over the head left him either dead or dying. And he may have escaped in Arthur's yacht. Isn't that right, Pauls?"

"Assuming Arthur actually owned one," she said, sitting down on Clarence's other side. With the four of them at the little table, that left no room for Rhys, who looked relieved. He sat down on the floor and began teasing Buck with a plastic bone. At first Pauley thought the background noise—excited yips and intermittent squeaks—weren't terribly conducive to a serious conversation. But maybe such everyday sounds would put Clarence more at ease. She really *did* mean to help Jem get to the bottom of Arthur's death, and that meant drawing the complete truth out of Clarence, whatever it was.

"Do you know if Arthur owned a yacht?" she asked him.

"I saw him out on the water a couple of times. It was a big one. Twenty-five feet at least. All the bells and whistles."

"More like thirty," Pauley said. "A Sunseeker. Given how successful he was, it seemed likely. But there wasn't one berthed at Neptune Cove."

"I'll have to ask Hack about that, next time we talk," Jem said.

"If you're holding out on details to spare my feelings, there's no need," Clarence said, setting his jaw. "You said he was hit on the head. But with what?"

Jem winced. "We found some damp bread on the floor close to the body. Someone conked him over the head with a frozen loaf."

"Death by baked goods?" Micki shook her head. "That's mental. But maybe I should just be grateful it wasn't one of your ruddy pumpernickel loaves," she said, giving Clarence's hand a final squeeze before releasing it. "One of those things is heavy enough defrosted—it would make a proper cudgel frozen. And we Lathams just went through the strain of an accused murderer in the family. We can't possibly go through that again."

"It was the pumpernickel," Jem said quickly.

"Oh, God." Clarence passed a hand over his eyes.

"Jem. No. Tell me this isn't happening," Micki said urgently. "Or at least say Hack knows better than to accuse Clarence of murder."

"Hack isn't running the investigation. It's DS Conrad from Devon & Cornwall," Jem said. "I think we'll have to assume he'll be questioning Clarence at the very least. Maybe as soon as tomorrow."

"But Clarence is Mr. Clean. He's never put a toe out of line in his life. Well, apart from some *very* catty remarks," Micki added, glancing at her cousin, "but God will get you for that when the time comes. Otherwise, you've led a blameless life."

Something about the look on Clarence's face struck Pauley as a tad off.

"That's true, right?" she asked, keeping her tone as unconcerned as possible. "No unpaid parking fines or run-ins with councilmen who might hold a grudge?"

"Nothing like that. Never been arrested or cautioned. Haven't been in a fight since Year Eight," he muttered.

"And you're a mean, keen baking machine who's passed the pumpernickel to every man in the Isles of Scilly," Micki added.

From his place on the floor, Rhys snickered. They glared at him, and he resumed playing with Buck.

"Speaking of, erm, passing the pumpernickel," Jem said, putting on what Pauley thought was a forced smile. She, too, seemed worried about something. Was she also troubled by Clarence's demeanor?

He practically fell over when he heard the news, Pauley reminded herself. Then she had an image of her friend and business partner on stage with the Tidepool Players, delivering a short monologue with ringing confidence. *He's an actor. Not a professional, true. But still—an actor.*

"Was Arthur the only man in your life?"

Clarence nodded.

"Were you the only man in his?"

He gave a sort of pained laugh. "Not even close."

10

A SUNSEEKER, A SEWING MACHINE, AND SETI

Jem was working on a delicate way to frame her next question when Clarence seemed to read her mind. He qualified his previous statement.

"Now, don't get it twisted. I'm not speaking ill of the dead or accusing him of anything. It was fine. Arthur was in crazy high demand and completely up front about wanting no strings. He called it ethical non-monogamy."

"Meaning, you're not exclusive and no one lies about it?" Jem asked.

"I call it civilized," Micki said.

"I call it a recipe for mass unhappiness," Pauley retorted, though without heat. Jem couldn't swear to it, but she thought her friend was taking the notion that her dead crush could never have been hers with a fair amount of grace, all things considered.

"I call it none of our business," Rhys said lightly, eyes still on Buck, who'd paused the action for a pat break.

"Thank you," Clarence told him. It was the most directly and firmly he'd yet managed to speak to Rhys. A good first step, Jem thought, even if born of tragic circumstances. "Anyway, I knew most people wouldn't get it, and that's why I kept my mouth shut."

"But *I* mentioned Arthur to you," Pauley said, sounding a bit hurt. Maybe Jem had been too quick to praise her composure. "You're literally the only person I confided in. Because I thought you'd understand."

"Hey?" Micki sounded miffed. "Jem and I are sitting right here, love."

"I know." Pauley's big eyes with their black-winged eyeliner shifted from one to the other. "But, Mick, you're killer confident when it comes to men. And Jemmie's with Rhys now. I thought Clarence would understand because..." She tailed off.

"Because I've waited too long for Mr. Darcy to come out of that lake in his wet, white shirt and sweep me off to Pemberley, just like you?" He nodded, flashing a sudden smile that Jem found disconcerting. A moment ago, he'd looked on the verge of breaking down completely. But, of course, people reacted to grief in varied and often surprising ways. Pauley herself was still pinging from mood to mood, whether she knew it or not.

"So yeah, lovely, I get it," Clarence continued, patting Pauley's shoulder. "And I'm sorry I kept schtum and didn't clue you in to how Arthur liked shopping in the men's department. But he insisted we were only friends—friends who sometimes spent the night—and indiscretion was the unforgivable sin."

"So he was in the closet," Micki said.

"Not really. Just... private." Clarence sighed. "And not just about his sex life. Arthur was mysterious about everything."

"Where did he come from?"

"The city is all he told me. I assumed he meant London."

"He told me that he took early retirement from investment banking," Pauley said. "Is that what he told you?"

"No. I mean, yes, at first. Then one night, when we were a bit pissed, he said it was all a front. That he was actually a professional gambler who hit it big and walked away. I asked him all sorts of questions, because that sounded amazing," Clarence said. "But, of course, whenever I showed too much of an interest in anything he said, he turned to stone and clammed up."

"Or suddenly remembered a prior engagement and dashed off," Pauley agreed.

"I hope you don't think I'm just being nosy," Jem said, suffering a faint pang as she prepared her next question. Although she loved to dig up new facts and reveal hidden connections, it was still slightly embarrassing to use those skills on people she knew and liked.

"But when Conrad interviews you," she continued, "I can promise he'll play mind games and try to twist whatever answers you give. Like to this question: Where did you and Arthur meet up? Was it at Neptune Cove?"

"Not at first," Clarence said. "We met at a dance club in Hugh Town. When we started hooking up, he had a rule—never in the islands, only on the mainland. That was from May to late July. Then he flipped the script. Suddenly we could never meet up anywhere but Neptune Cove." He sighed. "I figured he was ashamed to be seen with me."

Micki made an offended noise, and Pauley looked equally appalled. From the floor, where he sat cross-legged with Buck snoozing in his lap, Rhys murmured, "Didn't I call it? Smarmy emmet always going about like he was God's gift."

"Speak only good of the dead," Pauley snapped.

"I didn't mind," Clarence said. His voice was light, but his eyes slid away from Jem's, making it impossible for her to gauge his sincerity. "The cottage felt like an upgrade, if I'm being honest. With that full kitchen, I could cook for him. And Bryher's so private. Even in the season, it's secluded. Out of season, you could shoot a cannon down the beach without hitting anyone."

"Except maybe Kenzie," Rhys said.

"When's the last time you saw him?" Jem asked.

"Saw him? In the Square, yesterday afternoon. He was doing a shop and hobnobbing with this one." Clarence indicated Pauley. "If you mean when's the last time I was alone with him, it was the Saturday before last."

"Two weeks ago," Jem said. "Did you spend the night?"

"Now you *are* sounding a bit nosy," Micki said. Under most circumstances, she was lighthearted and easy-going, but as they'd all discovered during Jem's last case, a fiercer side of her emerged when she perceived a threat to her family.

"I promise, Conrad will ask," Jem said calmly.

"I didn't." Clarence lifted his chin. "It's fine. I preferred to get back to the B&B. Bart's always up late on Saturday nights, so I gave him a bell and he ran me home. No questions asked."

"Was Arthur's cottage always immaculate? Barely lived in?"

"Yeah, he was a minimalist. Liked to keep things shipshape and Bristol fashion."

"But you never saw a yacht moored in the cove?"

"No."

"And he never claimed to own one?" Jem said, still stuck on the idea of Arthur Ajax leading yet another concealed life in another private world. She supposed it was possible he'd just been obsessively neat, and there was no second hideaway stuffed with all the usual accumulations of daily life. But her instinct kept insisting that no human being could live in such a sterile, impersonal environment.

"No. And I did ask him about the Sunseeker after I saw him aboard it," Clarence said. "He said it belonged to a friend. That he was just catching a ride."

Jem decided it was time to lower the boom and watch his face for reaction. "Did you know Arthur Ajax wasn't really his name?"

Clarence stared at her. "Come again?"

Should she mention the John R. Derry letters? In a flash,

Jem decided not to. Her gaze flicked toward Pauley, issuing a silent warning not to pipe up. She wanted to believe Clarence, she really did. Still, there was a discordance in his reaction, a false note she had yet to zero in on. Better to keep some key details close to the chest; that might make it easier to decide if he was being completely truthful or not.

"Arthur Ajax doesn't exist, apparently. There's probably someone out there with that name, but not in England. Hack said when the landlord brought over Arthur's paperwork—next of kin, home address, etc.—it was all phony."

Clarence let out his breath. His shoulders sagged. "So it really was all a lie," he muttered.

"What?" Micki asked.

"Everything. A guy like him retiring to the Isles of Scilly. Wanting to stay because he liked us all so much. Giving one-tenth of a damn about me," he said bitterly.

"Oh, cuz, I'm sure he did care, at least a bit." Micki offered him a reassuring smile. "But from the picture you paint, all he wanted from you was a little fun from time to time. Nothing wrong with that, if everyone's honest."

"I just don't agree," Pauley said flatly. "And, Clare, I know I had a thing for him, but now that I know how he treated you, I feel like I dodged a bullet. The *nerve* of him, treating you like a backdoor man. Saying if you let anyone know, he'd call the whole thing off!"

"What's a backdoor man?" Micki asked Jem.

"The opposite of Mr. Darcy or any Regency heartthrob."

Micki frowned. "That can't be right. I quite fancy a Regency rake. The greatcoat. The sideburns. If he came and went by the backdoor, so much the better."

"Not in my book. You know what I say to them?" she asked Clarence.

"Boo. *Booooooooo*. He was never worth it. Any man you're with should be proud to be with you."

Clarence managed a smile, though Jem thought his eyes still looked sad. To come at the question of Arthur's true identity from another direction, she said, "I wonder if he actually had a lot of money?"

He shot her a startled look. Pauley laughed. "Are you kidding? He was rolling in it. When he arrived in the islands, it was by private plane. He chartered a private plane to fly him, and him alone, from East Anglia to Bryher. And his luggage was Tecknomonster."

Jem frowned. "I never heard of a chartered flight for one man. And what's Tecknomonster? Is it like Gucci?"

Clarence and Pauley exchanged pitying glances.

"Poor thing's never really kept up when it comes to fashion," Pauley told him.

"Lucky her. I wish I could ignore style, but it calls to me. Always has." Clarence sighed. To Jem he added, "Look, maybe he was traveling incognito. Maybe he was in trouble somewhere and hiding out on Bryher. But at some point, Arthur was rolling in it. Everything he owned was top drawer."

"Yeah." Jem flashed back to those natty red-and-blue striped pjs. Then she saw the treasure chest full of jewelry. Some pieces had been made for men, others for women. Did the collection belong to Arthur Ajax? Was he prone to caching away secret things, like the John R. Derry letters and the jewels?

I have no proof the jewels are connected to the murder, she reminded herself.

She was on the verge of asking Clarence his opinion when she remembered Hack's glee at finding an Isles of Scilly crime to call his own. If Jem gave Clarence the inside scoop, he'd report her questions about buried treasure to at least a few people. And then the island grapevine would take over and before Hack could even start interviewing people, the witness/suspect pool would be contaminated. Jem couldn't knowingly do that to Hack. Therefore, she moved on to the obvious question.

"Who would have wanted Arthur dead?"

"No one," Clarence said.

"Just like that?" Jem blinked at him.

He stared back at her, unblinking. "No idea."

Pauley nudged him. "I know it's hard to think straight right now. But in hindsight, can you remember Arthur mentioning a row with someone? Or maybe someone else pointed out Arthur and made what in retrospect seems like an ominous remark?"

"No."

Jem held his gaze until he finally looked away. Not a muscle jumped in his cheek; not a bead of perspiration showed on his forehead. He was fiendishly hard to read.

"Well, my only guess pertains to the ripped fabric in the Janome Atelier 6," said Pauley, launching into an explanation about the cobalt silk and the fancy sewing machine. It seemed mostly directed at Rhys, still idly petting his snoozing pup, since Clarence did occasional sewing for the Tidepool Players and would understand the value of that make and model.

"Why would a bloke like that own a sewing machine?" Rhys asked.

"I own one," Clarence muttered. "Blokes sew, too."

"I know that. I mean why would Mr. Bespoke have a home set-up to do his own tailoring? He couldn't even fly to Cornwall first class; he had to charter his own plane. Yet we're meant to believe he was willing to hem his own trousers?"

"Some people sew because they enjoy it," Pauley said archly. "And they're the sort to own an Atelier 6."

"How many people in the islands sew because they enjoy it?" Rhys demanded. "Really, let's hear it."

"Oh. Well. Me. Clarence, obviously. Roger Pinnock—you remember him, the poor dear with the Romeo breeches? And there's Sally Carew in Hugh Town and Zara Lamphier on the other side of St. Mary's. Ruddy cow, that one, but very talented, damn her." Pauley paused to consider. "That's about it. Anyone else with a machine or a well-used sewing box only does it to pinch pennies."

Rhys looked quietly pleased with himself.

"What?" Pauley demanded.

"I think he means to say, if Arthur was truly an enthusiast, you would have known," Jem said, not mentioning how she'd recently used the same logic regarding dog owners on him. "And I reckon he's right. So maybe the sewing machine wasn't his. Perhaps someone else brought it over." As she spoke, the obvious scenario came into sharp focus. "Let's say Arthur was seeing someone else on the same terms he was seeing you, Clarence. Total discretion, no problems, maybe a bit of friction as a result."

"Ethical non-monogamy doesn't automatically mean friction," Micki said.

"No," Jem said thoughtfully. "But then people are always getting together under one theory and then trying to alter it midstream, aren't they? Arthur may have thought he was perfectly upfront and ethical. Most people do, really, to hear them tell it. But maybe Hookup Number Two didn't see it that way. Maybe there was trouble in paradise?"

"And the cobalt silk could have been the flashpoint," Pauley said, sticking fast to her angle. "Maybe Arthur ripped it, Hookup Number Two boiled over, followed him into the kitchen, found the first heavy thing to hand—the pumpernickel—and whacked him into next week."

"Into the afterlife," Clarence said, and sighed again.

"Exactly. Maybe it wasn't even on purpose. Killing him, I mean."

Jem shrugged. "Killing him with one blow might not have been on purpose. But leaving him to die on the kitchen floor sealed the deal. That makes it murder in my book." She gave

Clarence another long, appraising look. "C'mon, Clare. Pauley was head over heels for him, and she has an idea. If Roger Pinnock was keen with a needle and thread, he goes on my list. Is there anyone Arthur clashed with? Some kind of bad blood?"

"Everyone I talked to adored him," Pauley said.

Rhys cleared his throat.

"Except for Rhys, our other prime suspect."

"Hugh Town," Clarence said a bit too loudly, as forcing himself to answer. "If I'm being honest, Arthur wore out his welcome there. I used to think he'd left a trail of bodies, but that's, erm, not the best phrase, obviously. He'd definitely left a trail of hurt feelings."

"How so?" Jem asked.

"It's a small community," Clarence said. "Arthur was a catch, full stop, and I think some of the guys went into lifetime love mode. I don't know how clear he was about his no-strings policy. But to hear those blokes tell it... they were built up on promises and dropped like patchwork blue jeans."

"Ooof." Even a fashion/style neophyte like Jem had no use for patchwork jeans. "So I should put every single gay man in Hugh Town on my list?"

"All three of them." Clarence waved a hand. "Sorry, hon, I'm joking. There's at least twelve. The rest are very married to the men of their dreams and wouldn't be caught creeping."

"But these twelve are angry enough that I should consider them worth tracking down?" Jem asked.

"I don't know. All I can say for sure is, I met Arthur in Hugh Town, but we never went back. Remember how I said we started by meeting on the mainland? That was mostly Penzance, at Noughts & Crosses or The Hunger Dames. But one Saturday night we met up in Marazion at a club called The Brazen Head. Arthur touched off such a ruckus just by being there that—"

"Wait. When was this?" Jem asked, resorting to the notes app on her mobile to jot down the specifics.

"August. No—September. Anyway, I was sitting at the bar when he turned up. Some people quit dancing to have a gossip in the corner, throwing glances at us and pointing. Very mean girls."

"Which means he left a trail of hurt feelings in Marazion, too," Pauley said.

"He must've," Clarence agreed. "We got in a couple of drinks before a fellow called Uriah made a scene. Then it was bye-bye clubs, hello Neptune Cove under cover of night."

"You went all the way to Marazion for electronic bop and watered-down beer?" Micki asked.

"There are still people alive called Uriah?" Rhys asked.

"Yes, and yes. I rather like Uriah. Biblical name. But I didn't care for that bloke. He waited till Arthur was in the men's room, then pounced on me. Asked if I knew what I was getting into. I said I didn't know what he meant, and Uriah said, he's an imposter. Claimed to know for sure because he worked for SETI. Uriah said SETI was monitoring Arthur. Watching and listening in."

"SETI?" Micki frowned. "That's the men in black, love."

"I know that," Clarence said patiently. "The Search for Extraterrestrial Intelligence, thank you very much, I *have* seen *Ancient Aliens*. Anyway, in case I didn't make it plain, Uriah was three sheets to the wind. I didn't argue with him, or even pay particular attention. I thought he'd mistaken me for someone else. It wasn't until Arthur came back, saw him, paid the tab and stormed out that I realized they actually knew each other. Arthur wouldn't talk about it, but I reckon the whole thing shook him up a bit. Heaven knows Uriah looked dangerous."

"So you're telling me Mr. Cash and Flash got confronted at a club and basically ran for it?" Rhys sat up straighter to ask the question, jolting Buck, who whined softly. "Did he stand up to Uriah at all?"

"A few words passed between them. More about SETI. But I'm not the best witness, because I was cross about going all the way to Marazion only to turn around and leave again. And I was feeling a bit mortified, if I'm being honest."

"Of course you were mortified. You went where no man has gone before." Micki grinned. "You shagged an alien."

"If they're all like that in the sack, sign me up for intergalactic outreach," Clarence said.

They all chuckled, but Rhys seemed to find the remark particularly amusing. Clarence regarded him with wide, worried eyes, as if he'd made an irretrievable blunder.

He really doesn't get it yet, Jem thought. *Playing the shy guy is a dead end. Though I suppose if we had enough insight to see how counterproductive our survival strategies really are, relationships wouldn't be such a minefield.*

She was thinking about Clarence, of course—his tendency to pull his head and limbs into his shell whenever he encountered an attractive man. But as her eyes rested on Rhys, gazing down at his dog with unmistakable fondness, she suffered an unexpected pang. Maybe she'd be better off analyzing her own actions.

"Right," she announced, looking around the kitchen. "So here's what we know. Arthur Ajax was the nom de guerre of a man who had plenty of money, secretive ways, and a habit of breaking hearts—intentionally or unintentionally," she added, seeing Micki on the verge of speaking up again for the ethically non-monogamous.

"He lived in a very neat home, had a fancy sewing machine that might not have been his, and might have a yacht tucked away somewhere. I've taken note of two other oddities"—it still seemed best not to announce the John R. Derry letters or the treasure chest of jewelry to everyone—"but in general, the bad romance angle seems best. Clarence, I know tomorrow is Sunday, but I suggest you contact an attorney first thing. And when DS Conrad says he wants to chat with you, tell him not without counsel."

"Won't that make him look guilty?" Pauley asked.

He already looks guilty, Jem thought grimly. *Which means in the morning, I need to hit the ground running to figure this out.*

11

SUNDAY MORNING SLEUTHING

Pauley had always been an early riser. The Sunday after Arthur's murder, she rose even earlier than usual—just before dawn—after a fitful sleep. She wasn't mourning him. They'd never shared enough of a genuine connection to trigger that deep sense of loss, that awful pit-of-the-stomach feeling that screams something has been stolen away forever. But she did feel naggingly empty. There was a sore place inside, hard to ignore, like a ragged socket that had lost its tooth.

It must be so much worse for Clarence, she thought, padding into the shadowy kitchen in her *The Nightmare Before Christmas* slippers, each imprinted with Jack Skellington's grinning white face. *Assuming he didn't... that he wasn't the person who...*

She cut off that thought. While lying awake, she'd X-rayed her feelings to the atomic level, trying to decide why her friend evoked even a flicker of suspicion. It was his too-quick denial when Jem asked who might want to kill Arthur. Clarence had been worse than unhelpful. He'd been a stone wall. And you only built walls to protect something valuable. Or secret.

With that acknowledged, the Clarence Pauley knew would

never make an unprovoked attack on anyone, much less an intimate partner. Of course, it was true that people sometimes snapped. In a moment of blind rage or temporary insanity, even a good person might commit an atrocity. But *if* Clarence had clubbed Arthur in a fit of passion, she believed he would've called 999 and tried his best to save Arthur's life. He wouldn't have fled the scene, leaving him to die alone on the kitchen floor, then spent the aftermath pantomiming shock for his family and friends.

But just because I can't believe he's a murderer, that doesn't mean I can't believe he'd lie to us. Either he's ashamed of something—like letting Arthur treat him like an embarrassing secret—or he's keeping mum in defense of someone else.

Could that be it? Did he know, or suspect that he knew, Arthur's killer?

Flicking on the overhead light, she spared a glance at her small collection of cookery books before opening the cupboard. She withdrew the usual suspects: self-raising flour, caster sugar, and baking powder. Then from the fridge she got four eggs, butter, strawberry preserves from Hobson's Farm, and double cream. The butter would soften on the counter as she whipped the double cream and sifted the flour. And when those simple, heart-lifting tasks were done, she'd make what she always made when she felt a bit down: a Victoria sponge sandwich cake. If Jem was interested, they'd have it for tea in the afternoon. If not, she'd pop it in a tin and give it to someone. Maybe Clarence.

If I had a yacht, Pauley thought, cracking an egg against the flat countertop, *where would I hide it. Scratch that—why would I hide it?*

Holding the egg over the bowl, she pressed her thumb into the crack, puncturing the membrane. Then with a practiced motion she pulled it apart, spilling out the deep orange yolk amid a gush of egg white.

I'd hide it if I were a thief. A stupid thief who stole a

gorgeous flash yacht that anyone would recognize and didn't know how to unload it for cash.

But was Arthur—the man for whom she'd mentally tried on dozens of gorgeous jet-black wedding dresses—not only a liar and a thief, but a stupid thief? The possibility rankled.

As she continued with the baking prep, Pauley ran over her association with him from the beginning. The chartered plane had been a mad bit of boasting, of course, and the Tecknomonster luggage—seven thousand pounds a pop by her reckoning—was also what Kenzie would call a "flex." Especially in the Isles of Scilly. Arthur had always been charming, amiable, and very good company, but he'd kept his interactions short and sweet. Looking back, it was clear that he'd enjoyed his five-to-ten-minute conversations with Pauley, but that was all he'd ever wanted—just a cheery, impersonal friendship, and only in bite-sized portions.

Groaning aloud at herself, she touched the butter—still an ice-cold brick—and decided to soften it in the microwave. Filling a glass with tap water, she placed it in the microwave and pressed the button.

Two minutes later, the microwave binged. Pulling out the glass of boiling water, Pauley popped in the butter and closed the door without turning it back on. She counted to ten, then removed the butter and gave it a poke. Perfectly softened. Direct heat from the microwave could be disastrous, but left-over radiant heat did the trick every time.

Now. Back to the mystery. Did Arthur sew? No. And it's not Clarence's machine, so until we receive new information, we have to assume it belongs to Uriah. Or a third man.

As Pauley mixed the batter, she sifted possible approaches in her mind, trying to decide how she could best help Clarence and Jem. Pauley had never actually met DS Conrad, but by reputation he struck her as a cross between Inspector Lestrade and Colonel Blimp—equal parts incompetence and preening arrogance. Sure to fixate on the pumpernickel loaf, he would probably be infuriated if Clarence followed Jem's advice to lawyer up. The man was a shortsighted, vengeful bully. In which case, if he thought he was being deliberately thwarted, he'd probably decide to stitch up a case around Clarence, then call it a day.

But surely Conrad can't steer every part of the investigation, can he?

Hack or some other reasonable copper would point out that a man living on a remote island under an assumed name must be fleeing from enemies. Why did it have to be Clarence who killed him, or even some other aggrieved ex, like Uriah from Marazion? Suppose one of those mainland enemies had discovered him on Bryher, ended his life, and slipped away, making it look like a domestic murder? If the victim had died while in hiding, shouldn't the police's first step be to discover his true identity?

The yacht might be the key, she decided, pouring the batter into two twenty-centimeter sandwich pans. Her much-repaired cooker was feeble and quite elderly. By rights, it deserved a state funeral for its long service, but Pauley couldn't possibly afford to replace it as well. Therefore, when she wanted to bake on the Gas 4 setting, she cranked it up to Gas 7 to get the same effect.

Arthur flew here and took a ferry to Bryher. That means there's only two ways he could have owned a yacht—he bought it after he arrived, or he already owned it, and someone piloted it here on his behalf. If he bought it, it probably came through Jimmy Franks. She pictured the diminutive owner of Franks All Marine, who dressed and spoke like an American movie mobster, despite the fact he was born in Instow Village, which was in the north of Devon.

Jimmy owes Jem one for solving that case with the sunken boat. I've never been able to abide the man, but if I want my share of this case, I'll have to woman up and give him a ring.

Even if he didn't sell Arthur the Sunseeker, he might know where it's berthed, or how I might find it, she thought.

Once the pans were in the oven, it was time to hurry up and wait. Pauley put the kettle on—these days she was on a morning tea kick—and started the coffee maker for Jem, who would say and do things she didn't mean without her morning java. Then she kicked off her Jack Skellington slippers and started a series of contemplative yoga poses to start her day. She was just transitioning from Downward-Facing Dog (Adho Mukha Svanasana) to Warrior Pose 1 (Virabhadrasana 1) when a voice behind her said, "Sweet moves!" Just like that, her meditative contemplation dissolved in a yelp.

"Sorry!" Kenzie held up both hands, in one of which was a house key. "I was sure you heard me come in."

"Kenz! What are you doing here? Since when are you even up at this hour?" Pauley asked, pressing a hand to her chest to slow her pounding heart. The last time a woman had surprised her like that in Lyonesse House, she'd had a loaded shotgun in her hands and a murderous glint in her eye.

"I am up at this hour," Kenzie replied in an over-dramatic tone, "because Mum came home still half-pissed to find Randy Andy packing his gear. He was trying to make a clean getaway, but she mucked that up, and they started screaming at each other. Then off he went, one box in his hands, three left behind, and said he'd send a mate round to get them. Mum threatened to set it all on fire. But I don't reckon she will. The last time she torched a man's shirt to make a point, the council fined her."

Pauley nodded, keeping a rein on her sympathy until she could be sure of how the girl was really doing. When Kenzie was little, it had been easy to judge her true level of distress; now, sometimes, it was impossible. "And you're feeling..."

"Absolutely buzzin', clearly." Kenzie sounded a bit surprised to be asked. "High time he chucked it in. Go back to the mainland, bruv. You don't belong in our ends."

"Are you sure that's London slang?"

"Yes. God, it was on telly, how many times do I have to say it? *Moon Knight*," she said, punching the air and doing some footwork that was probably meant to denote street fighting. "Now if only Mum would clean herself up and kick the booze and behave properly, we could be ever so happy with no trouble at home."

"Mm-hmm. And naturally, it would be just that easy. Cup of green tea?"

"Fancy a coffee, if I'm being honest."

"You're already breaking into houses and boxing thin air. If you think I'm pouring a few hundred milligrams of caffeine on top of that, think again."

"If she won't be drinking it, I will," Jem said from the doorway.

She wore her sleep uniform—fuzzy socks and an oversized T-shirt—and looked lovely as always, even after a bone-rattling yawn. Pauley was too accustomed to her tall, slender, pretty best friend to suffer real jealousy, but from time to time she felt a tiny pang. Then she pushed it down into the basement with all the other bullshit, took a deep, centering breath, and got on with it. In this case, that meant opening the oven and testing her sponge cakes by inserting a toothpick into the center of each. It came away clean both times, which meant the pans were ready to come out.

"I didn't break in," Kenzie told Jem. "Pauley gave me a key. I could've knocked, but instead I let myself in to be considerate, because I figured you were both still asleep."

"Gave me quite a turn," Pauley said, tipping the cakes out on wire racks to cool.

"And you woke me up with your nattering," Jem said, yawning again. "But that's fine, because I need to make an early start on the case. Since Conrad got Mr. Atherton out of bed with threats about me, I expect to be called on the carpet first thing Monday. That means I can't waste a moment of today."

"That's another reason I dropped by, besides spreading the news that Randy Andy is finally out of my life." Kenzie accepted her cuppa, took a sip, and smiled at Pauley. "Cheers. Anyway, I had a think about the dead man you discovered last night, and—"

"Hang on." Jem swung around from the counter where she was doctoring her coffee. She must've been having a good morning, detective-wise, to make that catch before Kenzie finished her sentence. Usually she stared into the middle distance and communicated in grunts until the magic bean juice kicked in. "How do you know about us finding Arthur Ajax?"

The girl blinked at them. "How do you think? Randy Andy. He still carries a radio tuned to police channels. He scans them all the time like the loser he is. Mum told him to shut it off and listen to her properly, he said there was a murder at Neptune Cove, and Bob's your uncle, I figured out what really happened last night."

"Is Bob's your uncle another phrase from *Moon Knight*?" Pauley asked.

"No, it's quite old. From the Restoration, maybe," Kenzie said. "I just threw that in to make you OAPs happy. Anyway," she said, turning to Jem, who had sat down beside her and was sipping her coffee with rather formidable intensity, "can I assume since you tripped over yet another dead body, you'll be beating down the killer's door in the next two to seven days?"

"That's the plan," Jem said.

"Right. Then you're in desperate need of my input. I am an expert on Neptune Cove. Been going there whenever I need a bit of respite for the better part of a decade."

"Since you were four?" Jem sipped more coffee.

"The better part, not every last year. But, yeah, if you need the deets, I'm your woman. Information is my game."

"Who killed him, then?" Jem asked.

Kenzie snorted. "If I knew that, I'd be quoting you prices. But I knew him, though. Not well, but I knew him."

"Did you?" Pauley thought this might be one of Kenzie's flights of fancy, but it wouldn't hurt to find out. "In the sense that he... I don't know, found you lounging on his beach and told you to get lost?"

"Exactly. Thought highly of himself. Acted like he owned the place."

"Renting the cottage gave him exclusive rights to use the beach, according to Randy Andy," Jem said.

"Yes, but he didn't *own* it, right, so he had no business being such a sniffy twat. Once I climbed a tree and said, 'There you are, I am no longer setting foot on your beach,' and he whipped out his phone and rang the police." She rolled her eyes. "I slipped away long before PC Newt came around."

"Did anyone ever visit him in the cottage that you saw?"

"Clarence came once. Turned up at twilight, just as I was off to catch *Merry Maid*. And that funny little man... kind of a garden gnome..."

"Kenz," Pauley said. "Do you mean a local?"

"Yeah, from Hugh Town. He does the theater."

"Roger Pinnock?" Pauley asked, shooting Jem a glance. The "poor dear with the Romeo breeches," as they'd referred to him the previous night, had crossed their path during the same case that introduced them to Jimmy Franks of Franks All Marine Boating Superstore. Roger was someone Pauley could imagine owning a Janome Atelier 6, especially if the breeches affair had convinced him that sewing costumes from patterns would be a lifesaving skill in a pinch.

"Anyone else?" Jem asked.

"I didn't actually have the place under surveillance," Kenzie said, sounding nevertheless pleased at the intensity of their interest. "But looking like he did, there were probably other blokes." She scowled as she remembered something. "Marv saw him grilling steaks behind the cottage and said he was a dead ringer for Rhys. Which was mental."

"Extremely mental," Pauley agreed. The idea made her shudder. She loved Rhys like a brother, but if Arthur Ajax had truly resembled him, any desire she felt would've fizzled in an instant. "They were both tall and blond. But Arthur was a bit shorter, and not as broad through the shoulders."

"And not as handsome. Marv needs a new contact lens prescription," Kenzie said, apparently still offended on Rhys's behalf.

"So you were meeting Marv at Neptune Bay?" Pauley asked, keeping her tone neutral. Thank goodness Rhys wasn't present just now, or he'd have that jaw-jutting, nostril-flaring look that foretold an explosion.

"Not like that," Kenzie barked, waving a hand. "I mean, really. Marv and I are just friends. We put on that dance last night to make the girl he actually fancies a bit jealous. But then Rhys started beating his chest and acting like a lunatic, so we kept up the act just to egg him on."

Sipping her tea serenely, Pauley pretended to believe the girl's tale. It was a little too breezy to be true. So Kenzie and Marv had been slipping off to Bryher? She hoped nothing much had happened between them, but whether it had or not, the time had come to keep a tighter rein on the girl. Lissa was semi-hopeless at the best of times, and the breakup with Randy Andy would likely leave her debilitated for days, if not weeks. Pauley would just have to find a way to brainstorm over the problem with Rhys— that was, once she found a way to break the news.

"So what was Marv doing there, trespassing on the private beach?" Jem asked. "Or did he take your view that islanders can go anywhere?"

"He was looking for buried treasure. Even brought a lantern

and a spade." Kenzie sighed. "Such a child. It's been years since I could play that game with a straight face."

Either Jem's caffeine had just hit her nervous system, or that bit of info meant something to her. She sat up straight, putting her coffee cup down. "Marv is what, sixteen? Seventeen?"

"Seventeen," Kenzie said warily. Definitely a guilty conscience there.

"Don't you think if he was searching for buried treasure, he actually thought he might find some?"

"I hope not," Kenzie replied. "I mean, I love the islands, but look at all of us. Rolling in shipwreck gold, we ain't. Pauley's the heiress, and she had to flog a load of old clothes just to redo her kitchen."

"Fair point," Pauley murmured, but Jem's eyes still shone avidly. Either she was holding back on something, which would *not* stand, or she'd made a leap in logic that Pauley had yet to see.

"I don't suppose you ever noticed a yacht moored near the cove?" she asked Kenzie. "Not a Cuddy cabin boat but a proper Sunseeker with all the bells and whistles?"

"About as often as I've seen shipwreck gold. The most exciting thing I ever saw on the water was Kit Verran's ferry," the girl said sardonically.

"He was letting people off on the beach?" Jem asked.

"No. He just buzzed the cove. Sometimes he didn't come close enough for me to be sure it was him. Other times, I saw the blue and white awning and knew it was him."

Pauley met Jem's eyes. "What do you reckon?"

"It's obvious, innit?" Kenzie asked, again lapsing into counterfeit Londoner. "There's no way anyone wanted on or off Bryher that much, and Neptune Cove isn't on the ferry route. He must've been dating Arthur."

"Wait. You knew Arthur was gay?" Pauley asked.

Kenzie regarded her over her teacup. "Affirmative."

"And you think Kit is, too?" Jem asked.

"Hell-*oooo*." The girl looked at her. "Don't tell me you didn't twig, Lady Detective."

"No, I totally and completely twigged. Now—more coffee," Jem said resolutely, rising. As she crossed to the pot, she tossed a look over her shoulder that Pauley interpreted as, *Shoo off the kid so we can start sleuthing in earnest.*

12

THE LAST OF THE GENTLEMAN JEWEL THIEVES

"Whew! I was afraid she'd never go," Pauley said, returning to the kitchen after walking Kenzie out. "At least I convinced her to take the Victoria sandwich cake to Lissa."

"Think it will cheer her up?"

"Nope. Lis always goes to pieces when another man leaves." Pauley waved that aside. "What's the agenda for today? What are we tackling first?"

Jem grinned at her friend. She'd gone all-in on this junior detective notion. And that might turn out to be a huge advantage Monday through Friday, while Jem was at work on the mainland. With Pauley snooping for her on some aspects of the case, and Rhys poking around on others, who knew what they might accomplish?

"Give me a sec." Making a dash for her bedroom, she returned with a fresh journal and a brand-new gel pen. The journal cover was a reproduction of William Morris's celebrated "Bird" wall hanging. The gel pen wrote in dark-green ink, which complemented the journal perfectly.

"All right. Page one. Our victim, Arthur Ajax." Jem wrote

that out, then went back and put his name in quotation marks. "Or so we'll call him for now.

"Now for the men in his life. Clarence Latham. Left behind a pumpernickel loaf that became the murder weapon—"

"Is it?" Pauley interrupted.

"Is it what?"

"The murder weapon. I mean, it's only been twenty-four hours since he died. We can't be sure, can we?"

Jem huffed in frustration. "You're right. But look at it this way. If the blow to the head didn't kill him, it was probably intended to. And we can't wait around for Hack to slip us the official cause of death, because if we just sit on our hands and hope for more info, DS Conrad will stitch up Clarence right before our eyes. So, yes, for now, the loaf is the murder weapon. Next man in Arthur's life. Uriah," she wrote.

"No surname," Pauley said. "May live in or around Marazion. Clarence met him at The Brazen Head. Supposedly has something to do with SETI."

"Right. So those are confirmed men Arthur was seeing," Jem said. Shifting to the next page in her journal, she wrote,

POSSIBILITIES

Roger Pinnock (seen leaving Arthur's cottage)

Kit Verran (seen around Neptune Cove at odd times)

Marv Bennett

"Marv Bennett," Pauley cried. "You don't mean—you don't think Arthur—"

"No," Jem said hastily. "Nothing of the sort. It's what Kenzie said about Marv treasure hunting with a shovel and a lantern. Remember?"

Pauley looked at her blankly.

"When we left Neptune Cove," Jem said patiently, "to move Kenzie's party to Crescent Beach, there was a light bobbing on the shore. At the time, I thought of fairy lights. But it must've been someone carrying a torch or lantern. That could have been Marv, searching for treasure."

"And there is treasure," Pauley agreed. "Okay. What else?"

"That's up to you," Jem said. "I need to take a shower and make myself minimally presentable. I'll do the washing-up, too," she said, taking her plate and cup to the sink. "But while I'm at it, I need you to check your journal for me." From age nine, Pauley had kept a journal. The practice had evolved over time. What started sporadically, using little pink books with brass locks, had become a fixed nightly routine, now with fancy bullet point journals that offered ample room for sketches, stickers, and margin notes.

"Sure. What do you want out of it? Maybe a timeline on Arthur's movements?"

"Top marks. The date he first arrived. Which days you saw him on St. Morwenna, or in Hugh Town. Anything interesting that he might have said. Just look over the entries and see if anything jumps out."

"Right," Pauley said with naked enthusiasm, and dashed headlong off to her room. Still grinning, Jem made for the shower.

By the time she'd showered, dressed, and wrestled her almost waist-length hair into submission—the double bun was her choice for long sleuthing days—it was nine o'clock, which made it safe to ring Rhys. Like many artists, he liked to work into the wee hours and sleep until noon, but on days when he had something big happening—like transferring custody of the treasure chest to Hack—he might wake as early as nine o'clock. She'd found that if she waited until nine to ring him, he might actually answer and speak to her, as opposed to letting it go to voicemail—or barking out something incoherent before hanging up.

"Jemmie!" he said jovially, picking up on the first ring.

"Good God. Who's this? I want Rhys Tremayne."

"Ha ha. Can't a man be in a good mood?"

"What?" she asked suspiciously. "Do you think Hack will decide to let you keep the jewelry or something?"

"Oh, Hack's been and gone. He's very keen on this investigation. It's the first potential major crime he's had all to himself. DS Conrad can snap up all the murders and attempted murders, but potential grand larceny is all Hack's. And *of course* he isn't letting me keep the jewelry. He said there's a process for unclaimed valuables found in public places, and it takes about forty days, blah blah blah. Those rules only apply to lost valuables, not stolen goods."

"Stolen. So they're real?"

"The real deal. Estimated total value, one and a half million pounds."

"Where did they come from?" Jem asked eagerly. "Was it a smash-and-grab? Or maybe an inside job?"

"Bang. That's what Hack thinks. How'd you guess?"

"Something about the little bags. I'm amazed you got an answer so fast. I expected Hack to come by and collect them, then send them to a lab for analysis and tell us it would take four to six weeks, like everything else in the world. How did he know they were genuine?"

"He brought along an expert to look them over," Rhys said, still sounding unusually jubilant for—in his mind—the crack of dawn. "Quite the surprise for me."

"Well, yeah. On a Sunday morning, no less. Hack must be super-keen to solve this one all on his own. I wonder..." She stopped suddenly. Rhys said nothing, but she could feel his excitement transmitting through the mobile. Inside her, the invisible energy triggered an answering thrill.

"The expert was your AA bloke, wasn't it? The retired jewel thief?"

"Yes. Terry O'Dell. Apparently his criminal past is an open

secret, at least among law enforcement types. He consults on cases of theft. You should've seen him, all kitted out in a suit and tie."

"I suppose if you fancy yourself the last of the gentleman jewel thieves, you want to look the part."

"True. He had a little case of tools with him, and a pair of loupes, and even some kind of special phone app. After he verified that the jewelry was real, he compared the bigger gems to their certification papers." He chuckled. "Did you know diamonds have papers? With, like, identifying marks and whatnot?"

"Yes, I used to wear an engagement ring," Jem said, trying not to laugh at him. "I thought you proposed to Lissa, once upon a time. Didn't you get dragged through the four Cs tango?"

"I proposed. I didn't buy her a ruddy diamond. She would've counted herself lucky to get a Ring Pop."

"Shocking that she turned you down. What about Hack? Did he let anything slip about unsolved jewel thefts? Maybe around London?" she added hopefully, thinking of the John R. Derry letters.

"No, I badgered him a bit, but he was the proper close-mouthed copper. Thanked me for turning in the find and said he'd write me up for a commendation. To prove I'm a good citizen, in case I'm ever a big deal in the art world and someone digs up my temporary moral lapse," he said, meaning the time he'd found a roll of drug money lying on the beach and attempted to deposit it into his bank account.

It had been a stupid thing for Rhys to do, if you viewed it purely in black and white, but Jem understood the temptation. He'd been fighting to make ends meet for years. It was common enough in the Scillies, apart from a few wealthy residents on Tresco. And apparently this ex-thief Terry O'Dell belonged to the latter rarified group.

"So I guess we know a little more than we did before." She sighed.

"Don't give up just yet," Rhys said, still upbeat. "Terry left with Hack because that was what Hack expected. But the minute he was back on Tresco, he rang me and suggested we meet around noon for lunch."

"Oh. Well. Okay." Jem wasn't very certain what more an ex-jewel thief could offer—he'd already verified the gems as legit—but it wasn't necessarily a total waste of time. If she hadn't already had Roger Pinnock, Kit Verran, and Marv Bennett on her plate, she would've been willing to risk the price of lunch to find out.

"You sound unconvinced. But I'm not," Rhys said. "Terry sounded pretty pleased with himself. He said ordinarily he'd keep his nose out, but as my girlfriend's the Scilly Sleuth, she might appreciate the expert opinions of an old pro. In other words—he's dying to meet you and dazzle you with his special expertise."

"Is he?" Hearing herself emit a faint, self-satisfied chuckle, Jem cringed. When she'd accidentally started her amateur detecting, the response had been mostly discouraging, if not downright insulting. Maybe now the tide was beginning to turn.

"Where are you meeting?"

"The Garden Café," he said triumphantly.

"Oh! That's a bit spendy, don't you think? You'll have to pay fifteen quid just to enter the Abbey Gardens. And who knows what the menu's like."

"I get in free as Terry's guest. He's a subscriber or something. Goes there every day to visit the figureheads."

Jem made an envious sound. As a child, she'd visited the Abbey Gardens with her school group and found the Valhalla Museum perfectly magical. It was an open-air display of figureheads, mostly from the nineteenth century, that had been recovered from shipwrecks around the islands. Some were romantic female images; others were sword-wielding soldiers, fish, or birds of prey. Walking among them was like peering back into the age of wooden sailing ships, when not even the Admiralty could abolish figureheads, since common sailors believed a ship without one unlucky.

"If I haven't made it obvious, you're invited," Rhys said.

"I know, but I'm afraid I really can't. Kenzie came by first thing—"

"To apologize and thank you two for the party?" he broke in.

"Better. To mention someone she saw visiting Arthur at his cottage. Roger Pinnock."

"Crikey. I like that little wally. Hope he isn't a murderer."

"Me, too. But he's keen on sewing and he's been seen at the cottage, so it's a good lead. Don't forget that if we don't kick up some possibilities too strong for Conrad to ignore, he'll zero in on Clarence that much harder."

"True. But I'll bet Clarence and Roger—and that Marazion bloke, what's his face, Uriah—aren't the only men Arthur had on a string."

"There might be another one," Jem agreed. "Kenzie has the notion Kit Verran might have been making unscheduled trips to Bryher. Also worth a look." She decided not to mention Marv and his probable rendezvous with Kenzie on Neptune Cove. Rhys was in too good a mood to hear about his kid sister meeting up with a much older boy on a secluded beach. At least not until Pauley could winkle out the truth and decide if it was an emergency or just more of Kenzie's often unreliable narration.

Hope she got it right about Roger and Kit, Jem thought with sudden stab of unease. *Otherwise, I'm about to go and make a fool of myself. Again.*

When Jem disconnected from Rhys, she found Pauley standing behind her, recipe card in hand.

"Here you are," she said proudly, passing it over.

She was relieved to find it inscribed not with ingredients, temperatures, or techniques, but with all the salient facts about Arthur Ajax that Pauley had pulled from her journals. Reading it over twice, Jem absorbed the details, trying to decide what might be relevant to his true identity, or why he'd been killed.

"Arrived on the second of April. First time you ran into him in the Square, thirtieth of April. Thereafter, you saw him every two weeks, more or less, either shopping at the Co-op or having lunch in the Duke's Head," Jem said. "First saw him on the Sunseeker in June, then again in August. Both times near St. Mary's Harbor," she added, meaning the harbor that served Hugh Town. "Both times he waved, said his friend was below, then walked round the deck out of sight. To me, it doesn't sound like Arthur secretly owned a yacht. Just that he knew a man with one. Maybe Uriah."

"Or if not him, then another man, and another yet-to-be-determined journal entry." Pauley sighed. "But I really liked the idea of discovering Arthur lived on a yacht part-time. And I still say no human man could possibly live in a house that tidy—no books or newspapers lying about, no heaps of dirty clothes, no Blu-rays or junk mail."

"Perhaps that's why SETI was listening in. You and Clarence fancied the man who fell to earth."

Pauley openly scoffed. "This from you? Ms. Stargazer? Ms. There-Must-Be-Intelligent-Life-Somewhere-In-All-Those-Billions-of-Solar-Systems?"

"Just because I believe there's alien life somewhere out there doesn't mean I think it's here in England. I mean, if it is, it's in the government, clearly. But probably not. I expect we seem quite barbarous to any advanced species. With our pointless wars and starving children and whatnot."

"Be honest. Those flying Tic Tacs. That high strangeness at Rendlesham Forest. You're a believer."

"Fine. Do aliens exist? Statistically, they must. Do they

dwell among us? I'll get right on it. But first I want to know who killed Arthur Ajax. And if his real name was John R. Derry."

"As to that," Pauley said, gesturing toward the kitchen table, upon which sat her open laptop. "While you were chatting with Rhys, I did some garden variety googling. Come see what I got."

13

FRAUDSTERS, PSYCHICS, AND "JEN VIRAGO"

When Jem sat down in front of the computer, she was impressed with what Pauley had been able to discover. Deep searches for information often required guidance from a trained librarian to search specialized databases, home in on relevant journal articles, and chase down primary sources. But Google was perfectly fine when your subject was an international fraud. And John R. Derry was part of an international fraud ring who'd snagged the attention of CNN.com, the *Daily Mail* Online, and of course, *Bright Star*, who outshone everyone when it came to raking through muck and displaying the filth for all to see.

"Four hundred thousand results," Jem murmured, focusing on the first open tab: a CNN.com article headlined,

> TWO CHARGED IN $200 MILLION 'ANNUNAKI' ALIEN MAIL FRAUD CASE.

Dated March of that year, the article read:

Two men pleaded guilty today in a sprawling scheme to defraud British, American, and Canadian consumers. An intricate sting operation spearheaded by OLAF, the European Anti-Fraud Office, and bolstered by Scotland Yard and the FBI, spent six months collecting evidence on the fraudulent business practices of Live and Be Your Best direct marketing company. Government filings reveal that this business, based in the British Virgin Islands, used letters written by alleged psychic and self-proclaimed "Annunaki" John R. Derry to prey on the unsuspecting, including pensioners and disabled persons that investigators describe as "intellectually or emotionally vulnerable."

In the scheme, Live and Be Your Best promoted John R. Derry as a human-alien hybrid with special psychic powers. Targets were urged to write to him for free advice about love, health, and money problems. The company responded to these requests with bland predictions, analogous to a daily horoscope, and then hit the target with a barrage of "special offers." These included fraudulent "distance healing," phony romantic pen pals who turned out to be paid employees, and bogus investments run by Live and Be Your Best's subsidiaries.

American citizen Philip Church and Canadian citizen Simon Gauthier were top-level managers at Live and Be Your Best. Although Church and Gauthier claimed to have been bribed and coerced into their criminal acts, essentially doing the bidding of a mastermind, they have been charged with raking in over 200 million pounds from close to 2 million victims. Mr. Church, 41, admitted to writing the original letters, then creating templates so that subordinates could personalize new letters for future dupes. Mr. Gauthier, 39, admitted to handling the operation's finances, including the creation of fraudulent cryptocurrency tokens he dubbed Aliencoin...

Intrigued by the mention of a mastermind, Jem skimmed the middle of the article, which was mostly sad capsule stories of the people who'd lost everything to the scheme. The article was vague about pending arrests, or even if the investigation was still ongoing, which made Jem assume it was. Reading between the lines, it seemed that the person who'd orchestrated the fraud and profited the most had got away scot-free.

> It remains unclear if John R. Derry, a small-time "psychic advisor" who briefly ran a metaphysical shop in Putney, will face any charges in conjunction with the international scam. Through his lawyer, he issued a statement insisting that while he leant his name and face to the operation, he merely licensed his brand, and cannot be held responsible for the impact of services that Live and Be Your Best provided or purported to provide.
>
> Mr. Derry's popularity in the tabloids and on daytime chat shows, however, was not inconsiderable in this period. He gave interviews to tabloid reporters, usually around holidays like New Year's and Valentine's Day, and dispensed general advice about love and money to chat show audiences. Nevertheless, Mr. Derry claims through his counsel that he is not under indictment and does not expect to be, writing in an open letter to the *Telegraph*, "I never penned a single fraudulent letter, nor did I receive any proceeds from this illegal and unethical operation. In fact, I consider myself one of the scheme's many victims."
>
> The operation's alleged mastermind, Derrick Christensen, now appears on the UK's Most Wanted list. Born to an American diplomat, he appears to have overstayed his visa in the United Kingdom for more than two decades. Christensen, who has a variety of aliases, will, if caught, face 15 counts of mail fraud in the UK. Additional charges of wire fraud, conspiracy to commit mail fraud, and money

laundering in the United States and Canada have also been filed.

"Derrick Christensen," Jem said. "That could be Arthur's real name. If he fled to the Scillies to escape the feds, that would explain how vague he was about his past." Something occurred to her. "Hang on. Shouldn't we do a quick social media stalk? See if he's on Instagram or Tinder?"

"I think you mean Grindr," Pauley corrected with a laugh. "And no, I haven't checked there, but that's about the only site I left out. Do you really think I fancied Arthur all those months without a deep dive online to try and fill in the blanks? He wasn't on Facebook, Twitter, or anywhere else. When I googled him, I got nothing. So I screwed up my courage and asked him. He said he was philosophically opposed due to privacy reasons."

"I reckon so, if he was on the run. Derrick Christensen," she said again, trying it out. "It's a far cry from 'Arthur Ajax.' I think if I had an alias, I'd probably pick something related. Jen for sure. Jen Virago?"

"Perfect," Pauley said with a grin. "But before you get too attached to the notion, click on tab number two."

Doing so, Jem found herself looking at a rogue's gallery of mugshots and police Identi-Kit composites. Most of the pictures were overwhelmingly male and almost uniformly terrifying. Apparently, you didn't get to appear on the UK's Most Wanted list unless you brought a cruel mouth, dead eyes, and a palpable aura of violence.

Except, it seemed, for Derrick Christensen. Jem had expected a mugshot or photograph, but it seemed that while overstaying his visa for twenty years, Derrick had become adept at invisibility. There was only an Identi-Kit drawing of him, and it could've been labeled "Generic Middle-Aged White Man." There were two eyes, a nose, and a mouth, as well as some light-brown curly hair, but none of them combined in any memorable way. The cheeks seemed a bit rounder than Arthur's, and the forehead a bit higher. It absolutely wasn't a positive identification, but neither did it rule him out.

"Huh." Biting her lower lip, Jem studied the image. "My gut says it isn't Arthur."

"Same. I don't know why. He could've dropped a stone and dyed his hair blond. And the other details fit—his money, that cache of letters, how secretive he was."

"But let's unpack that a bit. The letter scheme was obviously a huge deal. I know chartered planes and designer luggage is ultra-posh by our lights. But Arthur—I'm still calling him Arthur until I know for sure—must have been rolling in it. When the authorities pounced, he could've fled anywhere. Why come here?"

Pauley made an offended noise. "I'm sorry, did you just ask why a fugitive from justice would flee here—a sleepy seaside paradise—where no one would think to look for him?" she demanded, climbing upon her honor as a proud Scillonian.

"Come on, Pauls, be real. Derrick is facing life in prison. Wouldn't he go far away? Preferably some place with no extradition treaty with the UK?"

"Criminals always think they're smarter than everyone else. Maybe he wanted to hide in plain sight, sit back and laugh at the police."

"Fair enough," Jem said, thinking of some of the killers she'd helped catch, most of whom had been wildly deluded about their intellectual prowess. "But why rent a wee cottage on Bryher when he could've lived it up on Tresco?"

"Bryher is ideal for privacy," Pauley countered. "And if I were him, I'd be more worried about the people he left hanging out to dry. All the police will do is arrest him and try him. His co-conspirators want him dead, I shouldn't wonder. Which brings us back to Arthur."

"Yeah." Jem turned it over in her mind. "But do hits like that get administered with a loaf of pumpernickel?"

"Maybe. Especially if the killer wanted to be clever. Make it seem like the opposite of a professional hit."

Jem pinched the bridge of her nose. It was only ten o'clock, and she already felt like she was losing herself in a hall of mirrors. Every possibility seemed to throw back a confirmation *and* a denial.

"Right. Moving on for now," she said, refocusing on the articles Pauley had found by clicking on the third open tab. This story, dated 2 January of that year, was on *Bright Star*'s webpage. The headline read,

> "ANNUNAKI" JOHN R. DERRY CLAIMS HE CAN PREDICT YOUR FUTURE IN THE COMING YEAR.

Eagerly, Jem studied the photos, but they were even more of a letdown than the UK's Most Wanted. The story included three photos of John R. Derry at different ages, and in none of them did he resemble Arthur Ajax. The most recent showed a smiling man with a dark mustache and salt-and-pepper hair sitting at a bistro table outdoors. He didn't even look like Jem's idea of a fraudster, much less an alien psychic. She thought he resembled somebody's favorite history professor.

"So what exactly is an Annunaki, when it's at home?" Pauley asked. "And you needn't pretend you don't know. Clarence isn't the only one who tunes in to *Ancient Aliens*. You had it on last week."

"Only for laughs," Jem protested. "In history, the Annunaki were just another pantheon of ancient gods. Sumerian, in this case. Pretty much forgotten by the modern world. But then a bloke from Switzerland wrote *Chariots of the Gods?* and theorized that the Sumerians weren't fantasizing about gods, they were describing actual beings. Alien overlords, in his view.

According to his book, the Annunaki married human women, and after the pure-bloods flew off, they left their hybrid children behind to rule."

"Oh, yes, you absolutely watch only for laughs," Pauley said. "That's how you reeled that off without missing a beat. Stargazer."

"Shut it." Jem returned to the article.

> A psychic whose space alien heritage grants him special powers has predicted the big events coming this year. John R. Derry, 52, was born on Earth to a human mum and mysterious alien dad.
>
> "My dad was only passing through, but when he saw my pretty mum, he fell hard," says John, who grew up in Milton Keynes but now lives outside London in Putney. "It was meant to be strictly hush-hush, but by the time I was seven, I could look at a person and have a viewing of their future. Mum told me Dad was one of the Annunaki. They have been coming to Earth since the dawn of man. They helped build the Great Pyramids in Egypt. And by calling on their power, I can answer your questions about love, money, and work..."

"I can't read any more of this nonsense," Jem announced, closing the tabs and standing up. "Let's go to St. Mary's. Kit Verran lives there, and so do Roger and Marv. Before my head hits the pillow tonight, I either want one of them as my prime suspect, or a brand-new lead."

14

COLD DEAD EYES

It was a lovely day to be out on *Bellatrix*. The sun dazzled on the waves as a brisk northwesterly wind ruffled the sea. Overhead, gulls glided and cried, while out toward the horizon Jem spied a dorsal fin. As she watched, the dolphin leapt in a silver flash, then vanished back into the deep.

She'd officially packed away her sundresses for the rest of the year. Now when she went out on the boat, it was always in jeans or chinos, and always with a mac. Pauley, being gothic by nature and frou-frou by choice, didn't own jeans, even black ones, and didn't like macs. As the temperature dropped, she shifted to longer, thicker skirts, long-sleeved blouses. Today, for added warmth, she'd put on a black velvet coat with military flourishes on the cuffs and shoulders. Her vibrant magenta hair was in pigtails, and the twin black ribbons made her look especially fetching, at least in Jem's opinion.

I'm glad that losing her fantasy about Arthur Ajax didn't crush her spirits. Maybe in the course of that day's sleuthing, they'd run into an eligible man. Preferably one who was single, attractive, not exclusively into men, not a thief, not a liar, and actively seeking a thirtysomething girlfriend for fun and romance.

When I think of it like that, it makes catching a killer seem like the easier proposition, Jem thought. *I need to make her spend a week with me in Penzance. At least there, the numbers are more in her favor.*

Kit Verran had rented a house overlooking Carn Morval Point. To look at St. Mary's on a map, a visiting skipper might head for Rat Island and the Quay, which seemed like the most obvious place to tie up and come ashore. But even in the off-season, no one got a space there without express permission from the harbor master, and Jem knew better than to even ask. The *Scillonian III* was still running—and would be until November—and every local who owned a boat was out enjoying the good weather. Therefore, Jem headed for Porth Cressa. It was a sure thing, it wasn't too hard to get to shore—even for a woman in voluminous pseudo-Victorian skirts—and once they were on terra firma, it was only a five-minute walk to Kit's home.

"Digs to die for," Pauley said. As they traveled the old beaten path, a breaker crashed beside the eighteenth-century stone house, throwing up rainbow arcs of sea spray. "Don't tell anyone, but I've always had an illicit passion for Bond House. Usually only the best sort of holidaymakers stays there. Can't think how Kit got in."

"When did he come?" Jem asked, looking over the house, which oozed colonial respectability. Ten white windows faced the sea; five dormer windows peeked out from the roof.

"In the spring. Right before you did, I think. Bought the ferry business off Mr. Fry, renovated both boats, launched an app, and revitalized the whole thing," Pauley said. "Thank goodness. Mr. Fry was getting positively dotty, taking fares to the wrong port and forgetting to run his route sometimes. Bart thought he was in the catbird's seat—that we were so used to anything goes, he could lurch in with a lick and promise and do quite well."

"Is it weird that we keep using Bart?" Jem asked.

"He comes when we whistle." Pauley shrugged. "And heaven knows he needs us. But Kit's trade is humming. In the beginning, he worked seven days a week, but now he has a small staff and takes Sundays off. Would you look at that? Picturesque." She sighed, indicating a stone fence so old, it seemed mortared by moss. "I wonder if I could disguise the grittier sections of Lyonesse House's fence with heaps of greenery. Vines don't take long to proliferate, and I think there's a sort of sauce you can daub on stones to make algae grow. This is the look I should strive for."

Jem agreed, though she declined to say so. Her role, as she saw it, was to be a cheerful supporter of Pauley's renovation dreams, not another critic. But it was true that Bond House had aged gracefully while Lyonesse House, at least from some angles, looked like a neglected wreck.

"Should we go around back to knock?" she asked. Among islanders, it was considered friendlier to call at the rear like a neighbor, instead of at the front door, like a satellite TV flogger.

"Look, there's Kit," Pauley said, pointing toward the private garden.

"Where?"

"In the battery."

Stepping off the path, she led Jem up the hill toward a line of five eighteenth-century iron cannons in a miniature park. The exhibit was well maintained, the cannons spaced a few feet apart on a bed of gravel and roped off with a low chain. A pile of cannonballs and a plaque fronted it, surrounded by what appeared to be freshly potted evergreens. As they drew closer, Jem spied Kit Verran sitting on a gardener's bench, pruning a yellow shrub.

"Hiya, Kit," Pauley called. "How's the witch hazel?"

"Oh, you know. Queen of winter, some say," he called back, rising. Stripping off his gloves and leaving the tool behind, he smiled as he approached them. "Just got done sorting my Christmas Box," he added, indicating the potted evergreens. "That's my favorite, if I'm being honest."

I know him, Jem thought, realizing she'd seen him around the Scillies many times. Always as a face in the crowd—drinking a pint at the Kernow Arms or getting an ice cream in the Square. Plain-faced but pleasant-looking, with a shaved head and a smattering of faded freckles across his cheeks, he wasn't the sort who caught her fancy. Nor was there anything about him to latch onto with particular distaste. Of medium height and build, the only thing that hinted of his success—apart from living at Bond House, of course—was his upscale island wear. Most people Jem knew gardened in grubbies, but Kit wore a polo shirt with a designer logo, pressed trousers, and what looked like *very* spendy trainers.

Oh, Bart, he's obviously crushing you. For some reason the idea made her a bit sad, for all the big man's slapdash ways.

"How's the kitchen reno?" he asked Pauley.

"All done."

"Now then, Jem Jago. How's the sleuthing trade?" he asked her, smiling. "*Bright Star* owes you a follow-up of a more, shall we say, appreciative nature."

"I wish I could say we were murder-free around these parts," Jem said.

He regarded her with polite interest for a beat, and then his eyes widened. "Hang on. Did someone die?"

"Yesterday," Pauley said. "Did you get an alert?"

"Never carry a mobile on Sundays," Kit replied. "Now—who died this time?"

"An emmet on Bryher called Arthur Ajax," Jem said, watching his face for even a flicker of reaction. What she got was something more of a blaze—eyes widening, mouth falling slack, nostrils flaring.

"You can't mean it."

"Yeah. Knocked me for six, I can tell you," Pauley said gently, as if trying to gauge his need for sympathy. "I tried to keep a lid on it, but I was mad for him. Guess I was the last one to realize he didn't date women."

"No, he didn't. He dated men," Kit breathed, sounding slightly dazed. "Men in plural. The extreme plural. All the men he could manage and all at the same time, the right bastard. I expect one of them cottoned on to his tomcat ways. Stabbed him in the heart."

"Well, actually—" Pauley began. Jem silenced her with a sharp glance.

"What?" Kit regarded them in turn. "Oh, it's like that, is it? Jem Jago puts on her deerstalker cap and pops over to see if I did the deed?"

"Something like that," she said lightly.

"And that's your intern?"

"Unpaid intern," Pauley said.

"Unpaid sleuth, sticking her nose in for the public good," Jem said. "I don't suppose we could go inside? I've never set foot in Bond House."

"I have, but it was years ago," Pauley said.

"By all means. Never been a murder suspect before. Why am I meant to have killed Arthur? Because he didn't know the meaning of fidelity?"

"Actually, we're just looking for background," Jem said as she and Pauley followed Kit toward the back door, which was bright red. "Pauley and I found the body during a birthday party, if you can believe it. We went to Neptune Cottage looking for help with a cake, and there he was, dead on the floor." She shot Pauley another look. Rolling her eyes, Pauley responded by miming zipped lips.

"And you're quite sure it was murder?" Kit asked, opening the door onto the great room. Far across the way, Jem saw the front door they'd bypassed; apparently some walls had been knocked down to create one magnificent living space.

"I love it," Pauley cried. In the center of the room, she spun about, taking it in with obvious delight. "Jem, you should've seen the original floor plan. Poky front room, little study, and a formal dining room that was like a prison cell. *This* is a revelation."

"You can see why we get on," Kit told Jem. "Girl speaks my language."

"Is this leather?" Pauley asked, feeling the deep brown sofa as a buyer might stroke a horse.

"Vegan leather."

"I suppose it's a furnished let?"

He laughed. "It was meant to be, but I couldn't bear it, so the owners and I reached an agreement. I signed a year's lease on very favorable terms with the stipulation that I could redecorate. I made sketches and submitted swathes and chips, of course. They'd already knocked down the walls but were exhausted by the prospect of really turning Bond House into a showplace. So I did it for them."

"And you did it brilliantly," Jem said, though in truth she wasn't as over-the-moon as her friend. She liked the wood floors, polished to a warm glow, and the small dining set in the corner —either William and Mary or Queen Anne, she could never quite recall which was which. But the sheer volume of seafarer curios was hard to take, even for her. Colored glass bottles, salvaged buoys, antique life rings mounted on the wall, a ship's wheel repurposed as a chandelier. The pièce de résistance—or the fatal overreach, depending on your point of view—was a replica shark suspended from the ceiling.

Following their dual gaze, Kit asked, "Love it or hate it?"

"It ties the theme together," Pauley said politely.

"Definitely something you don't see every day," Jem said.

He let out a burst of good-natured laughter. "It's vintage marine taxidermy. Such a trophy! Look at those dead glass eyes. Makes me want to sail to the Algarve and acquire a few more. But never mind all that. Come see the kitchen. I'll show you a trophy I earned rather than bought. Then I'll put the kettle on, and you can interrogate me to your heart's content."

Kit's kitchen, fairly expansive by old house standards, charmed Jem more than the great room, though she would never have chosen such a kitchen for herself. At her Penzance apartment, the cupboards hid a multitude of sins. Kit's pots and crockery were displayed in wooden racks, every piece on display, and he had no pantry, only baker's shelves. At a glance, she could tell that he liked Steel-cut oats, whole-wheat flour, currants, dried pasta, and long grain rice. She didn't want just anyone privy to her pantry, which usually included Pringles, nacho cheese dip, and Jaffa Cakes.

As she took in the room, a bright spot in the wallpaper leapt out, despite the tall shelves in front of it. Without dragging them out of the way, it was impossible to see the complete outline, but Jem thought she understood what she saw. The wallpaper, which was anywhere from fifty to a hundred years old, judging by the antiquated rose pattern, had faded to almost white after years of sun exposure through the east-facing window. But recently something large had been removed from the wall, leaving a field of unfaded red roses.

"There was another mounted fish on that wall, wasn't there?" Pauley asked, clearly noting the same contrast. "A swordfish, wasn't it?"

"Right. When I took it down, it left a sort of reverse-hole, though I've done my best to hide it. Really must get those paper hangers in," Kit said apologetically, gesturing for them to sit.

"Did you bin the fish?" Pauley asked as he filled the kettle.

"Nothing so permanent. Just relocated it. That," he said,

pointing at a small, framed certificate hung beside the wall calendar, "is a trophy I snagged by merit. The free monthly paper known as *Cornwall Etc.*, a journalistic endeavor almost as dead reliable as *Bright Star*, recently named Kit Verran's Ferry Service the best new business in the islands category. I think the three people who run that paper"—he grinned—"were a bit shocked when I rang them up and requested a printed certificate. Usually, honorees are content just to be named. But life isn't just about visibility on almighty Google. It's about milestones you can look at or hold in your hand."

With the kettle heating on the cooker, he began gathering tea things, asking in a nonchalant tone, "If you don't mind my asking, and I don't care a fig, just so you understand, how did you know about me and Arthur?"

Jem spoke up quickly to head Pauley off. In the future, they'd need to make a game plan before diving head first into an interview. Being upfront risked offending Kit—he might not be pleased to hear that a teenager had (1) declared him gay and (2) ascertained through trespassing and low-key spying that he'd demonstrated a curious interest in Neptune Cove. So instead, she replied, "We heard it through the grapevine. Didn't want to speculate if it was true, or any of the details."

"But you'd like to, wouldn't you? Fair play. Here's the story of your old mate Kit and dreamy Arthur Ajax. He was a bint. I couldn't bear his ego or his sleeping around, so I told him to stuff it. The end."

"I don't want to name any names," Pauley said, sounding determined to get her share of the interview, "but we know another man who was seeing Arthur. He said it was a no-strings relationship. Discreet to the point of total secrecy."

Kit made a contemptuous noise. "Arthur didn't want a relationship. He wanted something new every day of the week. But he tailored the approach to the man. With me, he pretended to want a stable relationship. I found out later that with others, he had a line about ethical non-monogamy. He used that on the men he didn't want to be seen with, for one reason or another."

Now Pauley made a noise, more of fury than contempt.

"Ah, sorry, love. The man in question is a friend of yours, is he? Do him a favor and don't repeat what I said. Arthur was a victim of his own looks. Gorgeous blokes are always cruel. Diva behavior is a given." Placing an empty mug in front of Jem, he added, "Don't think I'm a stalker, but I've seen your beauty king boyfriend around Hugh Town. Rhys Tremayne." He half-sang the name, as if it were too special to merely speak. "Tell me the truth. He's a handful, isn't he?"

Startled, Jem found herself staring at Kit in amazement. "No. I mean—not like that. He's not a diva." She looked at Pauley. "I mean—he's not when my back is turned, is he?"

Pauley snorted. "He's an idiot sometimes, but he's a hundred percent true and good."

Kit set an empty mug in front of her. "I heard he punched a bloke in the face last year."

"He's getting better about things like that," Pauley said loyally.

"I'm sure," Kit replied in a tone that suggested he didn't believe her but was too polite to push the topic. "Anyway, Arthur and I broke up—oh, I don't know. Three weeks ago. Maybe four. I heard he was stringing along that little pillock man and decided enough was enough."

"Pillock?" Jem repeated. "You mean Roger Pinnock?"

"The very one." Opening a strange-looking packet in front of them, he plucked out something that looked like a miniature brown cake of soap. "These little jewels are better than brownies. Nothing but dates, seeds, and a hint of cocoa. Try one."

Pretending not to hear, Jem said, "Was Roger on the pretend stable relationship train, or the discreet non-monogamy train?"

"Oh, it was supposed to be a deep, dark secret," Kit said,

nibbling on his faux brownie. "Except little Roger was in love, God help him. He 'accidentally' spread the news about him and Arthur all over the islands. I heard about it down the pub. In the theater. On the ferry. I half expected to see it on telly. When I confronted Arthur—"

The kettle whistled. Breaking off to fetch it, Kit filled the teapot and carried it to the table. Then he sat down between them, still taking bird-like nibbles of the date/seed/hint of cocoa bar. Jem suspected he was the sort who ate purely to live and found people who took sensual pleasure in food completely mystifying.

"Anyway," he continued, "when I confronted Arthur, he lied, of course. Swore I was mad, and Roger was in fantasyland. Then there was a knock—oh, I forgot to say, we were at his cottage at Neptune Cove. In the middle of the row, a knock on the door. Arthur didn't want to answer, of course, so I marched over and threw it open. There he was on the doorstep, burning with rage, and cold dead eyes, just like my stuffed shark."

"Roger?" Jem and Pauley said at the same time and in the same incredulous tone. They knew Roger Pinnock. While it was easy to imagine the earnest little man overcome with emotion, whispering about his clandestine romance to anyone who would listen, it was impossible to imagine him as Kit described.

"What? No, not him. Uriah. A big, bearded monster from Marazion. Arthur had broken his heart, and he wanted a bit of his own back."

15

"THERE'S NO TWELVE-STEP PROGRAM FOR THIEVING"

For his meeting with ex-cat burglar Terry O'Dell, Rhys piloted one of his no-frills, hard-used runabouts to Tresco. In daylight he was as good a boatman as any, though unusually scrupulous about checking the weather and water conditions before going out. His younger brother had drowned in a boating accident; he knew better than most that the sea could be as deadly as a wildfire, appearances to the contrary.

It was a perfect day on the water. On the big yachts, some of the emmets wore coats, but Rhys stuck to his post-summer uniform: T-shirt, windcheater, and shorts. It was the windcheater that made it post summer. Many people treated winter in the Isles of Scilly like a Yorkshire January, but for him, it never got cold enough to necessitate long trousers. If he wore them, it was usually to satisfy a dress code.

Of course, there was no dress code at the Garden Café, a place that catered to Abbey Garden guests in need of nibbles and a sit-down. But his host, Terry, had made it clear he expected Rhys to turn up in a jacket and tie. That was why his one and only suit rode behind him in the runabout, zipped into one of his late mum's old dress bags. His good shoes—a pair of black Steve Madden Oxfords—also rode with him, lovingly cradled in the very box and tissue they'd come in. Rhys didn't part with things easily. Not shoeboxes; not tissue paper.

But I cleared out all that junk from the living room. Really thought Jem would be more excited to see that, he thought as Candlewick Castle, a Civil War-era pile constructed from the pulled-down stones of King Charles's Castle, came into view. *Maybe she thought I wanted to keep Buck's training ground up year-round?*

That seemed hard to believe. Surely she realized he wouldn't expect her to tolerate a doggy obstacle course for a living room for more than, say, six months out of the year. Depending on how Buck performed in the showings.

I don't know why I'm so sure I can get her moved in when I can't even get her overnight.

The fact was beginning to feel frustrating, no matter how he tried to apply well-worn slogans like "one day at a time," "easy does it," and "progress not perfection." He knew she would deliberately and determinedly risk life and limb to catch a killer. He'd seen her do it three times now, and fully expected her to do it again if the stars lined up. He also knew that she guarded her most secret self, the part he'd known when they were kids—the part she let him see now only by accident—with a ferocity it would take time to overcome. For those who didn't understand their history, it probably looked like a contradiction. But Rhys wasn't confused. Just increasingly... edgy.

On the foreshore he disembarked, wading through ankle-deep rollers and pulling the runabout behind him. When visiting Tresco, he preferred to alight near the castle for many reasons: it cost nothing, it was often deserted, and he could leave the runabout on the beach without worrying about it being stolen. There was always the possibility of boat-nicking scamps—like Jem herself had once been—but Rhys had a solution for that. Before walking away, he detached the outboard's small battery, dropping it into his backpack. Then he started up the beach with backpack in place, the bagged suit over his shoulder, and the shoebox under his arm.

If the reservations hadn't got mucked up again, Jem and I would be having brunch in Penzance right now, he thought. Wallowing in that image touched off a flood of captivating possibilities. Some of them were leftover teen dreams. Others were decidedly adult. Twenty years was too much to expect from any man.

Instead of whinging to myself, I ought to count myself lucky she moved away before we sealed the deal, he thought. *Back in the day, I was just your typical brain-dead adolescent. I might have ruined everything. I wouldn't have known what to do with her.*

A great many facets of life confused or mystified him, but there was one thing he knew for sure. The man he was today knew exactly what to do with Jem Jago. The only question was, did he accept their spot on the Egyptian House's waiting list—apparently there would be another opening in six weeks—or did he make a play to speed things along?

Along the island footpath leading to the Abbey Gardens, he stopped at a men's facility to drink from the water fountain and do a quick-change in a toilet stall. Hit of Lynx body spray—Ice Chill—shirt, trousers, shaking out a crease in one leg, necktie, jacket. Last, he traded his sandals for Oxfords, stuffing in his sockless feet with a grunt. His feet liked to be free—shoes as rarely as possible, and socks, never. But there was no point in dressing up unless he went all the way.

All that accomplished, he breezed out of the stall with only a sidelong glance at the mirror. His hair could've used a trim, but there was nothing for it. He'd get it touched up before he made his move on Jem. And he *was* making that move, sooner rather than later. Somewhere between the footpath and the stall, he'd decided one of them had to take the big risk. It might as well be him.

Per Terry's instructions, Rhys mentioned the ex-burglar's name at the ticket office and was let in. He didn't fancy carrying box, bag, or backpack to the lunch, so he stowed them in a rented locker before heading deeper into the gardens.

The sheer lushness of the subtropical foliage never ceased to amaze him. The gravel path wasn't especially narrow, but it seemed so because so many broad green fronds encroached on all sides. Off the main beat, little branches diverted into cul-de-sacs and stone tunnels. He passed a cairn topped with an antique ship's wheel, lots of palms and ferns, and a mossy stone arch pointing at the sky. Echeverias grew through the old abbey walls, which crumbled so picturesquely that Rhys lost himself for a moment and stood, staring. He could paint that stretch of wall, with succulents pouring through a gap and a magnolia branch draped over the side...

The heat through his suit jacket pierced the moment. He really would've been more comfortable in his usual clothes. Shaking himself, he moved on. Overhead, the sound of a helicopter grew louder, prompting him to shield his eyes and watch the sleek white craft fly over. Tresco's private heliport offered island tours. He'd never been on one, nor did he expect to afford one anytime soon, but he'd seen aerial snaps of the Abbey Gardens, and they were spectacular. He couldn't blame a well set-up ex-con like Terry for spending his money, however he obtained it, on paradise.

A path with massive pink King Protea flowers on either side led him to a more structured area. Once he found himself on a neat brick walkway surrounded by squared-off hedges, he knew the café was close. Sure enough, on a bench out front sat Terry O'Dell—eighty years old, thirty years sober, and as a dapper as an MP in his pinstriped suit.

"Don't you clean up nice, lad," he said, rising. "Feels good to dress like a productive member of society, doesn't it?"

Before Rhys could answer truthfully—it didn't—Terry seized his hand and shook it, pulling him close for a quiet word in one ear.

"And looking respectable opens all the doors, mark my words," he whispered. Clapping Rhys on the back, he gestured toward the restaurant as if he owned it, saying grandly, "C'mon, let's get you sat down with a pasty and fizzy drink. Or would you rather a slice of cake?"

Feeling like a preteen in the company of an indulgent uncle, Rhys followed his host obediently, choosing a beef pasty and a cola while Terry ordered a pot of tea. At an out-of-the-way table, Terry poured himself a cup and stirred in some sugar.

"Didn't expect to find me consulting with the filth, now did you?"

"I did not," Rhys admitted. "It's kind of hard to think of the Isles of Scilly police as the filth."

"Oh, I mean nothing by it." Terry sipped his tea. Bald as an egg with masses of wrinkles around his eyes and mouth, he nevertheless had a sprightly air. It wasn't youthful, in that youth tended to be aimless and experimental, whereas Terry was anything but aimless. His faded blue eyes shone with the wonder of a child, yet it was tempered with the understanding that every person and object around him came marked with invisible expiration dates.

"Sergeant Hackman is the kind of copper I respect. Dedicated to the law and the greater good. He's not interested in power for its own sake, or for lording it over other people. He just wants to keep people safe. I'm happy to help." He smiled at Rhys over his cup. "But that doesn't mean I told him everything. If I'd done that, I would've directly compromised people who are still in the business. That's a bridge too far for me. These days, anything goes, but when I was coming up, there was honor among thieves."

Rhys wasn't sure he believed that, but he nodded anyway. "Sorry I couldn't bring Jem along, but as I said on the phone, she's chasing down other leads. But I promise, anything you're willing to tell me will go to her. We're meeting for dinner tonight."

Terry pointed at Rhys's pasty. "You should polish that off before it gets cold. Now. Where should I start?" He closed his eyes for a moment. "Right. The buried jewelry. I discovered the first cache on St. Martin's. Ten Cartier men's watches, all identical—steel bands, white faces, sapphire accents. Quarter of a million pounds, easy. Sealed in plastic bags and buried in a Lyle's Golden Syrup tin."

Rhys whistled.

"Pipe down," Terry said with a grin.

"When was this?" Rhys asked before finally biting into his pasty, which was delicious.

"Late spring. May, I shouldn't wonder."

"How'd you find it?"

"Oh, I was out with my metal detector. Like those blokes in that program, always pacing about, searching for treasure. Never thought I'd actually come up with something valuable. How's that pasty?"

"Perfect."

Terry nodded in satisfaction. "Anyway, when I opened the box, I had a pretty good idea of what I was looking at, so I reached out to some old mates. I won't be providing any names or identifying details, of course..."

"Hang on," Rhys said, holding up a hand so he could finish swallowing. "What do you mean, you knew what you were looking at? As in, stolen goods?"

Terry pulled a face. "Well, of course they were stolen goods, lad. But men like myself, professionals, never lift so much as a toothpick without getting a few things straight in advance." He counted it off on his fingers. "One, street value. Two, the possibility of a private client willing to pay close to actual value. Three, safe storage options. Four, an emergency fence on call twenty-four seven should instant liquidation become the priority."

Rhys took that in. "If that's how professionals approach theft, then it sounds like the person who took the jewelry and the Cartier watches did it on impulse. He—or she—didn't know what to do with the loot once he had it, and he was afraid of being caught, so he buried them around the islands."

"Top marks."

"But that's mental."

The old man waved it away. "Non-professionals always embarrass themselves. Once upon a time, there were thieves' guilds to prevent this sort of desperate flailing about. Did you know in America, some tragic bugger embezzled millions from a fruitcake company, spent half of it on baubles, then tossed his fancy watches in a lake rather than let the FBI find them?" He shook his head. "They found them anyway, of course. Went down in SCUBA gear.

"So being a curious sort of bloke," he continued, "very early the next morning, I went round the other islands to investigate. It took a few days, and the police boat must've passed me two dozen times, but no one stopped to ask me any questions. Why would they? Just a sweet old duffer out with his metal detector. And what did I dig up on Apple Tree Bay?"

"A cigar box stuffed with tiaras?"

"No. A very nice repoussé antique tin covered with pink and blue flowers. Meant for better things, I can tell you that. Inside it was a velvet pouch containing six cut diamonds, each one just over a carat, all acceptable in terms of cut and color. But the box was the real find."

"Because...?"

"I'll come back to that. Now I mentioned that I still keep in touch with some of the old crew. I'm too old to go shimmying up drainpipes or creeping into windows, but I have plenty of wisdom to offer. I enjoy being an old-timer in the program," he said, meaning AA, "and I enjoy being a sort of mentor to the new breed of burglar. Smash-and-grabs with guns!" He shuddered. "I hate to imagine a world where that sort of vulgar thuggery becomes the new normal."

"I get that," Rhys said carefully. "But, well, strictly speaking, if we're following the program as intended, isn't it 'a manner of living that requires rigorous honesty?'" he asked, quoting the *Big Book of Alcoholics Anonymous*.

The old man gazed at him fondly. "I miss that first year of sobriety. Everything seemed so clear. And, yes, by all means, honesty is key, so far as it goes. But I lie every time I assure my daughter that my grandson is going places. That he's clever, and nice-looking, and sure to succeed. The boy's a ruddy barnacle, but I can't tell her that. And I've already given up the bottle, haven't I? I was caught in the trade, did my time, came out promising not to take it up again. I've kept to that. Mostly." He refilled his teacup. "But there's no twelve-step program for thieving."

"So I take it you rang up your friends in the, erm, trade?"

"Chatted with them on the World Wide Web," Terry said proudly. "We have a secret Facebook group called The Expendables. You know? Like the movie? A bunch of old rapscallions seemingly too old and gray to worry about?"

Rhys nodded, trying not to laugh.

"I explained what I'd found and asked if some jewelry shop clerk or distribution manager had decided to pull the crime of the century. Turns out there were two possibilities. Both men, middle-aged blokes who'd worked their way up to a position of trust and suddenly tried to cash in. One had worked as an executive for a safe deposit company. He embezzled a cool million, then stole the contents of some boxes before doing a runner. The other was an insurance salesman by day and small-time thief by night. He knocked over a string of little shops, here and there, then disappeared when things got hot.

"Anyway, I had possibilities but nothing solid. That meant I had to approach the problem another way. What do you think I did?"

Rhys tried to take another bite of his pasty and found only crumbs. Taking a swig of cola instead, he turned the problem over in his mind for a moment.

"If I were you," he said at last, "I would've waited for the next antique fair on St. Morwenna and tried to find the vendor who sold those vintage tins."

"Right you are," the old man cried. "I did give you a hint there, mentioning the finer qualities of that lovely little repoussé tin, but never mind. I found the lady in question, and she recalled the buyer quite easily. A tall, handsome, blond man. For an instant, I thought she was describing you."

"But it was Arthur Ajax," Rhys said. "So which one was he? The safe deposit guy, or the small-time thief?"

Terry's eyes roamed around the courtyard. Leaning closer, he said in a whisper, "Don't look now, but I believe that woman in the straw hat is eavesdropping. Her chin jerked when you said 'thief.' Let us repair to Valhalla, my boy."

Obediently, Rhys followed Terry out of the bistro and into the collection of salvaged figureheads. Some, modeled on women from Greek antiquity, had the frozen curls and sightless eyes of an Elgin Marble. Others, depicting Regency ladies, wore empire dresses and ribbons in their hair. There was a fish painted gold and blue and one female figurehead that was, in fact, only a head. It was strange to imagine these carved people in their previous life, forever pointed toward adventure, bobbing in and out of the spray. Rhys wondered if they had all been found washed ashore, or if some diver had peered into the depths to a find a beautiful face serenely looking back.

"This one reminds me of my late wife," Terry said, leading Rhys to a rather matronly female figure with dark hair and a gold torque about her neck. She wasn't crowned, but something about her burgundy and gold-accented gown put Rhys in mind of a queen. "I'll be with her again one day. But sometimes it seems like a hell of a wait."

Rhys glanced about to be sure no one else was listening, then asked, "So which one was he?"

"The safe deposit guy."

"And his real name?"

"A.J. McArthur."

"Oh, for God's sake. He ran away and came up with an alias that's almost his own name?"

Terry shook his head. "Non-professionals always embarrass the trade. I reviewed his work. A glimmer of promise in the way he chose his targets. Some of these modern lads think the only way in is through the ceiling, but that can go very wrong with today's HVAC, I don't mind telling you. A.J. found weakness in neighboring buildings and broke in that way. With a bit of training up, he could have made something of himself. I had intended to approach him, you know. I hadn't worked out how to manage it without frightening the life out of him. Anyone who would resort to burying his treasures on beaches was afraid of discovery and in desperate need of guidance. But alas." He shrugged. "He's dead."

"Yeah. Look, Terry, I can't thank you enough. Now that we know A.J. McArthur was the victim, maybe we can look into his life and figure out who wanted him dead," Rhys said.

"I'm looking into that myself," Terry said mildly.

"What?"

The old man smiled. "I told you, I was trying to work out how to approach McArthur. I popped over to Neptune Cove a few times. Saw him go out on a gorgeous yacht. A Sunseeker. It took time, but I found out who owns it."

Rhys waited, ready to be amazed. But after a beat, Terry shook his head.

"Sorry, lad. I can't give you the name."

"Why not?"

"It's a matter of honor."

"Then the owner of the Sunseeker is, well, a thief?"

Terry didn't reply, but his eyes twinkled.

"Can you tell me anything more?"

"If I were Jem Jago, I'd try to locate that yacht. It's like a ghost ship," Terry said. "It's not berthed at Tresco, I can tell you that much. Or St. Mary's, near as I can tell. But from what I observed, when it came to his private life, A.J. McArthur had a very full dance card." He paused, then added, "Or in the modern parlance, he couldn't keep it zipped. So the owner of the Sunseeker might be the killer, or he might not. But if I decide that he did the deed, I'll give you and your girlfriend his name. Thieving is one thing. Murder is quite another."

"Thanks. But what do you mean, if you decide?" Rhys asked suspiciously. This was the sort of conversation he often had with Jem just before she did something dangerous.

"Now don't fret. I won't get into trouble. I'll be perfectly safe as long as I can shake off my grandson. When he was young, he was quite the little peeper. Maybe he saw me dig up one of the tins," Terry said. "For years now, he's barely wanted to know me, and now every time I turn around, the ruddy barnacle is right there, watching."

"Please don't risk your life. Or your grandson's," Rhys said firmly.

"Terry O'Dell. Last of the gentleman cat burglars," the old man said grandly. He laid a hand on his favorite figurehead, as if for luck. "Don't worry about me. I'll be in touch."

16

POSTIE WITH THE MOSTIE

"Uriah from Marazion," Jem said again. Pauley, walking beside her along the road up from Bond House, waited eagerly for an announcement from Jem—namely, that they were chucking Roger's interview, climbing aboard *Bellatrix*, and chugging off to visit the club Clarence had mentioned. But Jem just kept walking slowly, stumbling a couple of times over uneven asphalt, her head in the clouds.

"But we know Roger," Pauley said for the second time. "He's, like, this tall"—she measured a height in the air close to her own diminutive stature—"and composed entirely of clotted cream. Newsflash, he didn't kill anyone. But *Uriah* sounds dangerous. And according to Kit, he looks dangerous. And according to Clarence, when Uriah said something threatening to Arthur, Arthur skedaddled. Arthur wasn't a total lightweight. I reckon he could've held his own, unless he thought he might actually be hurt."

"I know all that. It adds up to a lot of hearsay," Jem said vaguely.

"Hearsay on Uriah, but hearsay on Roger, too."

"But we'd be mad to skip Roger just because we like him. And Pauls, remember, it's a two-hour boat trip to Marazion."

"And?"

"And that means if you want to come home again, I'll have to spend an extra four hours on the water just to get you to Lyonesse House and me back to my apartment in time for bed. I can't possibly miss work tomorrow. And even if I could snap my fingers and instantly transport us to whatever that club was called—"

"The Brazen Head."

"Right. Even if I could do that, we're a couple of women—"

"What? No."

"—and picture it: two ladies strolling around a gay men's joint saying, 'Hiya, amateur murder inquiry, do you know someone called Uriah? No? Cheers. What about you, sir? Know a dangerous-looking, broken-hearted man called Uriah?'"

"I don't know what being two women has to do with it. Women go to gay men's clubs."

"I'm not saying we wouldn't be tolerated, but it's far from ideal. Coming in as intruders and trying to convince total strangers to open up to us."

"Then we're going to see Roger?" Pauley didn't care if the question came out in a faint whine.

"Yes. Unless there's any chance you think that fancy sewing machine actually belongs to Clarence, and that's what he's lying about."

Pauley stopped dead. "Lying?"

Jem also stopped, turning back to face her. Judging by her expression, she had no intention of taking it back. And although Pauley prided herself on being a loyal friend, she found herself unable to argue. At least not on the grounds that after learning of Arthur's death, her friend and business partner had spoken and acted like an honest man.

"Fine, so something's off. Maybe he's just embarrassed to

have it all come out. Or maybe—maybe he knew some real dirt on Arthur but was afraid to speak ill of the dead."

"I hope it's something like that. I wonder how the interview with DS Conrad went? If Clarence decided to go in without a lawyer, heaven knows what happened."

"Micki hasn't texted me," Pauley offered.

"Well, I've texted her twice now to see what's what, but she hasn't answered."

"I wonder if they're still at the police station. Why don't we drop by and have a peek?" Pauley asked. "Then we can double back to Old Town Road and see Roger," she added with a sigh.

With that seemingly decided, Pauley followed the lower Strand along the left-hand lane, Garrison, which led to St. Mary's Police Station. In the process of casually looking over to ask Jem what sort of name The Brazen Head was, she realized her friend wasn't there. Instead, she'd taken the right-hand lane, into Hugh Street, and was marching toward the post office.

"Oi! Wrong way!" she bellowed.

Jem, now meters ahead, jumped. "What are you doing over there? *This* way." She pointed ahead of herself as if Pauley was the idiot. "I saw someone you have to—that we should say hi to."

Someone you have to—what?

As Pauley hustled down Hugh Street to catch up, that incomplete phrase and Jem's midstream amendment suggested a possibility. An aggravating possibility: a set-up.

"Pranav!" Jem called to a small knot of people having lunch at a wooden picnic table on the post office lawn. "Hiya!"

It was a mixed crowd—two men, two women. All heads turned. But only the dark man in the pink shirt and cargo shorts stood up and waved.

"Hiya right back," he said, flashing a friendly smile as Pauley and Jem drew closer. Instantly she categorized him as cute—pleasant features, warm eyes, a nice-looking bloke from his thick black hair down to his trainers. He was easy to read, too, at least in this situation. Although he seemed receptive to Jem, his uncertain expression made it completely obvious he had no idea who she was.

"Maybe you don't remember me. Once I brought my boat in at high water and was about to wade ashore up to my chest," Jem said. "You were delivering the post by boat that day, and you took mercy on me and—"

"Oh! Right, right." His voice jerked up a bit high on the *i* sounds.

"Did he go on about how he loves being a water postie?" one of the women at the table asked. "Because he *loves* being a water postie. Poor thing."

"Why poor thing?" Jem asked.

"Drones, I reckon," Pauley said. "Apparently they're doing a good job getting mail delivered around the islands."

"Exactly." He turned to her. "Look at you. You're—you're amazing. I mean, the coat. I love that coat."

Pauley smiled. "Pauley Gwyn." She put out her hand. "I live on St. Morwenna. Lyonesse House."

"Oh, sure. Special delivery from Spain." He shook her hand gently. Men sometimes did that when they didn't want to come off as collegial or merely polite. His slow release seemed to say, that wasn't just a social exchange. Holding your hand, even for a moment, was a privilege.

"What was it?" he asked.

"Hmnh?" He *did* have nice eyes, large and liquid, with those perfect eyelashes men were often blessed with.

"In the package from Spain."

"Pran!" one of the men at the picnic table called. "We never ask. You know that. You're bringing down the profession."

"Never mind that," she said. "It was Marais tiles. For my kitchen backsplash."

He nodded as if that were the most interesting possible response in the world.

"Anyway," Jem interrupted, beaming in a way that Pauley would've found infuriating if she'd been able to focus upon it, "my name's Jem Jago and this is Pauley Gwyn."

"I already said that."

"Fine. True. Pauley Gwyn, this is Pranav Dhillon, who heroically spared me from a wet slog inland."

"Go, Pran! She remembered *your* name, mate," one of the men said.

"Pleased to meet you," Pranav said, nodding at Jem, and gently shook Pauley's hand all over again. Between Jem's botched intro, the unnecessary second handshake, and the murmurings of the lunchtime peanut gallery, it should have ranked high on the Cringe-O-Meter, but it didn't. Pauley found herself wishing she'd brought a parasol. It was always easier to flirt when you had a parasol to spin.

Set-up! her brain screamed. *This is all a set-up because Jem thinks I can't get a man on my own!*

She sent back, *He's cute and I bloody well like him, so shut it*, with such brute force, her brain retreated into shocked silence. But Pauley barely noticed. Instead, she heard herself asking, "Do you ever do the roto post?"

"Yes." Although not a tall man—around five-foot-eight by her estimate—Pranav drew himself up proudly. "My dad owns a helicopter tour service in Hampton. Practically grew up at the Thruxton Aerodrome. I had a private pilot's license before I joined the Royal Mail, and now I have my commercial license as well. That's why I love being a water postie," he added, sparing Jem a quick glance. "I never handled a yacht till I came here."

"Pranav," Pauley said, trying out the name and finding that she liked the feel of it. "I know we're interrupting your lunch. But can we sort of lure you away for a few minutes? Only there's something you might..."

The lunch group erupted into *ooohs* that sounded exactly like Kenzie and her school friends.

Pranav snapped, "Be quiet, you deranged—*ooh*ing things. You're all so completely horrendous I can't even think of what to call you," he added, grinning over his own lapse. "Come along, ladies. There's another table on the other side of the facility."

The second picnic table, placed in the shade of a tall tree, proved more private. The moment Jem saw they were alone, she launched into a quick recap of how she and Pauley had discovered Arthur's body that ended with, "Of course, I'm not a police officer. I expect Sergeant Hackman and the murder squad from Devon & Cornwall wouldn't appreciate me saying too much about what we saw inside the cottage. But I have a question that touches on the Royal Mail. Would you be willing to answer it?"

"I mean, sure." Pranav's quick gaze darted back to Pauley, lingering on her face. "Anything to help."

"It seems like Arthur might have stolen someone else's post. A lot of it."

"From another resident in the islands?"

"No. From Putney, actually."

"When you say a lot, do you mean three letters? Ten letters?"

"Maybe fifty or a hundred," Pauley said. "A wicker hamper's worth."

"Wow. From Putney? Did he come from there?"

"We don't know. Maybe not," Jem said.

"Well, that's strange. I suppose I could check in the system. There's a mechanism for people to report stolen letters," Pranav said. "Usually they aren't actually stolen, just mislaid or misdirected. And usually, it's one or two pieces. Were they all meant for the same address, or...?"

"I don't know if we should—" Jem began.

"They were all meant for John R. Derry," Pauley cut in,

deciding to go for broke. Partly because getting in on Jem's sleuthing routine was fun. Partly because she had no intention of letting this attractive postie with the naked left hand think Jem had all the agency, and she was just a ride-along. "He might be retired now, but he used to be—"

"Oh, I know who he is," Pranav said, voice going up a bit on the *i* in *is*. "There was an internal incident bulletin about some delayed post being sought by the Met. Mr. Derry used to get letters and parcels from all over the world. We were meant to be on alert for a misdirected tranche that was never delivered. Maybe the dead guy had it."

"Maybe," Jem said, giving Pauley the side-eye for piping up. "And now the letters and the entire crime scene are under mainland control, so I suppose everyone will be happy. I've been wracking my brain about how Arthur might have come to be in possession of those letters. One is that he stole them directly from John R. Derry's home. But he has so many. It doesn't seem possible that he could have taken them, day by day, without being caught. But what about taking them in one fell swoop from the route carrier, or the sorting center? How hard would it be to steal a tranche like that?"

"Oh—hard. Right up on impossible," Pranav said without hesitation. "Unless you worked there. Then I reckon it could be done, if you were willing to risk prosecution over a lot of fan letters and requests for psychic readings."

"Yeah." Jem sighed. "Just doesn't seem worth it, looking at it that way."

"So do you go up in the chopper a lot?" Pauley asked.

"It's not a chopper," Pranav corrected with a grin. "Not to sound like a stodger, but if you want to be up on your lingo, you call it a heli. And sadly, no. Not to deliver mail. The Windracers—drones—are going like gangbusters, chasing us all out of a job, I shouldn't wonder. But no worries. I still get up in the sky. My brother in Penzance has a heli tour service. He just invested in a new Airbus, which means I can take up the old Bell 212 whenever I want."

Pauley made an involuntary sound of delight. Pranav's eyes—so expressive, they really were his best feature—widened in answering pleasure. "You'd fancy a ride, wouldn't you?" He followed what sounded like a completely impulsive question with a nervous laugh, looking quickly at Jem, as if recalling her existence. "Both of you, I mean? For the, erm, case? Somehow?"

"That sounds wonderful," Jem said. "But I can't think of any way it could—"

"It would be perfect for the case," Pauley cried, jumping in again. "There's a mysterious yacht I'm—we're—trying to track down. I think we might have better luck from the air. If... if you're offering, I mean," she added, suddenly feeling a bit nervous. Pranav's stare was intense, and she'd caught herself gazing back just as hard.

"I am offering. Of course I am," Pranav said, as if astonished there could be any question. "We came into the office for a half-day's training. It's already finished, but, of course it's too late to get back to Penzance and fly this afternoon. But tomorrow's my day off, if you're free."

"Sorry, I have to work," Jem said.

"It's perfect," Pauley said.

Jem looked at her, raising an eyebrow.

"What? We've been wondering about the Sunseeker. It's a loose end. A big one," Pauley told her. "And you said it yourself, you have to go to work tomorrow and unruffle Mr. Atherton's feathers. Leave this to me. I'll report back like a good little detective."

Jem's gaze shifted from Pranav back to Pauley. Her lips curved only a little, but Pauley saw the look of self-satisfaction her friend was trying to suppress. So this *had* been a total set-up. The question about the John R. Derry letters was one Jem could've phoned in. At some point, perhaps on the day Pranav had given her a ride in the post office's delivery boat, Jem had decided he was just the sort of man Pauley needed in her life.

"Fine," Jem said with a sigh, relinquishing control with a visible effort.

"Well done, you," Pauley said, and meant it two ways.

17

"BECAUSE YOU'RE CONGENITALLY INCAPABLE OF RESISTING A PUZZLE"

All in all, Jem departed St. Mary's Post Office wrapped in the warm glow of accomplishment, even if she'd learned nothing concrete and had no idea whether a helicopter tour of the Isles of Scilly would advance her investigating one whit. Pauley and Pranav had met. They'd clearly hit it off, to the point where even his workmates felt free to hoot at them from the sidelines. And Pauley was carrying herself anew, moving with the saucy little strut that only came out when she felt especially triumphant.

On the way down Garrison Lane toward the police station, Jem very much wanted to interrogate her friend on her reaction to Pranav Dhillon, who frankly looked more fit and attractive than she remembered. But before she could phrase the question in a way more likely to be answered than tossed back in her face, Pauley said, "Look, there's Clarence and his lawyer. And Hack. And a troll in an overcoat."

Shielding her eyes against the sun, Jem saw DS Conrad, blocky and red-faced in his tan coat. From this distance, no one looked happy—not Clarence, not the lawyer, not Hack, and certainly not Conrad. In his case, that was a relief, since a pleased expression on his stony face would surely bode ill.

As they hurried down the lane to meet their friends, Jem realized the lawyer wasn't a lawyer at about the same time Pauley did, based on her gasp. The tall black woman dressed in a smart pinstriped suit, her straightened blond hair pulled back in a bun, was Micki. She'd borrowed the snazzy professional togs from somewhere and crowned herself with a wig, but it was definitely her under all that. The angrily dejected look she shot Jem spoke volumes. No need to pretend—the jig was up.

"Ms. Jago," Hack called. "And Pauley Gwyn, her faithful companion. To what do we owe the honor?"

"Just looking for Clarence," Jem said neutrally. She'd come to know Hack well enough to interpret his warning signals. When he called her "Ms. Jago" and spoke in that semi-formal way, he was putting her on her guard. Not really necessary, given Conrad's presence, but then again, sometimes when her back was up, her mouth lost control of itself.

"How are you today, Clarence?" she asked, pasting on a smile.

"Couldn't be better," Clarence said, grinning back defiantly.

DS Conrad eyed Jem the way a dog eyes a flea. "I should've known you'd turn up, Ms. Jago, despite my explicit warning. Mr. Latham has been instructed not to leave the Isles of Scilly until our inquiries are concluded. His cousin, Ms. Latham, has been advised of the same. She is also now fully aware of the perils of trying to interfere in a police investigation."

"I never lied—" Micki began.

"You implied time and again that you were his legal counsel," Conrad broke in, a flare of satisfaction in his piggy little eyes. "You'll get your day in court, and quite likely a considerable fine when the judgment is read. I look forward to giving evidence. No one hates bogus attorneys quite as much as a magistrate. They're usually moved to make a little speech for the entire court's edification."

Micki threw Hack a withering glance. He pretended to be absorbed in watching a gang of kids cross Hugh Street.

Jem could imagine what had happened. Clarence had declined to secure counsel, probably for monetary reasons—the B&B he owned with Pauley was still hemorrhaging cash, after all—and Micki, bold as brass, had accompanied him into the interview room as his lawyer. Hack had either raised the alarm, or accidentally given the game away. Jem knew that he liked Micki as much as any of her friends, and probably would've discreetly shooed her away, had it been possible. But when he was on duty, not to mention in the presence of superiors from Devon & Cornwall, there was only so much irregularity he could turn a blind eye to.

"I hope you don't get the sack tomorrow," Conrad told Jem conversationally. "But if you do, it will probably be down to your friend's behavior. I didn't realize you and Ms. Latham were part of the same amateur obstructive unit until you turned up, right on cue. Now I'll need to ring Mr. Atherton again and give him an update."

Jem suffered that choking spasm in her diaphragm that came from swallowing words that really, really wanted to come out. Only the fear that verbally striking back might somehow worsen Micki's situation—would she really be fined?—kept her from launching into a long, profane speech about what category of person Conrad belonged to, and where he could go to learn more about himself.

"You might as well take the rest of the afternoon, Hackman," Conrad added as he turned to laboriously tread back to the station, like a boulder rolling uphill. "I'll be using your office for some time yet."

Now it was Hack's turn to look as if he were injuring his thorax via self-censorship.

Jem, Pauley, Clarence, Micki, and Hack all stood regarding one another mutely until Conrad disappeared back into the police station. Then everyone spoke at once.

"Micki, why did you—"

"If Hack hadn't stared at me like he'd seen a ghost—"

"I told you it wouldn't—"

"How dare he threaten you with—"

"I didn't mean to give you away, it was—"

"Oi! Enough!" Jem cried. It was her impatient Londoner/stern librarian voice, and it got results. Everyone went silent, though the resentful and defensive stares spoke volumes.

"Clarence," Jem began, looking him in the eye. "Are you all right? What happened?"

"I probably said more than I should have." He sighed. "I was fine as long as Micki was acting as counsel. The questions were respectful. But once the jig was up, that copper turned dirty. All but accused me of beating Arthur to death. Called me his prime suspect right to my face."

"I told him to hire a lawyer," Micki all but screamed. The ferocity of her words made her wig slip into her eyes. Ripping it off, she threw the blonde thing on the ground, where it lay like a deflated golden retriever. "Now I'm in for a telling off and a fine."

"I'm sorry for that," Hack said in tones Jem thought suitable for hostage negotiation. "But you can't come into my station in a half-arsed disguise and not expect me to do a double-take. Give a man some warning."

"If I had, you'd have told me not to do it!"

"Yes, and then there'd be no telling off and no fine, now would there?"

"Jem," Clarence said pleadingly. "I don't suppose you've figured out who the murderer is?"

"No," she admitted. "But don't lose hope. I've barely begun.

I've even expanded the operation," she said, trying to lift his spirits. "Rhys is interviewing an expert. Pauley will see one tomorrow while I'm at work. And we're off to interview a suspect now."

"Which suspect?" Hack asked.

"Roger Pinnock," Pauley said.

Hack and Micki burst out laughing. Clarence eyed Jem with something like dread. "Please don't do that. He's a nice fellow. You'll give him palpitations."

"I have to," Jem said. "As for you two"—she looked sternly from Hack to Micki—"I have a pretty good track record for identifying suspects, so I'll thank you not to scoff. We're all still on for dinner tonight, aren't we? Lyonesse House? Eight o'clock?"

There were general murmurs of assent. Hack glanced over his shoulder at St. Mary's Police Station as if reluctant to let Conrad dismiss him. Micki kicked the blonde wig before picking it up and tucking it into her handbag. Clarence still looked worried.

"Clare," Jem said suddenly. "If you know something more about Roger, now's the time to tell me."

She tried to hold his gaze, but he only shook his head. Resigned to whatever he was hiding, Jem sighed and turned to go, Pauley on her heels.

Roger Pinnock's house on Old Town Road, a rather lovely mix of old stone and black shingles, had a doorbell that chimed like plucked harp strings. The sound put Jem in mind of a magic wand being waved. The first time she pushed the button: nothing. The second time, the patterned curtains at the front window—yellow birds on a white background—twitched. The third time, she heard a soft squeak in the vicinity of the front window, as of a small man shifting his weight on a loose floorboard.

"He's totally ghosting us," Pauley murmured.

"Isn't that suspicious in itself?" Jem asked.

"If pretending not to be at home indicates criminal behavior, our entire nation is lawless. But it's no good trying to get you to pack it in, because you're congenitally incapable of resisting a puzzle. You quit Wordle forever and went back to it the very next day."

"The American spelling is incorrect. At least for UK players. So the answer to that particular puzzle was just wrong," Jem said. "But I got over it. Because I'm mature."

"Because you're addicted. Fine. Let's do this." Making a fist, Pauley beat on the front door so energetically, it sounded like a police raid. "Roger! Roger Pinnock! We know you're in there! Open the door!"

More twitching of the curtains. Then from inside, a man called, "I'm not well! Please let me rest."

"Roger, it's me. Jem Jago," she said, trying to play good cop to Pauley's human battering ram. "I'm sure you know Arthur's dead. We just want to talk."

"I saw it on telly," came the voice from behind the door. "Nothing to do with me."

"Then you won't mind answering a couple of questions. Come on, Roger," Pauley urged. She pounded the door again, probably for no other reason than to startle him some more. "Open up and let's get this over with! You know you can trust us. We've stuck by you before."

Silence. Then: "I would. Only I'm not well! I don't want to alarm you. But I fear it's contagious."

"What've you got?" Jem asked, still striving to be the good cop.

"A pox. A small pox."

"*Smallpox*?" Pauley burst out. "I'm ringing 999."

"No, no, there's no need," Roger said hastily. "I think they eradicated that. Moderate pox. Nothing to worry about. But contagious. I'm sure it's contagious."

Jem and Pauley swapped glances. Pauley shrugged, but her fists remained balled for another volley against the door if Jem wanted it. They could keep insisting until Roger gave in, or perhaps tried to flee out the back. Jem decided to cut to the chase.

"Roger, you left your fancy sewing machine at Arthur's cottage. I don't want to go to DS Conrad about it, but I will if you don't open this door and explain why it was there."

Silence again. Then the door opened and there stood Roger Pillock, short and slightly doughy, with no pox on his pale skin but a hurt expression on his face. "Clarence sold me out?"

18

SEX, LIES, AND MEASURING TAPE

"I wish I had something better to offer you," Roger said, setting down a plate of gingersnaps. Their empty mugs were already before them, awaiting the tea currently steeping in the porcelain teapot.

"This is lovely," Jem said, eating a biscuit to prove it. "And because I don't think you believed me the first time, I'll say it again. Clarence didn't point to you as a suspect. He never even mentioned your name."

Roger's round face looked sad. His forelock flopped in his eyes. Pushing it away, he said, "I wouldn't blame him if he had. I mean... I'd blame him, because he promised not to. But I wouldn't hate him for it. He's a good man."

"Yes, and that's the only reason I beat down your door," Pauley agreed. "Because he *is* a good man, and he's been unfairly targeted."

"I wonder... was it a source of friction between you?" Jem asked as Roger poured the tea.

"Was what a source of friction?" The question arrived just a little late. And issued from the lips of someone clearly braced for more.

"Seeing the same man. Clarence had a sort of—what was it? Ethical non-monogamy thing happening with Arthur. Who had a supposedly legit— Hang on. That sounds judgey. I mean to say, Arthur had a supposedly exclusive, boyfriend-boyfriend arrangement with someone else in town. Who wasn't best pleased to find out about you. Or Clarence."

"Or Uriah from Marazion," Pauley said.

Roger sighed. "I was in over my head. When it all blew up, I behaved badly. Clarence understood, bless him. I doubt anyone else could." Seating himself on the other side of the table, he gazed down at his mug. Blowing on the tea to cool it, he sent the white foam scudding like clouds across an uneasy sky.

"I can see why you might have felt swept away," Jem said. "Arthur was gorgeous. I didn't know him, but everyone says he was charming and interesting, too."

"Too right. All of the above." Roger pushed away his forelock again. "I met him after a Tidepool Players workshop. He said he thought of himself as a natural actor. Maybe he was," Roger added, lips quirking sardonically. "At first, I could hardly believe he was giving me the time of day. I sort of worshipped him, really. And looking back, I think he soaked up the admiration like sunshine."

"Yep," Pauley said tightly.

"He was very clear with me. No promises, no expectations, just hookups. On his terms. Once I tried to turn the tables and he laughed at me. Said he had another man over and if I was lonely, I should arrange the same. But he was only needling me, I see that now. He knew I'd fallen for him," Roger said, voice trembling, "right from the first. He always knew, and he enjoyed pretending that we had a no-commitment rule, and he was holding me to it."

Roger took what Jem thought was a forced sip of tea, probably to give himself a break to compose himself. Then he continued in a steadier tone. "At that time I didn't even know about Clarence, or any of the others, specifically. They were just faceless men I was competing with. That I needed to outshine. I bought Arthur presents. Cleaned his cottage every time I was over. I pretended it was for my comfort, that I was an unbearable neat freak who couldn't bear a grain of dust, but of course I was really just trying to prove my worth. To make him love me."

"The Janome Atelier 6," Pauley said. "Why did you bring it over?"

"To impress him." Roger gave a half-hearted laugh. "I knew he liked the finer things, and that's the priciest thing I own. He'd bought some rather exquisite pajamas online. Cobalt blue, very striking. But the fit was a bit off. He thought because they were silk, there was nothing to be done. I said I could tailor it up beautifully, right before his eyes. I actually thought that was the night he'd fall in love with me. But it was the night everything went to hell."

"When was this?" Jem asked.

"Friday before last. Nine days ago."

"What went wrong?" Pauley asked.

"I was working on the pajamas in Arthur's bedroom when someone knocked. I thought he went to answer it. But what he must have done was peek around the kitchen door to see who was on the step, because he rushed back and told me to hide in the closet. Like a French farce. One lover popped into the closet, so the other lover doesn't see, while the hero smooths it over with lies.

"Of course, I did it," Roger added, again with that sardonic smile. "Stopped sewing, left the pajamas on the machine, and ducked into the closet. It had louvered doors, so I could see bits of what happened next. The other man burst into the bedroom —I expect he just walked into the cottage when Arthur didn't answer, since the front door was never locked—and shouted something like, 'You betrayed me.' Maybe not those exact words, but along those lines."

"Did you see who it was?"

"No. I saw his windcheater. Red. And his trousers. Tan. Then he yanked Arthur's pajamas right out of the machine. I clapped my hands over my mouth to keep from screaming."

"Could you tell if the other man was white or black? Old or young?" Jem asked.

"Did he limp?" Pauley asked.

"Have a certain odor? Maybe a cologne? Cigarettes?" Jem added.

"No idea. My brain wasn't functioning to its full capacity. Sorry, Jem, but I've never been good under pressure. Still," Roger said carefully, as if he might be on the verge of saying something foolish, "I did hear Arthur call the man by name. Uriah."

Jem's mouth dropped open. She looked at Pauley, who seemed equally stunned by their mutual ineptitude. They'd doggedly asked all the wrong questions, then stopped. Fortunately, their witness had volunteered the critical detail on his own.

"Right. Uriah. You're the third person to mention him," Jem said. "Clarence said he made a scene at a bar in Marazion. Threatened Arthur in a way. And Kit Verran said—"

"Kit!" Roger cried. "Him, too? Oh, never mind. I don't know why I care. It's just a reflex. You tell me the name of another man Arthur was sleeping with and my leg kicks, every time."

"Kit told us he was in the process of confronting Arthur when Uriah turned up looking dangerous. That means he went to Neptune Cottage at least twice," Pauley said. "And the third time? Maybe he killed him."

Jem turned that story over in her mind, trying to see it from every angle. Something seemed not to ring true, but she decided to wait and chew it over after finishing with Roger.

"Tell us the rest of the story," she urged.

"Well. While I hid in the closet, feeling like a gormless twit, Arthur ordered Uriah to get out. He was furious over the pajamas, I reckon. And being told off, of course. I'm not sure how it happened—maybe Arthur tried to walk Uriah to the door—but somehow, they wound up outside. Still shouting at one another. I only caught bits of it. Arthur called Uriah mental. Psychotic. A sociopath. I didn't hear anything else from Uriah. It seemed like the louder Arthur got, the quieter Uriah became.

"Anyway, I waited in that closet for a long time. Long after all the hubbub died down. I was expecting Arthur to come and say the coast was clear. But he didn't. Then the bedroom light went off, and I heard some rustling. I had the sudden, awful idea that Arthur and Uriah had made it up and gone to bed together. So I pushed open the closet door. It creaked a little, and Arthur sat up. He was alone. He'd gone to bed, you see. Forgotten about me in the closet. Forgot I existed."

Pauley groaned. "The cheek. How did I never see what a bastard he was?"

Roger continued, "He looked at me and said, 'God in heaven, are you still here? Why? Go home. I expect the pajamas are ruined, but you can see about them later.'" As he repeated those words, a blush rose from his cheeks to his hairline. "Like I was a servant. Not even that—servants are paid. I felt so..." He put out his small white hands, staring at them as if they belonged to someone else. "So angry. I don't think I've ever been so angry in my life."

He paused, but Jem didn't rush to fill the silence. Neither did Pauley. After what felt like a long time, Roger took up the story again.

"When I'm tailoring clothes to fit someone, I keep a soft tape measure around my neck. You know. Pink. One hundred and twenty inches. Three hundred centimeters. It was still around my neck when I went in the closet. My fingers kept going back to it, fiddling with the ends, the whole time I hid there in the dark. I thought, I should just tie this around my neck, secure it to the clothes bar, and fall forward. It wouldn't take much self-control to keep from clawing at the tape. Before I knew it, I'd black out, and this whole humiliating life would finally be over.

"I tell you that," Roger said, taking a gulp of breath, "to tell you the rest. No one else knows what happened that night. No one but Clarence." Suddenly he blinked, looking from face to face. "He really didn't tell you?"

"He told us nothing," Jem said.

"We swear," Pauley said.

"All right. When I opened the closet door, Arthur sat up and said—what he said. I felt... rage. The next thing I knew, I twisted that sewing tape around his neck and squeezed for all I was worth. And I couldn't even do *that* right," Roger said, beginning to cry. "Couldn't make him love me, couldn't behave with common human dignity, couldn't commit murder. He tore the tape out of my hands like it was tissue paper and threw me across the room. I landed on my shoulder. It's still sore." He touched the spot.

"Roger, that's... that's a lot," Jem said.

Pauley asked, "Do you think you would've killed him? If he hadn't been strong enough to fight you off?"

"I don't know. I wasn't thinking. Not with the human part of my brain. They say there's a reptile down deep that only knows hate and fear. It was in control."

"I assume you left the cottage as fast as you could?"

He nodded. "I never went back for the machine. I didn't dare. I spent the next day waiting to be arrested. When that didn't happen, I was relieved—for about five minutes. Then the bottom dropped out. I found myself breaking into tears everywhere, for no reason. It happened backstage at the theater. Clarence got me to confide in him. And he told me Arthur had him on a string, too. That the whole thing made him feel... small. That's how I felt, too. Small."

No one spoke. After a moment, Roger wiped his eyes and said, "Thank goodness I didn't kill him. Not just because I don't want to spend the rest of my life in prison. But because it wouldn't have freed me. When I heard he was dead, do you know how I felt? Just as miserable as I did when he was alive. Nothing changed. As if all that pain inside me had nothing to do with him." He stopped as if considering his own words. "Maybe it never did. Anyway... now you know why I didn't want to come to the door."

Jem stared into the man's red-rimmed eyes. "Roger. Tell me the truth. Did you and Arthur make up? Did you sleep over at the cottage, wait till he got up to make breakfast, and crack him over the head with a frozen loaf of bread?"

His look of shock and disbelief was too authentic to be faked. Jem had seen him perform with the Hugh Town troupe. He wasn't that good an actor.

"A frozen loaf of bread? Really?"

"Yes."

"And that *killed* him?"

"It seems so."

"After the way he fought me off, I assumed someone shot him, or stabbed him." He seemed to picture the scene, shuddering in a way that Jem found reassuring. No matter what he'd done in a fit of impassioned despair, Roger could still be repulsed by actual murder. That meant he wasn't beyond hope, at least in her book.

"Do you reckon it was Uriah who did it?" he asked.

"He's next on our list," Jem said. But something about the idea still shifted about uneasily in her mind, refusing to settle, assuring her there was more to the story. The Janome Atelier 6 sewing machine and the torn cobalt silk pajamas were crossed off. But the phantom Sunseeker, the buried treasure, and the John R. Derry letters still remained.

19

MISSING PERSON

In the course of Jem's many cases—make that three cases—she'd learned there came a point when a council of war was necessary. She called it a council of war because it sounded serious, and dangerous, and reminded her of the stakes. Someone had been murdered. With an incompetent—in this instance, DS Conrad—at the helm, it was a good bet that the killer would walk free. A personal friend might find himself stitched up, too. So having hit the point where she'd pondered the physical clues, chased down some suspects—although they hadn't managed to track down Marv Bennett—and gathered what intel was available to a citizen snoop, it was time to sit down with her friends and hash it all out. Preferably over a nice meal and a bottle of wine.

That night's dinner at Lyonesse House was unusual, in that Pauley didn't play amateur chef and dazzle them with a choice of savory dishes. After all, she'd been fully booked playing amateur detective. But she always had a frozen casserole ready for emergencies—in this case, a mushroom, lentil, and potato jumble—and couple of bottles of red. Hack brought a loaf of brioche; Rhys brought a two-liter bottle of soda, a can of dog food, and Buck. He also brought some unexpected news: the true identity of Arthur Ajax, who would forever thereafter be known as A.J. McArthur, amateur jewel thief.

"I need to confirm this," Hack said, taking out his mobile. Despite the fact he was out of his police uniform and in his off-duty uniform—hibiscus shirt, cargo shorts, and sandals—his attitude snapped back to official business. "I can't believe O'Dell sat on this when he was face to face with me this morning."

"Don't name and shame him, all right?" Rhys looked worried. "Blimey, I should have thought this through. I was so happy to bring Jem the news, I forgot I'd have to account for how I got it. Terry wanted to help without getting involved. He's all about protecting his mates."

"Protecting career criminals?" Pauley asked.

"Honor among thieves, he called it."

"It's not surprising." Hack seemed to be taking it better than Jem had expected. "Snouts are always finicky about what they'll say and when they'll say it. Once we confirm the vic's real name, we shouldn't have to revisit how we got it." With that, he headed toward the library, phone in hand.

"You two don't seem as thrilled about McArthur's identity as I thought you'd be," Rhys said, whistling for Buck, who was on his hind legs, trying to climb into the kitchen rubbish bin.

"I was hoping he'd be Derrick Christensen," Pauley said.

"Me, too," Jem admitted.

"Who's that?"

By the time they finished filling in Rhys on the John R. Derry scam, as well as the international fraud investigation, Micki and Clarence turned up with the pudding.

"Jam roly-poly," Clarence announced, placing the covered dish on Pauley's new butcher block counter. She was checking the casserole's center temp—her dotty old cooker often left layered dishes cold in the middle—while Jem uncorked the wine.

"We have tentative confirmation," Hack announced, returning from the library. "Based on appearances, A.J. McArthur is the man in the morgue. It will take some time for forensic certainty, but Conrad's convinced. Every person on his team has been called back in for a miserable Sunday night," he added with a grin, "to try and work out what sort of enemies might have followed McArthur to the Isles of Scilly. Maybe he had a partner in crime who tracked him down and did him in."

"A partner?" Rhys frowned. "You think? I figured he was a solo operator, given how he had no clue how to fence the goods he stole."

"Ah, but the jewel heists were just part of it, in my opinion." Hack rubbed his hands together. "We're on my investigatory turf now, let me remind you, and here's what I—" He stopped. "Oh. I really can't say."

"Even though I handed you your big breakthrough?" Rhys began putting Buck through his paces, trick-wise, administering a Tasty Bite for each success.

"All right," Hack said. "But no talking out of school, any of you. While the team at D & C were getting confirmation, I rang up a friend who works in Manchester on the ECU—Economic Crimes Unit. He couldn't name names or firms, but there's a company that lost over three million pounds in liquidated assets. Naturally, right before the loss was discovered, one of their people went missing. I think it will turn out to be McArthur."

"You mean, he flew into the islands loaded down with cash? Good boy!" Rhys exclaimed. That seemed to startle Hack, until he realized the praise was meant for Buck.

"If he did," Rhys continued, "and he treated his money the way he treated his jewels, you might never find it. Not unless you use ground penetrating radar on every island and rock within fifty miles."

Everyone chuckled at the impossibility of such a monumental task. Everyone except Hack, who put his head to one side and smiled his most piratical smile.

"Is that what you're planning?" Pauley asked, wide-eyed.

"Let's just say, it hasn't been ruled out. But this is all very preliminary, so remember, not a word of it leaves this room." Perhaps to signal the end of his willingness to entertain the topic, Hack drifted toward the covered dish Clarence had brought.

"I do hope it will be up to your standards," Clarence said in an impolitely polite tone. "Since you had no interest in tasting my pumpernickel loaf."

"I wish I had," Hack replied. "Then I could truthfully tell people I tasted a murder weapon. Or the nearest thing, if it came from the same batch," he added, lifting the cloth for a look at the goodies. Jem thought he meant to nick a piece, but Micki slapped his hand.

"What have you done to deserve any?" she demanded.

"Well. Aside from just giving all of you the inside scoop on the McArthur fraud investigation, I found you a barrister who's willing to prep you for magistrates' court," he said, unruffled. "She'll do it pro bono, as a favor to me. If you take her advice and comport yourself exactly as she says, you'll probably get off with a stern warning."

"Hack." Jem was impressed. "That's very generous of you."

"It would be, if I were doing it just for Ms. Legally Blonde," he said, winking at Micki, who pursed her lips as if unsure how to take it. "But the fact is, it will burn Conrad down to his uglies if she gets away without a fine. And Letitia Fetherton-Wright always gets results. Future QC, that one."

"What does that even mean?" Micki asked, still suspicious.

"Queen's Counsel. It's an honor bestowed on very distinguished lawyers."

"Oh. Well. Thank you, Hack." She inclined her head. "Why would Ms. Feathers-and-Whatnot want to help me?"

"Oh, that's easy. She hates the police." He grinned.

"But she likes you?" Jem asked.

"Everyone likes me. Except Conrad. And he's just wrong." Accepting a wineglass from Jem, he wandered away to observe Buck, who now lay quietly on the floor, playing dead. One eye was closed in eternal slumber. The other was open and fixed on Rhys, awaiting a Tasty Bite.

After the food was served and everyone was seated, Jem raised her glass and proposed a toast. "To Clarence," she said, smiling around the table. "And to all of us, who are going to prove his innocence by catching the real killer."

Most of them clinked glasses. Rhys, smiling politely, declined to bump his cola against everyone else's booze, instead murmuring, "Hear, hear."

"Thank you." Clarence gazed down at his plate as if his lump of casserole held all the answers. "Not sure I deserve this. Good friends. Loyal friends."

"What are you on about?" Micki asked around a mouthful.

Jem met Pauley's gaze. After interviewing Roger, they'd decided to let Pauley handle this. Of course, Hack's presence upped the ante somewhat. But as much as Jem and Pauley found Roger sympathetic and generally likable, his story had come as a shock. And as head of the Isles of Scilly Police, Hack needed to know Roger was capable of attempted murder, however ineffectual that attempt had been.

"Clare. As your friend as well as your business partner, I wish you'd told us everything," Pauley said. "It would've put my mind at rest. I lost a bit of sleep, you know, worrying over what you might be holding back. Jem was worried, too."

"Hang on." Micki looked from Pauley to Jem. "Are you *accusing* Clarence?"

"No," Jem said firmly. "We're putting him on notice that we know what he decided not to tell us. That someone in Hugh Town snapped and tried to kill McArthur."

"Clare, tell them they've got it wrong," Micki said.

"I can't," he said, still looking at his plate. "I'm sorry. Only... Roger was completely broken. He was too ashamed to even go back and get his sewing machine. I felt bad for him. Not bad enough to break it off with Arthur. I still thought I could win him over for myself. But I felt terrible for Roger, so I promised not to tell anyone. I thought I was doing the right thing. It's not as if I ever believed for a second... the man had a breakdown, that's all. If Arthur—sorry, *McArthur*—hadn't fought him off, I reckon Roger would've come to his senses long before..." He tailed off.

"Before he actually choked him to death?" Jem asked.

"Jem." Hack's ringing tone indicated that he'd taken back the full authority of his position. "Please tell me you don't mean Roger Pinnock?"

She nodded.

He turned to Clarence. "You can tell me everything now, or you can go with me to the station as a material witness and tell me there. Either way, you're on the record."

Note to self. Let everyone finish eating before going into confrontation mode, Jem thought once Clarence had related his version of the story, which matched Roger's in all respects. She and Pauley were fine, of course, and Rhys's interest hadn't stopped him from plowing through two helpings of casserole, two slices of buttered bread, and two glasses of the fizzy stuff. But Hack had put down his fork and taken up his phone—he was making notes with a stylus—and Micki seemed too infuriated by Clarence's lie of omission to eat another bite.

"On the brighter side," Pauley announced with determined cheer, "tomorrow I'll have my first ever heli ride. If there's a Sunseeker yacht berthed in a sleepy cove, I'll find it."

Jem expected Hack to object, or at least break into lecture mode, but he actually smiled. "Not a bad thought. It's the sort of thing Conrad will never order unless a higher-up overrules him.

He sees himself as an old-fashioned shoe leather detective. Air reconnaissance is flash. DNA is hocus-pocus."

"Who has a helicopter?" Micki asked Pauley, thawing slightly.

"A bloke Jem knows owns it. Well, his brother. She told him we're on the case and he offered to take me up."

"Who's this, now?" Rhys asked. Mention of "a bloke" had made him stop eating.

"Just a friend from Hugh Town," Jem said vaguely. "Nice fe—"

That was meant to be "fellow," but Pauley broke in with a new narrative.

"Old guy. Granddad. Experienced pilot. Very safe, very careful," she lied, emphasizing *careful* as if she found the trait particularly frustrating. "Of course, he didn't even want to take me up, he wanted Jem Jago, the Scilly Sleuth. But she has to go to work tomorrow and see how much trouble she's in, so I'm stepping up."

Rhys frowned. "An old man whose brother owns a helicopter? On the mainland? Like Penzance?"

"Not there. Maybe Porthcurno."

"There's no helicopter tours out of Porthcurno."

"What difference does it make?"

"You're riding in a chopper and you don't know where the heliport is?"

"It's not a chopper, no one calls them that, and why are you interrogating me?"

"He must think Granddad's making a play for you," Micki said, smiling at last.

"Maybe he is. What's his name?" Rhys asked.

"Rhys, come on," Jem protested.

"His name is Felix," Pauley declared. "Felix Catchpole. And he's seventy years old and very married and will you just stop?"

"If you want to worry about someone, worry about me," Jem said, trying to distract Rhys from googling the imaginary Felix Catchpole. "Mr. Atherton might sack me tomorrow. Since Micki's my friend, Conrad decided to take her lawyer impersonation as proof I'm interfering in his case. So now two complaints have been lodged."

Clarence groaned. "This gets worse and worse. I can't just sit around the B&B all day while everyone else does all the work. Isn't there something I can do to help?"

"Actually—there might be," Jem said. "We know McArthur was seeing you, and Kit, and Roger. Kit says Uriah turned up at Neptune Cottage. Roger says the same, but on a different night. And you met Uriah at The Brazen Head..."

"Uriah made two trips out to Bryher?" Rhys asked.

"Three, if he's the murderer."

"That's a long way from Marazion," Micki said.

"Yep. It bothers me, too. Then again, if he had a yacht..." Jem smiled at Pauley.

"I know how I can help," Clarence said suddenly. "I can go back to The Brazen Head. The bartender will probably remember me. If he knows Uriah, I can get his last name. Maybe even track him down and ask some questions."

"I don't know." Jem hated to squelch his newfound enthusiasm, but the idea hatched several scenarios, none of them good. "If he's half as tough as Kit makes him out, you could be putting yourself in danger. If he's not really a psychopath, but just snapped the way Roger did, you might spook him. Best case, you go all the way there and come up with nothing. Suppose the bartender doesn't recognize you, or the gay community is full of Uriahs?"

"Gay community?" Clarence scoffed. "Hon, we're talking about a tiny corner of the West Country. It's more like a knitting circle than a community. Maybe I forgot to say, but Uriah wasn't in The Brazen Head when Arthur—McArthur, damn it

—and I turned up. Madame Defarge saw us come in, put down her needles, and rang up Uriah. 'Get over here, he's back,' was probably all it took for him to come running."

Pausing for a sip of wine, Clarence seemed to envision the possibilities. Then he continued, "Maybe the murder news hasn't hit Marazion yet? If I go in and tell the bartender that Mr. Tall Blond and Rich will meet me there soon, maybe Uriah will magically turn up again."

"Not that it's my murder case," Hack said, eyes on his phone and stylus tapping. "And lucky for you, I'm so absorbed in my work, I didn't hear any of that. But if you think Uriah might have killed a man in cold blood, it's foolish to surprise him on his patch by accusing him of it."

"Yeah, Clarence." Jem gave him an apologetic smile. "Hack's right."

"I could go," Micki offered. "But only if you can wait a week. I'm working Monday through Thursday and singing Friday and Saturday night."

"Live?" Jem and Pauley asked at the same time and in the same hopeful tone.

"In the studio. Laying down background tracks for Tommy and the Knockers. I'm doing it gratis so they'll forgive me for... you know."

"Oh." Jem tried not to sound disappointed. At least Micki was singing again. But it was singing live she had a mental block about, not harmonizing vocals in a cozy recording booth.

"I'll go," Rhys said. "People were always saying what's-his-face looked like me. We're the same type, anyway, especially in a dark pub. If Clarence and I turn up for drinks around the same time as before, maybe that will flush Uriah out."

"But this is mental," Micki protested. "You're saying that if the murder news hasn't come to Marazion, the bartender will see you, mistake you for McArthur, and ring Uriah. But if

Uriah's the killer, he's the one person in Marazion who knows the truth. So he won't come."

"True," Rhys said, untroubled. "But while we're in Marazion, we can probably zero in on his name and address. And if he does turn up to confront McArthur... well, that means he's probably not the killer, doesn't it? Which at least strikes him off Jem's list." He smiled, looking pleased with himself.

Give that boy a Tasty Bite, Jem thought.

The jam roly-poly went over much better than the main course, now that Hack's report was filed, Micki had decided to forgive Clarence, and Rhys had put "Felix Catchpole" out of his head. Jem was just about to ask if she should uncork another bottle of wine when Hack's mobile rang.

"Hackman speaking. Yeah. That's right. Okay. Cheers. Why? Sent through when? No, no, you did right. At that age I'll take the family's word, even if it's only been a few hours. Terry O'Dell. O, apostrophe, capital D, e, l, l..."

Rhys groaned. "Are you kidding? I didn't really expect you to sit on it forever, but I assumed you'd last till morning."

Scowling at the interruption, Hack rose and walked rapidly into the library. Still talking, he closed the door behind him.

"Easy now," Pauley said. "You had to know Hack would be straight with PC Newt or whoever that was. As for your friend, if he's truly reformed, he won't mind so much."

Clarence exchanged a curious glance with Micki, then said, "I guess we missed whatever this is about. But... we're still on for Marazion, right?" He looked away shyly as he asked the question, but managed to get the words out without stammering or going mute.

"Yeah, of course. Tomorrow. We'll get Bart to pick us up around... what? Three o'clock? Hit The Brazen Head around five? I know it's a bit early, but otherwise we might not be able to get back to St. Morwenna by sundown."

"Perfect," Clarence said. Though still too shy to meet Rhys's eyes, he looked pleased with himself. In Jem's book, that was a victory, considering how overawed of Rhys he'd always been.

Down the hall, the library door opened. Hack returned to the kitchen mobile in hand. The look on his face—utterly blank —made Jem's stomach drop.

"What?" she asked, keeping her voice steady with effort.

"It seems that Terry O'Dell left Tresco around two o'clock in his runabout, a Chris-Craft Speedster," Hack said. "This is according to his adult daughter, Helene, who lives in Hugh Town.

"Apparently, Mr. O'Dell is a metal detector hobbyist and likes to comb the beaches for lost objects. Helene's son—Mr. O'Dell's grandson—wanted in on the action but kept being warned off, apparently. Today he seems to have been spying on his granddad." Hack shrugged. "I don't know if it was just a game, or if he thought his grandfather was up to his old tricks again. Thieving, in other words. Anyway, the boy followed him from island to island by using ferries, or by getting a ride in someone else's boat. When the kid reached Bryher, he found the Speedster at Neptune Cove, just sitting on the foreshore. No Terry O'Dell. That was five and a half hours ago."

"Is that so bad?" Micki looked around the table, studying faces. "I mean, he's a grown-up, and it hasn't been twenty-four hours. Maybe he holed up with a friend. McArthur wasn't the only bloke getting busy in Scilly."

Jem reflexively groaned at that, as did everyone else.

"Just something I'm workshopping," Micki muttered.

Hack said, "O'Dell is an elderly widower who lives alone. People look out for him. According to his daughter, he attended a seven o'clock meeting in Hugh Town every Sunday without fail. But tonight he didn't turn up, so the leader phoned her. Helene became agitated, which prompted the grandson to cough up the details of his follow-the-leader game, and how he found the runabout abandoned on the beach. PC Newt just located it, right where the kid said it would be. So we have a missing persons case. Terry O'Dell was last seen on the water, en route to Bryher, around three p.m."

Rhys groaned.

"Right. You know something more. Time for a full confession," Hack said. "Now."

20

PIE IN THE SKY

The moment was hours in the making, but it came off exactly as Pauley had planned. She was breezy. Spontaneous. Cheerfully gothic in an ensemble that was equal parts jet black and baby pink. It didn't take a mirror or a selfie for her to know her look landed perfectly. It was obvious from the moment their eyes met.

Of course, actually getting to that magic moment was a process. Step one: pack an overnight bag. Step two: lock up Lyonesse House. Step three: accompany Jem to St. Morwenna's quay to board *Bellatrix*.

On Sunday nights, Jem usually departed for Penzance around nine o'clock, but the group dinner and unexpected news about Terry O'Dell had delayed things. By the time they arrived at Penzance Harbor and tied up in Jem's rented slip, it was pushing midnight and there was plenty of yawning. Fortunately, the walk from the promenade to Jem's building was a stressless ten minutes. Even at the witching hour, Penzance was safe and serene.

"Or is it?" Pauley wondered as they started up the stairs to Jem's flat. "My theory is, your body generates a sort of increased homicide probability field. If I'm right, your mere presence warps the odds that a slaying will occur. You're the eye of the storm. And now that you've flitted from the islands to Penzance, people hereabouts are feeling a strange compulsion. Like contemplating steak knives, or suddenly googling household poisons."

Apparently too tired to dignify any of that with an answer, Jem unlocked the door. The living room was dark; on the sofa, a blanket-draped lump snored faintly. Tori Jago, Jem's little sister and flatmate, resided there full-time, sleeping on the sofa as there was only one bed.

"Remember, I have a double," Jem told Pauley. "You can either take the bathtub or kip with me, I don't mind. But if you elbow me in my sleep like you did when we were kids, I swear I'll elbow you back."

"Fine. But the minute I feel the touch of an ice-cold foot, I'm screaming blue murder."

"I'll sleep in socks."

"See that you do. Oh, hallo, Wotsit. How's kitty life treating you?" Pauley asked the cat who strolled across the room to meet them with studied indifference. Her eyes weren't yet accustomed to the gloom, but shorthaired, tailless Wotsit was mostly white and therefore easy to pick out.

"I like that. You get a sniff and a head bump. I get ignored," Jem said as the cat, having acknowledged Pauley's presence, pointedly turned away from her. "He doesn't approve of my weekends off."

"Of course he doesn't. He can always come live at Lyonesse House," Pauley said, not for the first time. "Unless you plan on renewing this lease for another year."

"Stop badgering me on that. I haven't decided if I can handle the commute," Jem said, also not for the first time. "Let's get some sleep."

The bed, although too narrow, was reasonably comfortable.

When Jem's mobile roused them at seven o'clock, Pauley awakened feeling rested, despite the suspicion she'd been elbowed a few times.

While Jem and Tori rushed through breakfast—hot coffee and cold cereal—Pauley did her morning yoga routine. As she finished up, the sisters hurried out to work, Tori muttering about missing the bus, Jem looking tight-lipped as she no doubt contemplated her meeting with the boss. Once they were gone, Pauley settled down with a cup of tea on her right and Wotsit on her left to swipe through the latest digital issue of *Vogue*.

She already knew what she was wearing, but putting out feelers for fresh inspiration never hurt. And as it happened, a photo spread on vintage Versace gave her the idea of adding a retro scarf-and-sunglasses combo to her ensemble. Pranav had asked her to meet him at the helipad at half-ten, which gave her time to pop by Questionable Taste, a second-hand shop.

Twenty minutes and twenty quid later, she had a sheer black scarf and oval-lensed sunnies with darling pale pink accents. When she gazed at herself in the shop's full-length mirror, she saw generous curves poured into a ruched black dress, black stockings, and patent leather granny boots. Baby pink laces kept the dress's plunging neckline under control—she was full-figured in more ways than one—and her parasol had a matching pink lace fringe she'd sewed on herself.

"Dita Von Teese? Please. You're going to kill," said the clerk, who was possibly on commission. Pauley decided to take the compliment as sincere nevertheless.

Not only will I kill, but I might also find the Sunseeker and nail a murderer, she told herself. Exiting Questionable Taste, she set out to find Pie in the Sky Helicopter Tours. It operated out of Penzance Heliport, which was located off Jelbert Way.

Because Jelbert ran adjacent to the waterfront, she'd imagined the heliport to be near the Promenade, but her mobile's navigation app soon disabused her of that notion. If she intended to walk, she was in for a long one, much of it along a busy motorway without a footpath. Sighing at the added expense, Pauley booked a ride via Uber—only recently available in the West Country—for the very first time.

It was a pleasant ride. The woman who picked her up in a red Ford Fiesta was cheery, had passionate opinions on the *Game of Thrones* finale—"Worst ending in the history of ever!" — and got Pauley to the heliport in record time. She alighted at precisely half-ten, only to realize she still had a way to go. On one side of the motorway was a KFC and a Tesco Superstore; on the other, a car park and acres and acres of green pastureland. The low office attached to the hangar was gray and faceless, with tinted windows. She didn't want to bumble in like a typical emmet, bleating about whether she'd found the right place. She wanted to catch Pranav by surprise and bowl him over.

Hoping she wasn't bollixing things up, she walked all the way around the office's south side. Completely alone under a clear blue sky, with no sound but her heels clicking on the pavement, she went as far as the footpath allowed, then cut across the lawn. There was the concrete helipad with its big painted H, a white helicopter parked atop it. And there was Pranav beside the aircraft, peering into what she assumed was a maintenance port.

Walking as close as she could without stepping onto the pad —since she knew her heels would click—she waited until he closed the metal door, then said casually, "I don't know why, but I expected something smaller."

He spun around with gratifying speed, a smile in place even before taking her in. Then his mouth went slack and his gaze traveled up her body, pointed toes to chiffon scarf.

She slipped off her sunglasses. Their eyes came together, *click*, as loud as her heels, and she knew every second of preparation had been worth it.

"Sorry," Pranav mumbled.

"Why?"

"You said something. No idea what. You look... amazing."

"Thank you. So do you," she said, twirling her parasol for emphasis. He was slightly more dressed-up than she'd expected —tan chinos, button-down shirt, red windcheater. Maybe it was just her ego basking in his praise. Or maybe standing beside a six-ton machine—one he could in fact propel into the sky at will —somehow made his cheekbones stand out. Either way, this date was already worth the price of an Uber.

"What I said was, I imagined a smaller heli. A two-seater. But that's silly, isn't it? If your brother does tours, he'll want to carry more than one person at a time."

"Exactly. Well." He bounced on his toes, looking eager and just the tiniest bit nervous. "The bird checks out. Weather conditions are perfect. Ready to earn your wings?"

"Sure."

Climbing aboard was slightly tricky from a modesty standpoint—the ruched dress, her sexiest, hadn't been designed for anything but standing still. Still, once she was settled in the front passenger seat, she was surprised to find nothing but clear plastic beneath her feet.

"That's so you get the best view," Pranav said, climbing into the pilot's seat. He put on a headset, adjusted the microphone, then passed its clone over to her. Through it, she heard him say, "Fasten your seat belt and take a deep breath. We're going up."

Blades overhead whirling, the helicopter rose smoothly as Pauley, equal parts afraid and entranced, watched the world under her granny boots drop away. She glimpsed the big red fire engine parked beside the open hangar and the single carriageway that was Jelbert Road. Then the heli picked up speed, climbing higher as it did, and Pranav radioed a quick assurance back to someone at Pie in the Sky. Pauley didn't process the actual words; she was gazing at St. Michael's

Mount, looking like a fairy-tale castle surrounded by the silvery sea.

"I like to travel around ten thousand feet," Pranav's voice said in her ear. "But as we come in around coves and whatnot, I can get as low as five hundred."

"No need to get that low to pick out a Sunseeker."

"No, but we might need to come in for the name. Or better still, the WIN," he said.

"Listen to you." She flashed him a smile. "Good point. I didn't even think about the watercraft identification number."

"It wasn't that long ago I aced my skipper certification course."

"I hope you can always be a water postie. No matter how reliable the drones get. Oh! There's a big yacht moored at the jetty. See it?" Pauley pointed with her foot. Penzance's long stone and metal fingers reached into the sea, like slender trees blooming with boats. "Can we swoop in?"

"Swooping—now," he agreed, banking hard and laughing at her gasp of surprise. "Sorry. But you can't expect me not to show off a bit."

"It's all right. Jem and her mysteries are turning me into a sort of quasi-thrill seeker."

"Oh, yeah? Fancy a roller coaster? A log flume ride?"

"I've never set foot in an amusement park."

He made a shocked noise. "You have to come to The Flambards Experience with me. The Hornet Roller Coaster—you won't regret it."

"There!" Pauley pointed again, this time touching his shoulder to keep him from passing over the boat.

He grinned at her. "Sorry. Coming round again."

"Oh. I can already see it's not right. It's too aerodynamic and those gray accents are wrong. The one I saw McArthur on was all white and had a lot of miles on it."

"Good. I didn't want to end the search quite that fast anyway, if I'm being honest," Pranav said.

Same here, Pauley thought, and smiled at him.

The flight over patchwork Cornish pastures, many still quite green and carved into jumbled rectangles by ancient hedgerows, made Pauley's heart swell. There was something about the countryside that fed the soul, fulfilling a primeval need for verdant, peaceful places. Next came Land's End, that craggy granite headland, gateway to the English Channel and the Celtic Sea. It looked as callous and forlorn as those mismatched green and brown pastures had been lively and welcoming. Even from her helicopter seat, Pauley thought she could hear the waves crash, could almost feel the knifing wind.

"There's Longships Lighthouse," Pranav said after a moment. "Kind of pretty, don't you think? I feel wistful just looking at it. Can't imagine what it must be like to live there."

"No one lives there," Pauley said. The white froth around the jagged shapes of the Longships islet were hypnotic; sad and lovely and faintly menacing, all at the same time. It made her think of an armored plesiosaur breaching the waves, or a stone dragon, half-submerged. "It's automated now."

"Wow. You know your lighthouses."

"I live on St. Morwenna, remember? We've been trying to get ours back in tourist shape for ages."

"I always forget about Tremayne Lighthouse. No offense, but that thing's more of a saltshaker."

"Please promise me you'll keep that opinion to yourself." Already anticipating the day she'd have to come clean about the true identity of Felix Catchpole, she didn't want Pranav to start his acquaintance with Rhys by insulting the venerable old family home.

Soon, her familiar Isles of Scilly came into view, beginning with the Eastern Isles. They looked larger than she expected from the air. Certainly larger than she tended to think of them, since they were all uninhabited.

"Below us, we have the Scilly Heritage Coast," Pranav said in a mock tour guide voice. "Down there can be found Bronze Age cairns, traces of Iron Age settlements, and—"

"—and a Roman shrine on Nornour," Pauley cut in.

"Nornour. That's odd. So they all have individual names?"

"Of course they do! Great Ganilly. Little Ganilly. Great Arthur. Little Arthur. *Medium* Arthur, for heaven's sake. And —" She broke off, realizing he was teasing her. "Fine. You did know. I should hope so, if you've been delivering the post around these parts for... how long?"

"Six months."

"Oh, look, there's a proper yacht. All white, I think," Pauley cried, pointing at a shape moored just north of Ragged Island.

"Then let's go check it out." Pranav banked sharply again. This time, Pauley's gasp was of sheer delight. She hadn't had so much fun in ages.

They worked their way through the islands, islets, and rocks, falling effortlessly into the sort of easy rapport Pauley expected only from longtime friends. The sheer continuum of color astonished her; pools of turquoise encircled by a French blue and purples that were dark as a bruise. Most of the vessels they spied were sailboats or small motorboats; while commercial fishing around the Isles of Scilly was good, the industry mostly went dormant in winter, when storms made conditions too chancy.

Around St. Mary's they found three large vessels, none of which matched the image in Pauley's mind's eye. Nevertheless, she took down the names jauntily painted across their transoms: *Luck Be A Lady*, *Moonshot*, and *Mine All Mine*.

Next, they buzzed along the rocky edges of St. Morwenna and its conjoined twin, Penlan. It was a meandering survey full of natural beauty but not a single yacht. Then Tresco, virtually a yacht convention—at least compared to the rest of the Scillies—but none of them matching the older, all-white behemoth she remembered. She took down a couple of self-consciously clever boat names anyway: *Vitamin Sea* and *My Kids' Inheritance.*

"There's Candlewick Castle," Pranav said. "And there's Bryher across the channel. Is it too obvious to fly around Neptune Cove and Hell Bay?"

"Nothing's too obvious. We're not low on petrol, are we?" she asked, thinking of the likely expense for the first time. How much did a helicopter ride cost in practical terms, anyway?

"We're fine," he assured her. "Let's go a bit lower. Even if you don't see your yacht, you might see some dolphins."

Bryher proved no more revealing as far as the Sunseeker, though Neptune Cove was now crime-taped off in addition to Neptune Cottage. Pauley checked her mobile to see if Hack had sent any updates about the missing Terry O'Dell, but he hadn't. There wasn't an update from Jem, either, despite the fact that her meeting with Mr. Atherton must've happened hours ago. Not a good sign.

"There's Gweal," Pranav said as Pauley stared at her phone. "Let me get a little altitude—well. Would you look at that?"

Her head came up. On the far side of Gweal, one of the biggest of the Norrad Rocks, was an all-white Sunseeker yacht. Viewed from above, she estimated it was closer to sixty-five feet than one hundred. Score a point for Clarence; his guestimate had been right. It was an older design but still luxurious, thanks to the flybridge and sleek lines.

"No one's on deck," Pranav said. "Let's swoop in toward the transom."

For the first time since their search began, they found themselves looking at a boat without a painted name. The legally mandated WIN was there, of course, but quite small—too small to see with the naked eye. Pranav had to buzz the yacht a few times, allowing Pauley to snap various digital pictures with her mobile until she managed a good one. When she zoomed in, the code read:

GB-SSR-55-820-C-04

"Here comes another vessel. You recognize it? Looks like a ferry," Pranav said.

Leaning across the cockpit to look past him, Pauley saw Kit Verran's primary boat, *Sweetheart 1*, beneath them. No passengers sat on the benches beneath the blue canvas awning, but Kit had exited the pilothouse and stood on deck, waving up at them.

"That's Kit Verran. He runs a ferry service out of St. Mary's. *The* service, really."

"A bad day for trade by the looks of it. Do you reckon he's just friendly?"

"Nope. He's signaling us. Maybe he wants to tell me something about that boat," Pauley said.

"Tell you personally? So he knew you'd be up in the sky today? In a Bell 212?"

She felt like an imbecile. "No, of course not. I thought because I could see him, he could see me. I don't know why he's flagging us down if he doesn't know who we are."

"I suppose he might be in some difficulty. Should we land on Bryher and find out?"

"Sure, but it doesn't have a helipad."

Pranav chuckled. "I'm allowed to land this bird anywhere, as long as I cause no damage and disturb no property. That spit of land looks clear enough for our purposes."

He touched down gently on a bit of scrubby turf and shut off the engine. Removing his headphones, he hopped out and ran around to her side of the cockpit, handing her down like a Victorian lady. She liked the obvious pleasure he took in playing the gentleman. She would've brought out her parasol for some seductive twirling, but the wind was gusting too strongly. Besides, Kit's presence way out here was curious, which meant flirting could wait.

Pauley and Pranav got as close to the waterline as the granite foreshore permitted—they weren't wearing shoes fit to clamber over sharp, wet rocks—but it wasn't close enough. Thanks to wind and distance, they couldn't hear Kit's shouted question from *Sweetheart 1*'s deck, and he evidently couldn't hear them. Finally, he held up his mobile and pointed. Pauley brought out her phone.

"Better pray to the satellite gods," Pranav said.

Kit's local resident hotline was already saved in her contacts list. She rang it, and he picked up right away. The connection was crackly, but it held.

"Is that Ms. Pauley Gwyn, apprentice sleuth?"

"Good eye!"

"Surprised to find you in the whirlybird. Guess you found the yacht I've been curious about. It's been moored thereabouts, on and off, for weeks now. Weird, eh? No name on the transom. I thought that's what you were looking for, based on your flight pattern. The WIN, right?"

"Yeah."

"I already copied it down and tried to look it up. Led me nowhere, I'm afraid. You really have to be police or Coastguard to determine ownership using it. And now that Arthur's dead, it shouldn't matter, of course. Either that, or it matters more than ever." He gave what sounded like a forced laugh, even over the static-filled connection. "I'm afraid I wasn't entirely honest about how we left it."

"How who left it?"

"Me and Arthur."

"What do you mean?"

"Oh, you know. I tried to play it cool for you and Jem Jago. Said I realized Arthur's game and told him off. Then Uriah turned up at the cottage, fit to be tied, and I washed my hands of the whole business."

"Are you saying you kept on seeing Arthur anyway?" Pauley didn't explain that "Arthur Ajax" was really A.J. McArthur; that was surely privileged information for the police to reveal or conceal as they chose.

"No. I called it quits. But I only pretended it was a total break. The fact is, he still had his hooks in me. I wanted him back. I assumed I'd get him back one day. But now he's gone forever, and it's left me chasing ghosts. Like this boat."

"I still don't follow," she admitted.

"Then I'm saying it wrong." Another forced laugh. "Listen. I don't claim to be a sleuth, and I probably have no right to say this, but Uriah struck me as dangerous. I think he's the killer. And this is the yacht I used to see around Bryher, sometimes, on my route. I think it belongs to Uriah. So you'd better take care, Pauley. If he realizes you're poking around, he might do something crazy."

21

"JUMP, JIVE AN' WAIL"

Rhys had never been to Marazion specifically, but he'd been through the village countless times in his younger days, on the way to a beach, a girl, or a pub. Sometimes all three. It was a pleasant stretch of coastline, connected to St. Michael's Mount by the famous disappearing and reappearing causeway. The houses were old and blocky, some white, some yellow, some made of rough brown stone. Many of the front gardens were concrete, but splashes of subtropical color often appeared—a bristle of green fronds here, a stalk of purple allium there.

The Brazen Head, a small two-story pub, lurked at the east end of Turnpike Road, next to a hedgerow with a strange crawl space cut near the bottom. Spying it, Rhys thought instantly of a fairy story in an old book. He couldn't recall the story itself, only the pen-and-ink illustration of a curious boy on his hands and knees, peering into a child-sized entrance. The caption read, *John wanted to see who had called his name.*

"Don't you go nosing around in there," Clarence said, coming over for a look. "I reckon someone made it for a dog to go in and out. Unless you'd rather crawl into Narnia than walk into a gay bar."

The remark proved what Rhys already knew; Clarence had loosened up considerably during their two-hour trip aboard *Merry Maid*, courtesy of Bart the Ferryman. They'd been the only passengers—a fact that moved Bart to make several unprovable and no doubt slanderous allegations about Kit Verran—and it had been necessary to strike up a conversation. After some probing, Rhys discovered that Clarence, like him, hated one football club above all others. Bonding over sports was run-of-the-mill; bonding over sports villains was golden.

That discussion did the trick. Midway through their joint dismantling of Real Madrid, Clarence stopped looking at his feet and stumbling over his words. By the time they disembarked from *Merry Maid*—almost a mile's walk from their destination, but as close as Bart's ferry could get them—they were kicking remarks back and forth like old teammates.

"I've been in gay bars before," Rhys said, turning to look at The Brazen Head. "At least, it's a safe bet. When I was drinking, I followed the booze. And guys have hit on me since I was—I don't know. Seventeen, eighteen. I say I'm not interested. It's no big thing. But what do you reckon the name means? 'Brazen Head?'" He pointed at the old-fashioned painted sign swinging on hinges over the door. It depicted a man's head, bald on top, mustachioed, with wide eyes and lips parted as if speaking. The head, including the eyes and hair, was all one color—light brown.

"Haven't the foggiest," Clarence said. "Let's go in and ask."

On a Monday in the mid-afternoon, it perhaps wasn't surprising to find only a handful of people inside. A man sat frowning at a fruit machine, pint in hand, as if silently debating whether to spin again. An old woman perched on a stool near the taps, watching CNN with the audio muted and the captions on. A family of four occupied one of the tables, the adults splitting a plate of chips, the kids eating sandwiches.

Rhys whispered to Clarence, "Are we sure this is the right place?"

"Maybe Saturday is pride night," he whispered back, then led the way to the bartender, who was staring at his mobile. Flashing a smile, he put it away and asked, "What will it be, gentlemen?"

"Pint of bitter," Clarence said.

"You have Dr. Pepper?"

"In the bottle."

"Perfect." Settling himself on a stool, Rhys asked, "What's a brazen head?"

"It's a legendary device. A human-looking wise man made out of brass," the bartender said, positioning a clean pint glass under the tap. "In some stories, they made the whole man. In other cases, just the head. You could ask it any question and it would answer."

"Like Siri," Clarence said.

"Exactly like Siri." The bartender finished pouring, handed Clarence his beer, and pulled a Dr. Pepper from the mini fridge. "I love those stories, because they're completely random and ludicrous in the context of the times. Roger Bacon, a Franciscan monk, was meant to have constructed a brazen head with the help of the devil. In another story, one is found in a cave—in that case, the complete man—but his head is cut off by a frightened mob and carried about thereafter." Popping off the bottle cap, he passed Rhys his soda.

"Sounds a bit like a robot. Described by people who didn't have a word for robot," Rhys said idly, tasting his soda.

The bartender rewarded him with a mischievous smile. "And who would've left a robot sitting about in a cave to be discovered by relative savages?"

"Aliens. I've heard this song before," Clarence said.

"It didn't have to be aliens," Rhys said. "It could have been some ancient civilization. One that built itself up and blew itself up a long time ago."

"Why do you say that?" the bartender asked.

"Because you said it was human-looking."

"Top marks. Antediluvian civilization. Google it." Picking up a pint glass, the bartender began to polish it with a flannel. "And that will be five quid."

They spent the next two hours chatting amiably with the bartender. He gave no sign of remembering Clarence's visit in the company of A.J. McArthur but did offer a variety of opinions on Atlantis and dimensional portals. As afternoon became evening, the family of four departed and the woman watching CNN left. Then the telly was switched off, dance music came on, and men began turning up, singly and in pairs. Soon the bartender had his hands full and there was even a bit of half-hearted dancing in the middle of the room.

"People are giving us the eye," Clarence murmured in Rhys's ear.

Rhys glanced around. They *were* getting sized up from men all over the room, but not with the intensity he'd hoped for. "We need to cause a stir."

"How?"

"Hang on." Rhys plunked down some two-pound coins to snag the bartender's attention. It took a few minutes, but when he finally made it back, Rhys said, "Another bitter for him and one for you."

"Cheers, mate."

"Now—can you switch over to rockabilly music? Or swing?"

He looked pained. "Why?"

"Only we've learned a dance routine and he's shy." Rhys elbowed Clarence lightly for emphasis. "He says he's afraid to enter a competition. I say, if he can dance here in front of all these blokes, he can dance anywhere."

"All right. Give me a sec." He adjusted something on his phone, and the pub's music went from Kylie Minogue to the Brian Setzer Orchestra. The room erupted into cries of protest. "As requested. Godspeed."

Ignoring Clarence's deer-in-the-headlights expression, Rhys grabbed his hand and pulled him onto the pub's makeshift dance floor. His feet knew the routine—rock step, triple step, rock step—and for a few seconds he was doing them solo, as Clarence continued to stare at him in mute horror. Then he extended shaking hands, Rhys seized them, and they fell into a promenade and circle with reasonable grace.

"I don't know the woman's part," Clarence said.

"Don't look at me. Just improvise." Rhys dipped Clarence forward, then back, almost spilling him into the midst of some onlookers. The narrow save sparked appreciative laughter.

"Now Charleston," Rhys said, releasing him.

"God help me." Clarence started slow but rapidly matched Rhys's pace—first with bouncing steps, then slides, and then finally kick-crosses. Someone in the crowd whistled.

Knowing the watchers were on their side improved their mutual rhythm. Turns, twirls, swing outs—the faster and more expertly they performed the maneuvers, the more the patrons grinned and cheered. As Setzer's version of "Jump, Jive An' Wail" neared its end, Rhys said, "Big finish. Cradle swap."

"No bloody way!"

"Back-to-back with a flip."

"Oh Lord," the other man prayed, even as they turned in sync. Clarence was about as heavy a lift as he expected, but that didn't stop Rhys from catapulting the other man on his back, over his head, and smack down on his feet again, all to explosive applause.

"I can't... my heart..." Clarence gasped. Wide-eyed, he pressed a hand to his chest. "Did I survive?"

"You did and they love you. Me, too," Rhys said, sweeping

an elegant bow he'd learned for a Tidepool Players role called the Pransome Hense.

"Amazing," said one of the nearest onlookers, a middle-aged man in a hibiscus shirt. "Glad you two made it back after—you know. That ridiculous scene."

"You remember that?" Rhys asked, or rather coughed, since someone chose that moment to slap him on the back.

"Of course. Poor Uriah hasn't lived it down yet."

"Harry here gave him a ring to say you've come back," said another man, this one younger, with an impish smile.

"I did," said the aforementioned Harry, waggling his mobile as proof. "Sorry. I do fancy a bit of drama. Maybe Uriah will say sorry. Or maybe it will turn into round two."

"I'm not bothered," Rhys said, affecting nonchalance, though inside he was high-fiving, down-lowing, fist-bumping, and finger-gunning. He'd potentially pulled his sternocleido-mastoid during the big finish, but the impromptu Lindy Hop had flushed out Uriah. Jem was sure to be impressed.

They returned to their barstools to wait. The man in the hibiscus shirt had followed them to the bar and was asking politely how long Clarence had been swing dancing. Rhys pretended to have eyes only for Clarence—if he seemed completely absorbed in the other man, hopefully no one would zero in on him as someone looking for company—but really kept his eyes on the door. Within ten minutes, it opened, and a bearded man in a fisherman's hat and vest entered. He did so warily, eyes flicking around the room, and when his gaze alighted on Rhys, he stiffened.

Is he disappointed that I'm not McArthur? Or did he know I couldn't be, since he killed him? In which case, he only turned up because Harry gave him a bell, and it might've seemed suspicious to ignore it...

Uriah continued standing halfway inside The Brazen Head, door open behind him, until Rhys stood up and crossed the room to meet him. In the process, he glanced over his shoulder at Clarence, but the man hadn't noticed. He was deep in conversation with Mr. Hibiscus, who seemed utterly fascinated.

"Hiya," Rhys said. "I take it you're the bloke who had it out with Arthur Ajax a few weeks back."

"I was told he'd be here. Who are you?"

"I can't wait to tell you. But it's loud in here. Let's go outside for a bit."

Uriah scowled beneath his beard. Wild and long overdue for a trim, the wild reddish hair made him look menacing, especially with that floppy hat shading his eyes. He asked, "You his brother or summat?"

"No. Transplant from the north, are you?"

"Yorkshire." Glancing behind him, Uriah took what appeared like a reluctant step into the street. The caution wasn't unreasonable. He wasn't a slight man by any means—he certainly looked like he could hold his own in a brawl—but Rhys overtopped him and had a longer reach. He was ten years' Uriah's junior, too.

Under the creaking wooden sign, Uriah said, "You must be kin to him. So where is he?"

"Dead," Rhys said, and proceeded to explain. Try as he might, he couldn't gauge the other man's reaction. Uriah claimed to have spent the afternoon on the water, mobile switched off, which explained how he'd missed the news.

"Well, then. Poor Arthur. Sorry he's dead," he said. "Wish our last meeting hadn't been such a mess. But it was. And I still don't know what you're doing here, or what you want with me."

"You see my friend at the bar? Black bloke named Clarence? He was with Arthur that night. Said you told him to watch his step. That SETI was listening in. What did you mean by that?"

"SETI?" Uriah stared at him, then barked a laugh. "Seefoe!

That's what I said. SETI listens for UFOs." He pronounced the acronym "you-foes."

"What's 'seefoe?'"

"S, F, O. Serious Fraud Office."

"You work for them?" Rhys didn't mean to blatantly inventory Uriah, taking in his grotty trainers, bulging fisherman's vest, and fly-adorned hat, but he must've been both obvious and offensive, because Uriah snapped,

"Aye, I did, whether you believe it or not. I'm on sabbatical now. Living on my boat."

"What kind of boat?"

"Why in the blazes should I tell you?"

Rhys sighed. He was making a dog's breakfast of this interview, mostly because he was overeager. Did Jem find this so difficult? Impossible.

"I'm sorry. Let's take it from the top. My name's Rhys Tremayne. I'm a friend of Jem Jago. She's been mentioned on telly and in *Bright Star* once or twice. Called the Scilly Sleuth?"

Uriah stared at him as if he were babbling in Greek.

"Scilly as in, Isles of Scilly?"

"Heard nowt," Uriah said.

"Fair play. Only Jem's looking into the murder of Arthur Ajax. I mean, the man you knew as Arthur Ajax. Unless the Serious Fraud Office knew him by his real name?"

Uriah continued to stare at him.

"Are you sworn to secrecy now? Because you weren't then. You burst into that pub and talked until Arthur disappeared."

"First, I was three sheets to the wind. Arthur had stuck a knife in my heart. Second, this Clarence must have been half in the bag himself, since he didn't understand a word of it. I never said SFO"—he again pronounced it seefo—"was monitoring *him*. I said it was monitoring a man named Derrick Christensen."

It took a second for that name to register with Rhys, even

though Jem and Pauley had mentioned it only the night before. Trying not to sound too eager, he said, "So you had reason to believe Arthur was in league with Derrick Christensen?"

"In league?"

"Sorry. I mean, working with. Conspiring with—"

"In league's what you do with the devil."

"Right. You're the fraud expert. What would you call it?"

"I don't know. Because I don't know for certain Arthur was in criminal association with Derrick Christensen. I didn't even know of Mr. Christensen's whereabouts, or what he looks like. For all I know, you could be him."

"I'm not, I promise."

"How do you know about him?"

"I told you, Jem Jago is investigating the murder. She noticed that Arthur—his name was actually McArthur, if that matters to you—kept a wicker basket full of letters. All were addressed to John R. Derry."

"Oh, aye. I saw them. Saw something else in his cottage, too. A manila folder full of press clippings and stories pulled off the web."

"About John R. Derry?"

"Not about him personally. About the mail fraud and the sting operation," Uriah said patiently, as if Rhys might be soft in the head. "Some of the worst people involved were caught and prosecuted, but the man at the top scarpered."

"So you thought McArthur was—what? Admiring Derrick? Hero-worshipping him?"

"I thought he was sleeping with him," Uriah snapped. "Because that's what he did with virtually every man he met. Each and every one that would have him, anyway. I'm not sure you're up to this. Maybe you'd better give me this Jago lady's number."

"I'll do better," Rhys said. "Why don't I take you to meet her?"

22

A QUESTION OF PRIORITIES

Jem was just settling into her second bowl of ice cream—Moomaid of Zennor's Shipwreck flavor, bought at a Tesco Express on her way home—when her mobile buzzed. It was Pauley, wanting to FaceTime. Jem accepted.

"Oh! Look at you! What's going on?" Pauley asked. She looked flushed and happy, her magenta hair uncharacteristically askew.

"Spa night," Jem said, smiling at her green face in her screen's inset picture. The avocado mask was working its magic on her complexion while her hair dried in a towel-turban. Her fingernails had been buffed, filed, and varnished; her toes had undergone the same treatment and were now air-drying, held apart by foam spacers. "What about you?"

"I just got home," Pauley said. "What did you do with the WIN number I texted you?"

"Sent it to Hack. He said he'd get back to me if it yielded anything worthwhile. He's busy with the search for Terry O'Dell," Jem said. "If it goes on for much longer, they'll have to shift into recovery mode and start looking in the water."

"How's Rhys dealing with it?"

"I don't know. Haven't heard from him or Clarence yet. I reckon they're still at the pub in Marazion."

"Well, it's sad about Mr. O'Dell. I know he was just trying to help."

"You're feeling very generous this evening," Jem said. "Last night, you said he was an old crook looking out for crooks in general."

Pauley tossed her head. "Maybe. Doesn't matter. Ask me how I got home."

"How did you get home? Did Pranav land at the Tresco Heliport?"

"That's what I expected, but he said if he dropped me there, I'd have to take a ferry home. So he flew me to St. Morwenna and set me down in the gorse patch outside Hobson's Farm. I felt like a VIP."

"Then he's not entirely awful."

"Not entirely, no." Pauley grinned. "You did good, you cheeky monkey. Only there's something we need to get straight."

"If you mean to tell me off for setting you up when you have obviously had a perfectly lovely first date, I'm hanging up."

"No. Just this. For the time being, we'll need to weave a web of lies."

"Weave a what?"

"Web of lies," Pauley repeated. "As far as anyone knows, I went up in Felix Catchpole's brother's heli. It was fine, I found the Sunseeker and talked to Kit, but that's all."

"Pauls. Rhys is going to find out sooner or later. If you don't want him interfering, tell him."

"I know. But he's going to be unbearable," Pauley protested. "And this time... look at it this way. You know how sometimes you hear about a guy, and he's absolutely perfect on paper? Right job, right history, right everything? Then you meet him, and it's just—meh. Or worse, total repulsion?"

"Right."

"So Pranav is the opposite. He's lovely. He's hot. I can't wait to see him again. But on paper—he's a quagmire. Rhys will lose his mind. And I don't want to spend between now and Christmas fighting with him when I could be slipping off with Pranav whenever possible. *Christmas*," she added, singing the word. "The holidays! Now I can't wait."

"Back up," Jem said. "What do you mean, he's a quagmire? He can't be married. I know how you get about that. Men who cheat on their girlfriends give you hives. Men who cheat on their wives..."

"That's the thing. He's not cheating," Pauley said.

Jem blinked at her. "What? He *is* married?"

"All right, this is what happened. But I'm swearing you to secrecy in advance."

"Tell me."

"Promise you won't tell Rhys."

"It's not fair to expect me to hide something from him when I don't even know what I'm—"

"Jem!" Pauley broke in. "This is important to me."

"Fine. Proceed."

"Right." She took a breath. But while she seemed to try and assume a more sober bearing, her eyes sparkled the moment she said the postie's name. "After we talked to Kit, Pranav's brother, Dev, radioed from Pie in the Sky to tell him something about a broken turbine. Or a mended turbine. I don't know. Anyway, right before he signed off, he said, 'By the way, your wife's rung twice. Better see what's up.'

"Naturally, that burst my bubble. I mean, we hadn't called it a date, and we hadn't precisely *said* we were interested in each other, but some things are so obvious, they don't need words. I felt like I'd been punched. And Pranav sort of choked, like he hadn't expected his brother to say such a thing. He ended the call and apologized. Said Dev was a bit morally rigid and didn't like to see women deceived. So he deliberately mentioned Nora—that's the wife—because he knew I was in the cockpit and would overhear."

Jem nodded, amazed by Pauley's calm demeanor. Usually the mere suggestion of such situations got her back up.

"Pranav explained that he and Nora married ten years ago. They have a son, Michael, who's five. Not long after Michael came along, they started having problems. To mend things, they moved to Penzance for a fresh start. Bought a cute little house, did counseling, all that. But it didn't take. He says they just fell out of love. They're friends, of course. But the only thing they really have in common is Michael.

"Right when they started divorce proceedings, the economy took a turn. Nora was made redundant. Their student debt was crushing. They took bankruptcy because they thought it would help them save their home. Now they might lose it. They had to put the divorce on hold, because that costs money, too. So even though the marriage is over..." She trailed off hopefully, her big eyes pleading with Jem to empathize.

"They're still living together in the house while they try to get their heads above water? I mean—it's not unheard of," Jem said. "Especially when there are little kids in the mix. But." She paused, searching for a gentle way to make her next point, then gave up and just said it. "Since it's not unheard of, it's the perfect line for married men to use on prospective girlfriends. Especially ones who live in the Isles of Scilly and aren't likely to run into the wife in the shops."

Pauley surprised her by grinning. "That's what I said! Jem, I was so upset, you should've seen me. If I hadn't been on blinking Bryher, for heaven's sake, I would've stomped off and left him explaining to thin air. But I was stuck, and I had to hear him out. He's married. He's bankrupt. He's worried he'll be made redundant, too, if the drones do a better job delivering the post than people can. But he's not a liar. Ask me how I know."

Jem felt a rough wet swipe on her cheek and turned to see Wotsit, who'd crept up beside her. Having sampled her avocado face mask—which he wasn't enjoying very much, based on the emphatic way he was licking himself, as if to rid his sandpaper tongue of the taste—he tried to go for her Moomaid of Zennor.

"Tori!" Jem bellowed.

From the bedroom, her sister bellowed back, "I'm on the phone, aren't I?"

"Hang on." Giving Wotsit a lick of her spoon, Jem carried the bowl to the kitchen, washing what little remained down the sink. Shipwreck was a wonderful flavor, but she'd had enough. On her way home that morning, she'd imagined ringing up Pauley and pouring out her heart. But now she was beginning to think Pauley's heart was too full for anyone else's drama. At least for today. Besides, Jem's long afternoon of pampering had achieved the desired result. At the moment, she felt good.

"Now. Pauls." Jem sat down at the kitchen table, studying her friend via FaceTime. "If I know you—I think you called Pranav's bluff, or his potential bluff. You asked him to introduce you to Nora."

"Yes!" Pauley cried. "I said, listen, if you expect me to believe this story, I need proof. Take me back to Penzance and show me this isn't a lie. And he did. We had tea with Nora. She's lovely. Has her own boyfriend, thank you very much. It's really just a matter of time before the divorce goes through."

"Thank goodness. He told me he was single, you know," Jem said, suddenly recalling their first meeting. "I asked him in a roundabout way, but he gave me the strong impression he was a bachelor. I suppose I can't blame him. If he tried to tell the full and complete story to everyone he met, it really would be a quagmire."

"So. You see my point," Pauley said. "About Rhys."

"Yeah. But, Pauls. If you don't want him in your business, you need to put your foot down."

"I know. But that's easy for you to say, isn't it? All the time you were gone, he was my best friend. The boundaries got a little blurred. He has this crazy idea he's protecting me from the bad guys." She stopped to consider. "All right, a couple of them were pretty lowdown, now that I think about it. But mostly they're just blokes, and Rhys still finds reasons they aren't good enough, every time. I can't let him do that to Pranav. I just need to find a way to make Rhys like him *before* I tell him we're dating."

"This really will be a web of lies."

"I know. Will you help me?"

"Of course." Jem sighed.

"Oh! I can't believe I forgot to tell you. Pranav emailed some friends in Putney. They work at the mail-sorting center. They confirmed that a tranche of John R. Derry's correspondence was stolen from a storage locker. It had already been put aside to be given into police custody upon request."

Jem sat up straighter. "Wait. So they were stolen after the sting happened? Or before, while it was still quietly unfolding?"

"After," Pauley said. "Everyone knew it was a mail fraud case. The police had already impounded—is that the word?—or taken charge of tons of mail. Like, literally tons. These were stragglers that came in after the fact."

"Weird. I was assuming the letters were kept as part of a scheme to suppress the fraud," Jem said. "Why risk taking them after the jig was up? When the police already had plenty?"

"Pranav says the person who took them was never caught, but it was definitely a Royal Mail employee. No one else would have had the access. In which case, they were either involved directly with the scam, or bribed by someone. McArthur, I guess."

"But A.J. McArthur was from Manchester, not Putney." Another possibility danced on the edge of Jem's consciousness.

Just as she reached for it, her mobile vibrated, and a text from Rhys appeared. "Just a sec."

The text read,

Jackpot. Bringing you a surprise. Be there soon.

"Oh! Looks like Rhys and Clarence's trip to The Brazen Head paid off," Jem told Pauley. "Apparently he's coming to brag about it in person."

"Who's coming?" Tori asked from behind her, startling Jem into almost dropping her mobile.

"God, you're a walking jump scare. Rhys."

Tori, in pajamas, her brown hair up in twin pony-poofs, goggled at her. "He is? Tonight?" She gave a low whistle. "Tonight's the night?"

"Please. Look at me. I'm a walking jump scare myself." Jem pointed at her avocado-green face. "He's coming to talk about the case."

"Why don't I believe you?"

"Because you're a snotty little runt?"

"Please. And after I tenderly gave your giant feet a pedicure. Hiya, Pauley," Tori added, focusing on Jem's mobile screen. "As you see, my big sis has it together. Call it a resignation, call it being sacked, she's treating it like an opportunity."

"Get out of here!" Jem cried, swatting at the air.

"Oh! Shit! Sorry. I just assumed you—sorry!" Tori retreated back to the bedroom and shut the door.

"Jem." Pauley was staring at her. "What is she talking about?"

"Nothing earthshaking," Jem said, and was pleased to realize she meant it. "Only I had my meeting with Mr. Atherton, first thing. He was very displeased and disappointed. He kept using those words. First to be roused out of bed on Saturday. Then to be told that despite an official warning, I was back to my old tricks on Sunday. And put a good friend up to posing as an attorney and getting herself brought up on charges."

"But you didn't!"

"I know. Conrad lied about half of it and put the worst possible spin on the rest. He even told Mr. Atherton that I said I didn't give two figs about the Courtney's reputation. That I had my own reputation—my own brand, if you can believe it—and any library associated with me would just have to learn to like it."

"Oh!" Pauley began with mild curses, rolled into moderate ones that sounded like they came from Kenzie, then exploded into showstoppers. "You should sue him for defamation! For slander!"

"I don't think I'd get very far. He's a decorated officer with twenty-six years of service to the Devon & Cornwall Police," Jem replied calmly. She'd already raged in similar fashion, hours ago, and now had the benefit of some perspective. "Look at Hack. He had a great career on the murder squad until he took on Conrad. Now he's Mr. Drink Driving Patrol in the Isles of Scilly.

"Besides," she continued, "even if I could kick up enough fuss to raise some doubt, it wouldn't change Mr. Atherton's mind. He's kind of a bootlicker, if you want the truth. He believes anything that any person in authority tells him. He's scared of his own shadow and thinks I'm mental for even dipping a toe in a murder case."

"But he sacked you? Can he do that? Can you take it before a tribunal?"

"No," Jem said. "He just told me off about how distressed and disappointed and displeased he was. All the disses. Then he said he wanted me to commit to him in writing that if I continued with the Courtney, I would no longer be involved in any open police investigations. Otherwise, he'd speak to the board about finding me a position in London or Birmingham."

"And what did you say?"

"I told him I was giving notice. Six weeks. I thought maybe he'd back off," Jem admitted. "But I was so furious, I didn't care how he reacted. Which was good, because he said he'd waive the notice and pay me out. That I should clear out my desk and expect a lump sum by the middle of next month."

Pauley took that in, staring at Jem with huge eyes. Then she ventured, "I should've guessed. You never do a spa routine. *And* you were eating Shipwreck ice cream. All the signs were there. But I just nattered on and on about Pranav..."

"I wanted to hear about your date," Jem insisted. "And thank goodness you met Nora and it's all okay. Besides, look at it this way. I have money coming in. I'm free to work on the McArthur murder as much as I want. And now I'm a free agent."

"You'll be able to find other work in the West Country as a librarian? A Special Collections Librarian?"

"Yes," Jem said firmly.

"Where do you think?"

"I don't know."

"How long will a search take?"

"No idea."

"You seem... very sure of yourself. Which is perfect," Pauley added hastily.

"I'm good at what I do. Very good at it. Any library would be lucky to get me. But I'm good at cracking mysteries, too," Jem said. "Mr. Atherton put it to me as a question of priorities. He expected me to prioritize him. But I'm prioritizing me."

There came a hard rap on the door. "Open up, Jemmie!" Rhys called.

"Jeez, I thought I had more time," Jem said. "I'll give you a ring later, Pauls."

"Right. And if tonight does turn out to be the night—text me," Pauley said with a mischievous grin.

Jem didn't dignify that with an answer, just ended the call. Opening the door, she was surprised to find not just Rhys, but a bearded man in fishermen's gear. He gaped at her—robe, turban, avocado face mask—as Rhys burst out laughing. As usual, he closed his eyes, pressed both hands to his chest, and simply roared.

"Damn you!" she told him. He was too busy marinating in his own amusement to care.

"I'm Uriah Shaw," the stranger said, putting out a hand.

"Hallo, Uriah," she said, shaking it with a sense of disbelief. "A couple of people have made you out to be the boogeyman. So much so, I'm surprised Rhys would bring you to my home." She glared at him, still recovering from his laughing fit.

"It's all right, Stargazer. He's all right. I reckon little Roger's been lying to you. Him, or Kit. Listen to what Uriah has to say."

23

"THE HELL YOU WILL"

Jem retreated to the back of the apartment to wash her face, finger-comb her semi-dry hair, and change into a T-shirt and yoga pants. As she changed, she noticed that Tori, too, had ditched her pjs for real clothes, and had even put on a little make-up.

"What's up with you?" Jem asked. "I didn't plan on telling Pauley about the Courtney tonight, but I'm not about to give you the keys to the street, just because you blurted out the truth."

Tori looked up from her mobile. "Trying to get my mate Lila to answer a text."

"Why?"

"Because three's a crowd, that's why."

Wotsit let out a sharp meow.

"Sorry, Wotsit, I mean, three humans are a crowd. You're exempt. You grace us with your presence."

"For your information, there are two people waiting in the living room. Rhys and a bloke we used to consider a suspect. So you don't have to leave." Inspired by her sister's face, Jem paused to pick up a lipstick. It was a peachy pink she liked very much but hadn't worn in ages. Applying it, she smiled at herself in the mirror, pleased by the effect. Was it the mask treatment that had her cheeks glowing?

"Oh, yeah, I can see how you're all business," Tori said. "Go on. If I can't get Lila to meet me down the pub, maybe I'll catch a late movie."

"It's not necessary," Jem said, but she wasn't quite sure she believed it. Either way, she checked her hair in the mirror before leaving the bedroom. People, including Rhys, were always on her to "take down her hair," but when it was in the process of air-drying, it wasn't shown to best advantage.

Oh, well. It's not worth the breakage and split ends to blow-dry it. And I mean to hear Uriah's story, not pose for glamor shots. Maybe he'll say something that blows this puzzle wide open.

"Where's Clarence?" she asked, returning to the living room. She sat next to Rhys, who'd taken more than his fair share of the sofa, and opposite Uriah, who'd settled in the armchair. "Don't tell me you ditched him?"

"Of course we didn't ditch him," Rhys said mildly. "He chose to stay behind at The Brazen Head. Too busy chatting up a bloke called Jonathan to be bothered with anything else. Anyway, Uriah, the floor is yours. Tell Jem what you told me."

"Right." Uriah clasped his hands together, took in a deep breath, held it, and seemed to struggle inwardly for a clever opening statement. Then he let it all out in a rush and said, "It's my belief that Derrick Christensen is living in the West Country. I thought Penzance or thereabouts, but now I think he's in the Isles of Scilly. Problem is... I think a lot of things. Which is how I ended up on sabbatical."

"What do you mean?"

Uriah sighed. "Listen. I'm a forensic accountant. I'm quite skilled at my job, and since I've been with the Serious Fraud

Office, I've assisted on several high-profile cases. I'm proud of my CV."

Jem, who sensed a *but* coming, nodded helpfully.

"But sometimes I can get a bit... excited. That's how I ran into difficulties in London. Fancied myself as a sort of private investigator. I thought I could branch out. Get away from the desk. Go out in the wild and get my hands dirty."

"Oh," Jem said. In the recesses of her brain, a well-worn GIF about feeling personally attacked began to flash.

"So I took it upon myself to confront a man connected to a case. In my private time. Not criminally. Not even rudely," Uriah said, looking from Jem to Rhys as if that were the most important thing. "It's not my fault people have always found me too intense. Even intimidating. I don't know why. Well, presently, it might be the beard, but even clean-shaven." He shrugged. "So the suspect—I mean, the man in question—complained to the police that I had harassed him. It was the worst complaint about me. But not the only one."

"So they put you on sabbatical?"

"I call it sabbatical," Uriah said. "Actually, I got the sack. But I used the severance package to buy myself a very nice fishing boat."

"What kind?" Jem interjected.

He blinked at her. "Abermarle 31. Dual console."

"Nice. Don't suppose you have a picture of it?"

Uriah fumbled for his mobile, swiped through his camera roll, and came up with a picture of him standing on the deck. He looked miserable and vaguely threatening, but it was definitely him and clearly thirty feet, max.

"Thanks," Jem said. "We're looking into a sort of ghost ship with an unknown owner. A Sunseeker. Ring any bells? No? All right, sorry to interrupt. You bought a fishing boat."

. . .

"Aye. I find fishing therapeutic. And my solicitor thinks he can get me reinstated, next time the tribunal meets. As long as I promise to change my behavior.

"Anyway," he continued, clearly unaware of Jem's visceral reaction to his story, "I came to the West Country to rest up and recharge. Then I met Arthur and went right off the deep end." He made a stabbing thumbs-down gesture. "Rhys tells me you know all about him and his ways, so I won't bore you. Point is, I was still on the job in a sense, even though I wasn't. I found a wicker basket of letters in Neptune Cottage. Those John R. Derry letters. And I asked him straight out, 'Are you part of the space alien scheme?' He said no. That his property was none of my business and he'd thank me not to go snooping again."

"But you did," Jem said.

"But I did. The next time I spent the night, I checked between his mattress and the box spring. Tucked in there was a manila file full of clippings..."

"Hang on. Why did you think to look there?"

Uriah blinked. "Well, that's basic technique, wouldn't you call it? Check between mattresses. Peek in the freezer. Examine shoes for hollow heels and tables for hollow legs."

"You should be taking notes." Rhys winked at her.

"Shut it."

Investigators really check heels on shoes? Jem fully intended to write down Uriah's top tips. Just not in front of him.

"As I was saying," Uriah continued. "The folder contained some newspaper clippings about the fraud bust, and some internet search data that had been printed off. The search stuff was all about Derrick Christensen. Including his profile from the Most Wanted page."

"What did you do?" Jem asked.

"I confronted him, of course," Uriah said. "I asked if he knew Christensen. He denied it. Told me to get out of his place and never come back." He sighed. "It didn't help that I stewed over the question for days first. I rang some people in London to try and feel out whether the police had any leads on Christensen. Got myself all worked up. Then I showed up at the cottage, unannounced, and naturally Arthur wasn't alone. He had another man there, who wasn't best pleased to see me on the doorstep."

"Kit Verran," Jem said, remembering the ferry owner's account. "What happened next?"

"The other man left. Said he didn't want to be involved in a scene. Arthur barely heard me out. He was cruel," Uriah said. "I left feeling awfully low. Like a great fool. But I couldn't get it out of my head. The basket of letters was strange enough, but the file—the file seemed like blackmail. Or the beginnings of blackmail."

"When did you see McArthur next?" Jem asked.

"Down the pub. Marazion." The man gestured vaguely to the east. "He'd brought a new man with him—Clarence, your friend. Someone gave me a bell and said, hiya, that fellow you've been mooning over has moved on. Cheeky git. Still, I came to see for myself. Drunk and hurt and still working the case. You understand that, right? How once you home in on a mystery, you can never let it go?"

Jem, hoping fervently she had less in common with Uriah than she feared, nodded.

"So I said, if you know Derrick's whereabouts, put a flea in his ear. Seefo is monitoring him closely. Someone's always watching. Someone's always listening. That's what I said, and Arthur decided to leave," he said. "Clarence got the whole thing garbled, like a game of telephone. He thought I said SETI was listening in."

"Personally, I'm kind of crushed aliens aren't involved," Rhys said. "I know Jem is. She's a true believer."

Shooting him a look that promised pain at a future moment of her choosing, Jem leaned back against the sofa cushions.

Closing her eyes, she tried to view all the various nuggets of information as puzzle pieces, spread out before her.

"Don't sweat it," she heard Rhys tell Uriah as she refined the image in her mind's eye. "Groaning and writhing is all part of her process."

Arthur was killed in the morning by a man who slept over. Which man? He was still seeing Clarence, but I'm sure it's not him. He'd already broken Roger's heart. Roger claims he never went back after being left in the closet...

Jem opened her eyes. "Uriah, when you met Arthur at Neptune Cove, how did you get there?"

"On my boat."

"How often did you visit him there?"

"Four or five times."

"How many other men did you see there?"

"Just the one. My age. Bald. Kit, you called him."

"Suppose I tell you someone else claims you were there. That you barged into the bedroom, found some pajamas on the sewing machine, and ripped them out from under the needle."

"I'd never do that." Uriah looked appalled. "You could ruin something that way."

"But Roger claims Uriah was there," Rhys said.

"Yes. Well, no," Jem said. "He heard the name Uriah spoken. What he saw was part of a man wearing tan trousers and a red jacket."

"Half the males in Britain. Check."

"He assumed McArthur was calling the intruder Uriah. Is it possible he actually just used that name in a sentence? Suppose the intruder was really Derrick. Is it possible that McArthur mentioned Uriah to say, this fellow in Marazion is on to you?"

Rhys and Uriah seemed to consider that. Finally, Rhys said, "It's either that, or Roger's lying. I mean, he's an actor. And a doughy little guy. What sounds more believable to you? That he tried to strangle McArthur with a length of measuring tape? Or he snuck up behind him and conked him on the head?"

"The way he told the story, he was so gutted by McArthur's callous disregard, he fled the cottage and never went back. Never saw him again. Then confessed it all to Clarence because he needed someone to understand."

"Was he eager to talk when you and Pauley showed up on his doorstep?" Rhys asked. "You didn't say."

"No, he pretended not to be home. Not very well, though. We saw the curtains moving," Jem said, replaying the scene. "Then he talked to us through the door and said he was ill with —well. Smallpox. As in a rather smallish pox. He had to know it wasn't going to work. I thought he was just having a mini breakdown."

"Or playing the role of a frightened bloke who couldn't hurt a fly," Rhys said.

"It could be." Jem had told herself Roger wasn't a good enough actor to pull off such a complex scene. But who could say what depths he might plumb, if his life and freedom were on the line?

"Maybe he played me," she admitted. "Maybe he dreamed up the story about being stuck in the closet. Maybe Uriah was never there at all that night, and it was McArthur who pulled the silk pjs out of the sewing machine." Realizing all that must seem like gibberish to Uriah, she turned to him, expecting a confused face. Instead, the bearded man looked transfixed.

"I'd really like in on this murder investigation," he breathed.

Yikes. Is this how I seem to Mr. Atherton?

"Well, as a matter of fact, you can help," Jem said. "Just ring whatever contacts you have with the authorities and tell them everything you told me. That they need to look for Derrick Christensen in the Isles of Scilly. I remember that composite image. Curly brown hair, blue eyes, nondescript sort of everyman. I reckon a person can disappear in Hugh Town if he keeps to himself. But if investigators make a thorough check of rented properties and new home purchases, they should be able to close in on him without much trouble."

"Unless he sails away on the Sunseeker first," Rhys said. "What? I'm trying to help, not cheerlead."

"Right. Um. About my contacts in London." Uriah took off his fisherman's hat and squeezed it between his hands. "I already tried. No one got back to me. I'm persona non grata just at the moment. Ow!" He drew back a finger he'd stuck with the sharp end of a fishing fly, popping it into his mouth to stop the bleeding.

"You've been so much help," Jem said in her most grateful and positive voice. She stood up, smiling, and gave Rhys a quick sidelong look to make sure he did the same. "I can't thank you enough for coming here and telling us everything." Taking his unstuck hand, she pumped it enthusiastically—and with finality.

"But the investigation..."

"Too rich for my blood," she declared, flashing what she hoped was a rueful grin. "I intend to ring up DS Conrad of Devon & Cornwall, first thing tomorrow, and turn what little I've discovered over to him. That's what you have to do sometimes, Uriah. Step back and get out of the professionals' way."

Nodding dejectedly, Uriah allowed himself to be maneuvered out the door. Once over the threshold, he suddenly asked for Jem's number, but Jem countered by asking for his. She actually entered all the digits correctly into her mobile—as opposed to merely pretending—but expected to delete it before long. *After* she'd located Derrick Christensen herself and handed the information to Hack on a silver platter, of course. If a Most Wanted fraudster had chosen the Isles of Scilly as his bolt-hole, Sergeant I. Hackman deserved the collar and the acclaim that followed.

"What was that I overheard?" Tori demanded, emerging

from the bedroom with bag in one hand and phone in the other. "There's no way you're giving Conrad anything."

"Of course not. I just had to throw that poor bugger off the scent. He could get himself hurt tagging along."

Rhys folded his arms and hummed a little tune.

"What?"

"Nothing. Feels ironic, that's all." To Tori he said, "Are you off, then?"

"Well spotted. Meeting Lila down the pub. Then we're going back to her place. I'll catch you kids tomorrow. Unless you two are planning to make a day of it, now that your time is your own again, Jem?"

Jem's jaw dropped. Tori, looking abashed at her second moment of indiscretion, scooted for the door, crying, "Sorry! Foot in mouth disease. Later!" The door slammed.

"What does she mean, your time's your own?" Rhys asked.

"Just what she said. Mr. Atherton wasn't best pleased, I gave my notice, he waived it. I am now unemployed."

"Oh. Well. I'd say sorry, but... you seem okay." He moved closer, taking both of her hands in his. "The boss got your back up, didn't he?" A smile spread across his face. "Didn't know who he was dealing with, am I right?"

She shrugged, entranced by the scent of him—soap and Nivea Men mixed up with the masculine odor that was pure Rhys. "I doubt Mr. Atherton wanted it to play out that way. Who knows, maybe he did. But the West Country's a big place. Plenty of collections are purely online. I'll find a better job."

"Did you know I've never had a proper job? Working a hundred percent for someone else. I think if I did, and I lost it, I'd be knocked back on my heels. But it doesn't scare you."

She shook her head.

He released her hands, dark-blue eyes holding hers. "Do I scare you?"

"Not you. Us."

He slipped his arms around her. Melting against his big, broad chest, she let the fear careen around inside her, like a trapped, panicked animal running into walls. Determined, she waited it out. Slowly, it faded away.

"Rhys," she murmured.

"I'll sleep in the bathtub, Jemmie."

She looked up at him and smiled. "The hell you will."

24

PILLOW TALK

"Rhys," Jem said softly.

Like Buck the dog's way of simultaneously playing dead and angling for a Tasty Bite, Rhys opened one eye. "I wasn't asleep."

"You snore when you're awake?"

"I only snore around cats. Not that I was snoring. You're trying to entrap me."

"Imagine blaming poor Wotsit when he's not here to defend himself."

"He's sitting on the chest of drawers, watching us right this minute."

"Oh!" Jem sat up, reflexively grabbing for the duvet. Rhys sat up, too, laughing.

"Gotcha. Didn't want your innocent fur baby to see, eh?"

"Of course not." Relaxing, Jem lay back down against him, skin on skin. Rhys's body cranked out BTUs like a five-thousand-watt electric fire. It felt delicious. "If he'd seen, he would have been scarred for life."

"Not by round one. But in round two—yeah, we got a little wild." His fingers traced the back of her neck, a tantalizing touch. "You know, I used to have this all planned out. Mind you, I was sixteen, and the entire scenario depended on my dad not realizing he'd left us alone at my place."

She grinned. "Let me guess. We did it in your grotty little bedroom."

"Of course. After I picked you up and carried you up the stairs. Very white knight and fair lady."

"I would've loved it," Jem admitted.

"I thought about carrying you in here," he added, gesturing around her bedroom. "Only I pulled something in my neck, doing the Lindy Hop's big finish with Clarence."

She giggled. "You sound like Roger. After he told this horrifying story about trying to strangle McArthur and getting flung across the room, he touched his shoulder and said, 'It still hurts.'"

"Speaking of Roger. If you want my opinion, he's the killer. This Derrick Christensen stuff is interesting, and I guess it's important in its own way, but it's a red herring."

Jem made an unconvinced sound. "I know he told me himself that he snapped. In a moment of humiliation and despair, I can see it. But let's tell his story another way. He said he thought McArthur would fall in love with him after he tailored the silk pajamas..."

Rhys shook his head.

"What?"

"We're a daft, ignorant breed, men."

"Oh, I think unrequited love has mucked about with many a brain, male or female. And Roger had never been in love before. Never been in any relationship at all. Most of us get to make stupid mistakes as kids and have the numptiness walloped out of us," Jem said. "Roger was learning on the fly with nothing but romcoms and sappy telly to guide him. Of course he thought, I'll show McArthur this stupendous sewing machine, I'll work my magic on his spendy new pjs, and voilà—love at last."

"But maybe McArthur became irritated for some reason?" Rhys ventured.

"Yeah. That's another way the pjs might have got torn out of the machine. Maybe Roger was insisting on sticking around to play tailor when McArthur wanted him gone. Rip, they're ruined, and Roger's mortified. But suppose it went down differently. Suppose Roger swallowed his pride, took the blame, said sorry, and went home. Then the morning after his next sleepover, he slipped up behind McArthur and cracked him over the head. Revenge served cold. No physical risk."

"Exactly." Rhys sounded pleased.

"Except here's one part of the scenario I can't swallow."

"Lying to Clarence afterwards as a sneaky alibi?"

"No."

"Acting like a fluttery fool to you, and even throwing in that stuff about the measuring tape, to convince you he was admitting everything?"

"No." Jem grinned at him. "The part I can't square, no matter how I think about it, is this. I looked up that sewing machine after Pauley told me about it. It costs eight hundred pounds."

He whistled.

"Used. New, they cost well over a thousand. I can't believe Roger would've left that machine behind. If McArthur pulled the pjs out and told him to get lost, surely Roger would've bundled up the machine and taken it with him. Or if he left it then, surely he would've taken it with him after the murder. That sewing machine was the only physical evidence connecting Roger to McArthur."

"Maybe after the murder, he was too wound up to think clearly. Palpitations. Regrets," Rhys countered.

"But in our scenario, the whole thing was premeditated. He slept over with the intention of ending McArthur's life."

Silently, Rhys seemed to consider that for a moment. Then he began running his fingers through Jem's long brown hair.

"Don't try to distract me."

"But it works so well. So who does that leave us with? Kit Verran? Derrick Christensen?"

"Yeah. My first choice is Derrick. He's a big-time scammer. He defrauded plenty of vulnerable people on fixed incomes, then ran away with the cash and left his lieutenants holding the bag. If he's living in Hugh Town and likes to date men, it's not surprising that he went for McArthur. The guy was a walking thirst trap."

"And you think—what? They compared notes about scamming? Terry O'Dell said he was in touch with other thieves on the web. They had their own little community, from the sound of it."

"I don't know," Jem admitted. "McArthur was obviously a talented amateur, but in over his head. Something made him decide to hide his loot by burying it around the islands."

"Maybe talking to Derrick made him realize how slipshod he was," Rhys suggested.

"Maybe." Jem couldn't muster any enthusiasm for that scenario. After reading about Christensen's successful escape from the authorities in three nations, it was hard to imagine him sharing the truth about his Most Wanted status with McArthur. "Uriah said something interesting about snooping..."

"Oh, not Uriah. He's as bad as you are about solving crimes. I mean, as keen," Rhys said quickly when she shot him a look. "Clearly, he's not very good at it. And after attempting my first interview tonight, I have to admit, it's harder than it seems. But Uriah's not our killer."

"No. It's just—Pauls and I snooped on McArthur. Uriah did, too. Do you think McArthur might have snooped on Derrick? Like, discovered that tranche of John R. Derry letters, stolen from Putney's mail sorting center, and took them?"

"Uriah did say the manila folder seemed like the beginning of a blackmail file." Rhys sat up straighter, stretched, and folded his arms behind his head. "Check your mobile, would you?"

"Why?" She'd silenced it some time ago.

"Because I know Hack will text you right away if he finds any trace of Terry. I'm still hoping they'll find him alive. And I did warn him to be careful," Rhys added. "But the last of the gentleman jewel thieves reckoned he could take care of himself."

Jem retrieved her mobile and checked the screen. There was nothing from Hack. Only a text from Pauley, more than two hours old, that read simply,

???

She sent back,

Tonight. ❤

Jem expected no immediate response, given the time. But a few seconds later, a GIF reply came back: Snoopy, doing his happy dance.

"Nothing from Hack at all," she replied, returning the phone to the bedside table.

"I know the police already talked to Terry's grandson, but I doubt he was any help," Rhys said. "Terry called him a barnacle. He thought the kid must've seen him dig up some of McArthur's treasure and decided to shadow him. Hoping to find treasure of his own, of course."

Distantly, that rang a bell for Jem. She held up a finger, closing her eyes and following the thread back to a previous conversation. An early morning discussion, when she'd been absorbed in consuming caffeine.

"Terry's daughter is Helene, right? Do you know her?"

"No. Wait. Sort of. She came from the mainland to marry Steve Bennett. Known him forever. Bit of a prat."

"Father of Marvin Bennett?"

"Who on earth is Marvin Bennett?"

"The kid you frightened to death at Kenzie's party. Remember? For dancing too close?" As his eyes widened, Jem added, "I just remembered something Kenzie said. She saw Marv at Neptune Cove not long ago. He was carrying a spade and looking for treasure. She thought he was behaving like a child. But apparently, he knew something she didn't."

"Marv," Rhys repeated in a faintly sinister tone. "Right. Tomorrow, first thing, we're talking to Terry's grandson, Marv. Maybe he'll cough up something for me that he didn't tell the police."

"So you're setting the agenda?" She raised an eyebrow.

"Sorry. I mean, if you'd care to run the two of us to St. Mary's tomorrow in *Bellatrix*..."

She laughed. "Of course. The thing with Kit waving down Pauley and, erm, Felix, worries me. It's probably too much to hope the Sunseeker will still be moored near Gweal tomorrow, but we can certainly go find out."

"What are you on about?"

"Oh! Sorry." Cupping his face, she kissed him, enjoying the rough beard stubble against her palms. "Pauley had a good day up in the helicopter." Not wanting to give him time to focus on the pilot's identity, she quickly recounted their finding of the Sunseeker, and Kit's appearance on *Sweetheart 1*.

"Honestly, on a Monday afternoon, I'm surprised he had time to be out on the water in his main ferry. Even in the off-season," Jem said. "Either he's letting Kendra take over more of the route on *Sweetheart* 2, or... well. He was acting out of character."

"Sounds like he was trying to help. Taking down the WIN

number and warning Pauley that the owner might do something crazy."

"True. Except he told her the owner was Uriah. Did he really believe it? Or was he just doubling down on the story he told about big, bad Uriah looking to get revenge on the man who broke his heart?"

"I reckon Kit neglecting his business, even a little, is suspicious," Rhys admitted. "That's why Bart loathes him—from the moment Kit turned up in the islands, he hit the ground running. Worked seven days a week all summer long. Rented Bond House and fixed it up. Just a good citizen. Everything Bart's not."

"Bond House is coming along," Jem agreed. "Except he has a thing for trophies. There's a taxidermized shark displayed in the great room. Ghastly thing. But in the kitchen, he hung up a framed citation for best new business from *Cornwall Etc.* magazine. So, yeah. Neglecting the ferry service is a red flag."

They continued batting ideas back and forth until Rhys got up for the call of nature. Exiting the bathroom, he checked his cargo shorts, which lay where they'd been discarded in the middle of the hall. Withdrawing his mobile, he checked it, answered a text, and returned to bed. The moment he dropped his phone on the mattress, it vibrated.

"Look at this." Grinning, he showed Jem the screen. The first text, from Pauley, was three question marks, as it had been for Jem. Rhys had replied with his standard affirmative, a green check mark. Pauley's reply: the same Snoopy dance GIF.

They started kissing again, which led to caressing, which led to a passionate stirring that didn't frighten Jem in the least. Now that she'd given in, all she wanted to do was let herself succumb all over again. To luxuriate in letting go.

Rhys said, "I love you, Stargazer."

Pulling him down to her, Jem wrapped her legs around his waist and squeezed him tight. "Prove it."

25

INTERNATIONAL MASTERMIND, PUMPERNICKLER, AND PHANTOM YACHT OWNER

Jem awakened around five the next morning wrapped in resplendent warmth. Rhys was on his side, snoring gently, the duvet pushed off the bed so she could see every superb inch of him. Wotsit, who'd apparently wandered into the bedroom during the night, was perched on the windowsill, regarding her and Rhys with inscrutable eyes. Perhaps he, like A.J. McArthur, was plotting blackmail?

She imagined Derrick Christensen, a faceless mannequin in her mind's eye, inviting McArthur to his home. No, not a home —the Sunseeker. Surely Derrick, like McArthur, placed a high value on discretion and didn't want to meet in public. He was an international fugitive, after all, and even in Hugh Town—quite large by St. Morwenna's standards—neighbors took note of comings and goings. Therefore, Derrick using the yacht for trysts made sense.

But Derrick bribing a Royal Mail employee to steal a tranche of John R. Derry letters, and then keeping them in his possession where they might be discovered by prying eyes, made no sense at all. It was true that many criminals became obsessed with trophies, but...

She sat up suddenly.

Trophies.

Easing out of bed, she moved quietly across the room, snagged her robe off the hook, slipped into it, and went to the living room. Using her laptop, she pulled up the UK's Most Wanted list online, clicked on Derrick Christensen, and studied the artistic rendering.

Kit's head is shaved. I assumed he did it because he was going bald. Maybe he did it because curly hair is just about his only memorable feature.

Could she ring Hack? Yes, though he was probably still fast asleep after a long day of fruitlessly searching for Terry O'Dell. If he turned his investigative arsenal on Kit, could he determine if there were holes in his background? Did he have an employment history, a housing history, a family somewhere that would vouch for him?

Hack wouldn't be able to undertake the search, Jem thought. *He'd be obligated to turn it over to Conrad. And I think it's safe to assume that if Kit masterminded a huge fraud, and got away scot-free when the hammer fell, he managed to create a fairly believable new identity. He certainly chose to hide in plain sight. Like Rhys said—from the minute he arrived in the islands, he's played the role of model citizen. And unlike A.J. McArthur, he at least selected a new name a little less obvious than Arthur Ajax.*

Even as she thought it, it occurred to her that men named Christopher or Christian were often called Kit. And the first syllable of Verran was virtually the same as Derrick.

Good grief. It's him. He had the nerve to take his ferry out to the Sunseeker he owns and pretend to be surveilling it. He even told Pauley the WIN number was useless, and she ought to stay away because the owner was probably a killer. Slick, lying, bold-faced fraudster.

"Rhys!" she called. "Get up! I'm making coffee."

"So?" she demanded after laying out her case, point by point.

Rhys smiled at her sleepily. He was fairly serene for a man who usually slept late and wasn't accustomed to being driven out of bed—much less presented with murder theories—before six in the morning. She thought she knew why, and in any other circumstance, she would've taken time to bask in a certain smugness. But the sun was coming up, and time was of the essence.

"I think you're probably right about Kit. Sneaky of him, pretending to surveil his own boat. But he had no clue Pauley was catching a ride in a helicopter. How would he know to stakeout his own yacht? And why bother when he could just pilot it to Ireland? Make up an excuse, put Kendra in charge of the ferry for a few days, and get rid of it? If he knows how to avoid the FBI, he knows how to make a boat disappear."

"I have a thought. Take a sip of coffee first."

Rhys obeyed. "Not bad." He took another. "What's your thought?"

"Maybe Kit had no idea that a helicopter was looking for the Sunseeker. Maybe he was doing something else with his ferry yesterday. Like shuttling Terry O'Dell's body from wherever he was killed to the yacht."

"Oh." He sighed. "God, I hope not. But that would make sense, wouldn't it? Damn. Poor Terry."

"I know. And now the question is—are we too late? Did Kit wait until the helicopter flew away, then board the Sunseeker and sail away?"

Rhys thought about it, fortifying the process with more sips of coffee. Then he said, "There's no way around it. We need to ring Hack."

That proved easier said than done, as Hack didn't pick up when she called. Nor did he respond to her voicemail. Only when she texted him in all-caps did he return her call, in tones furred with sleep.

"What do you mean you've caught the murderer? Whose murderer?"

"Sorry. Bit melodramatic, I know," she said, switching to speakerphone so Rhys could hear. "Are you quite all right?"

"I worked twenty hours straight yesterday. O'Dell's family is frantic. The old duffer had friends all over the world, as it turns out. They're all six hundred years old, but they know how to call, and email, and tweet, and Facebook about how the IoS police isn't getting it done. Plus, I'd rather not leave a nice old ex-con to die of exposure if there's any chance of bringing him back alive."

"Well, of course you wouldn't. Listen. I—make that we—think we know who killed McArthur. We, because it was a team effort. Pauley, Rhys, Clar—"

"Jem. Thank the Academy later. Just tell me."

"Sorry. It's Kit Verran."

He snorted.

"No, hear me out." Hoping he wasn't too sleep deprived to follow her reasoning, Jem sketched her case again Kit. As the explanation dragged on, touching on framed certificates and the price of a Janome Atelier 6, Hack sighed and yawned. Finally, he broke in with, "I'm going to stop you now."

"Why?"

"Because you're asking me to believe two wanted men, completely unconnected, each coincidentally decided to hide out in the Isles of Scilly. Not only did they pick the same place, they met up and had an affair. Oh, and then one murdered the other. Do you have any grasp of statistics? Probabilities?"

"It's strange. I know. But strange things happen every day."

"Now you want me to believe Kit, a grinding normal bloke who's already beloved around Hugh Town for simply not being Bart, is an international mastermind, pumpernickler, and phantom yacht owner. All because you have a hunch he might have stolen some letters."

"Arranged to have some letters stolen."

"Of course. Pardon me. It's mental, Jem. It's embarrassing."

"Hang on," Rhys said. "I know you're worn out, Hack, but give her the benefit of the doubt. It's circumstantial, sure, but the pieces come together."

For several seconds, Hack didn't answer. Then he said, "You two had a nice sleepover, I presume?"

Jem signaled for Rhys not to reply. Taking the call off speaker, she put the phone to her ear and carried it into the living room.

"Listen. I'm so sorry for waking you. I know I must sound quite mad. But it'll take a couple of hours for me to get back to the islands on *Bellatrix*. When I'm approaching St. Mary's, why don't I give you a bell? We can go to Bond House. Or better still, we can just see if *Sweetheart 1* is docked. If Kit hasn't fled—"

"Jem. It's Tuesday. Surely you have some work to do."

"No, actually, I don't, as a matter of fact. The Courtney and I have parted ways."

"Oh. Well. I'm sorry to hear that," he said stiffly. "But I reckon it had to happen."

"Hack—"

"This is what I'm willing to do," he cut across her. "Today at noon, PC Newt and PC Robbins and I will begin the recovery mission for Terry's body. Fire & Rescue will be sending a helicopter to help us search. If a white Sunseeker is glimpsed around Gweal or anywhere else, I'll send someone to check it out. I'll even bring you in tomorrow, or the next day, and let you officially lodge a statement about Kit. But not until Terry's body has been returned to his family."

"Hack—"

"Not good enough? Call Devon & Cornwall. The McArthur murder belongs to them." He rang off.

Jem returned to the kitchen, uncertain how to feel. She'd never known Hack to be so caustic or unkind. Then again, overwork and lack of rest could do that to anyone. And not so long ago, he'd been very much in the running to get serious with her. She'd chosen Rhys—and now, without meaning to, awakened Hack out of an exhausted sleep to rub it in his face.

"I know," Rhys said when she picked up her coffee mug. "I should've kept my gob shut."

"It was already going off the rails," Jem said. "Maybe he's right. Maybe I've become so used to running around, sticking my nose in and deciding what I want to believe, I think I can solve any mystery just off a hunch. Could be I'm turning into poor Uriah." She sighed.

"You really believe that?"

"No. I think Kit is bloody Derrick Christensen. He changed his name around, shaved his head, and opened the best island ferry service St. Mary's has ever seen. Then his boyfriend threatened to blackmail him. And so he killed him."

Rhys nodded. "So which authority do we try next? There's always your friend and mine, DS Conrad."

"We're taking *Bellatrix* back to the Isles of Scilly. If *Sweetheart 1* is still docked, we'll assume Kit hasn't scarpered. That the Sunseeker is still moored somewhere around the islands. If we find it, we'll... I don't know. Ring Hack again. Call Scotland Yard. Tell *Bright Star* that Meghan and Harry are aboard and ask them to send a fleet of paparazzi."

Rising, he placed his hands on her shoulders and kissed her forehead. "Even if Kit took the boat and ran, you still cracked it."

"It's not enough," Jem said. "Let's bring it home."

26

MAYDAY

It was a cloudy, gray morning on the water when Jem and Rhys set out on *Bellatrix*. It took a little while for the boat's small engine to warm up, but once it did, they were soon humming along the familiar sixteen nautical route from Penzance Harbor to St. Mary's. Rhys looked a bit disheveled—hair slightly squashed on one side, heavy beard stubble coming in—which only made her love the sight of him even more. She was no fashion plate, either—hair in a double bun, blue jeans, windcheater, and trainers. But they'd set out at a gallop, without time for all the usual morning niceties, to see if the man they knew as Kit Verran had fled the Isles of Scilly. If not, Jem's plan was simple—keep him in sight, whether he ran his usual ferry route on *Sweetheart 1*, or even if he sailed for Ireland in the Sunseeker.

"What if he's in the wind?" Rhys said.

"In the *wind*?" She looked at him.

"Heard it in a film. You know. What if he's run off to do more crimes someplace else?"

"We take it as an admission of guilt and ring Hack. Go and find him, if need be."

"I didn't like his attitude."

"Yes, well, if you'd kept your lip zipped, I reckon it wouldn't have turned so ugly." She gave him a sidelong smile. "Not that I didn't appreciate you speaking up for me."

"Maybe we should ring PC Kellow," he said, referring to a junior officer with Devon & Cornwall who'd allied with Jem on a previous case.

"Honestly, if I think Kit is within reach and Hack stays dug in, I'll call Conrad," she said. "He'd drop everything and come running just to prove me wrong. And I don't care about his attitude or even if he tries to charge me with interference. I only care about Kit being caught."

Rhys put a hand on her shoulder. "Steady on. Net boats ahead."

"I see them." Eyes on the sea, she leaned back against him, and they passed most of the journey in companionable silence.

Jem's farsighted eyes were at their best first thing in the morning, but the instant St. Mary's Harbor came into sight, she picked up her binoculars, using them to scan the boat slips. Kit's first scheduled loop around the islands was still three hours away, *Sweetheart 1* was right where it belonged, bobbing tranquilly in the water, the pilothouse dark. Beside it was an empty slot—only lapping waves.

"*Sweetheart 2* is gone. Damn it! He's fled."

"Yeah, but we don't know when. He might be on the way to the Sunseeker right now. After he warned Pauley off, he probably figured he had time to make arrangements."

"You think?"

"Well, we know he's an arrogant son of a gun. Three national agencies were looking for him, and he didn't even leave England." Rhys chuckled, shaking his head. "The *cheek* of that man. He basically shaved his head, changed his name, and became Hugh Town's favorite son. Did he seem shook up when you interviewed him at Bond House?"

"No. He was perfectly at ease. Served tea and some horrible health food biscuits. Implicated Uriah."

"Right. So he's a cool customer. Just because he saw Pauley looking at the Sunseeker's WIN doesn't mean he'd panic and flee into the night with nothing but the clothes on his back."

"You're right," Jem said, envisioning the taxidermized shark with the soulless black eyes. "I reckon he'd clear Bond House of any trophies. Including that shark and his silly framed award. But where should we look for the Sunseeker? Even if he's still in the area, there's too many coves and rocks and berths." She considered her options, trying to think as Kit Verran might.

"All right. Everyone knows there's an island-to-island search going on for Terry. Yesterday it was Hack and his crew on the RIB."

"They probably started on land, since Terry's boat was found on the beach. Once they'd covered the inside of the five main islands, they would've shifted to the coast. Today they'll get back on the water and widen the circle. Call in helicopters to help."

"So let's say Kit went home to plan his escape. He couldn't take the Sunseeker. And he couldn't move it without abandoning *Sweetheart 1*. So he must've left the yacht near Gweal," Jem said with rising excitement. "I should've worked this out right away."

"It's seven o'clock." Rhys rubbed his eyes. "The fact we made it here on no breakfast and very little coffee is an achievement."

"Not in my book," Jem said. Opening her paperback pilot's guide to the Isles of Scilly, she began plotting a course for the Norrad Rocks, and Gweal.

~

Watery sunlight was leaking though the clouds as Jem guided *Bellatrix* west of Bryher. Just beyond Hell Bay, her Marine VHF radio crackled to life.

"Mayday," a voice croaked.

Jem swapped glances with Rhys, who picked up the radio mic. "This is *Bellatrix*. What's your vessel?"

Silence. Then: "Is that Mr. Tremayne?" in a tone so small and pathetic, Jem thought for a panicked moment it was Kenzie hailing them on channel sixteen. But, of course, she would never refer to Rhys that way.

"This is Rhys Tremayne. Who's this?"

"Marv. Marv Bennett." The words carried over the marine band on a ragged whisper.

"What's your vessel, Marv?"

"I don't know." The young man choked back a sob.

Jem gestured for Rhys to pass over the mic. "Marv. Are you aboard a white Sunseeker yacht?"

"Yes," he said, still in a whisper. "I was looking for Granddad. He's poorly. He might die."

"Terry's still alive?" Jem screeched into the mic.

"Oh. He's coming. Kit." Marv's voice rose, frantic. "Help us. Please, help us!"

The channel went dead. Jem's knee-jerk reaction was to try and hail him, but she squelched the impulse, gritting her teeth with the effort. Maybe Marv was injured. Without a doubt, he was panicked. The moment he heard Kit approaching, the wise thing would've been to switch off the marine radio, but perhaps he'd lacked the presence of mind. If she tried to raise him again, she might only succeed in alerting Kit to his young hostage's bid for rescue.

"That stupid kid." Rhys dug both hands into his hair, making it stand up in pure frustration. "I think I get it. Terry knew about the Sunseeker. He decided to do his gentleman cat burglar routine, creep around onboard, and decide if Kit was just a thief, or a thief and a murderer. But Kit must've caught him in the act and decided to hold him hostage."

"Wouldn't it have been easier to kill him?" Jem asked. She was pushing *Bellatrix*'s little engine to its limits, guiding the boat between Gweal Hill, which was part of Bryher, and the east face of Gweal. On the western side, God willing, she hoped to find Kit's Sunseeker, preparing to set sail. If it was already en route...

"I don't think Kit's a committed murderer. Look how he did in McArthur. He's a fraud guy. A white-collar criminal. Maybe he doesn't own a knife or a gun. When he realized he needed to get rid of McArthur, he just hit him over the head with the first thing to hand."

"Yeah. Well. I hope you're right," Jem said. "I suppose Marv knew about the Sunseeker, too. Just like he knew about the treasure. He must've been out searching for Terry on his own when he found the boat. And before he knew what was happening, Kit had nabbed him, too."

"Do you reckon he'll take Terry and Marv with him as hostages?" Rhys asked.

Jem sighed. "No. I think while he's preparing to leave, having a couple of human shields might be an ace in the hole. But once he's in international waters, he'll probably toss them overboard."

"But a fraud guy—"

"Kit's not a fraud guy anymore," Jem said, looking Rhys in the eye. "He's a murderer. The first time was probably hard. Now it's just numbers."

They followed the coast of Gweal in silence. Jem held her breath, hoping to see the white yacht still moored where Pauley had found it and wondering what she would do if it were already gone. Hack had been too irascible and depleted to listen properly at five a.m. Now it was barely eight, and he was probably still asleep.

I'll have to ring Conrad, she decided. *Much as I despise the man, I know he'll come running.*

"There it is!" Rhys whooped in excitement, pointing at a big white shape floating placidly on the silver sea. "That's good, right? Terry and the kid might be alive, right?"

From inside the Sunseeker came a loud bang. Like an engine backfiring—or a gun discharging.

27

XIPHIAS GLADIUS TO THE GLUTEUS MAXIMUS

The water was bracingly cold, but Jem barely felt it. After the initial shock of her feet first plunge, she set her jaw and began swimming toward the Sunseeker's transom. Her front crawl wasn't elegant, but her arms carved the water with big, sweeping arcs and her long legs kicked in relentless rhythm. Almost before she knew it, her hands grabbed the lowest metal rung, just below the waterline, and she began to climb. The wind felt icy, cutting through her zipped-up windcheater, and her bare feet slipped a couple of times on the rungs. Nevertheless, she hauled herself up with a death grip, teeth gritted, heart pounding, her vision narrowed with adrenaline.

Once on deck, she spared a glance for *Bellatrix,* now at anchor a few hundred yards away. Rhys's tall form was in the pilothouse, raising all the help he could. Forcing her gaze back to the Sunseeker's deck, her eyes ran along the yacht's luxurious accoutrements, searching for any sign of Kit. There was a built-in sofa with white vinyl cushions, a wet bar, and a daybed, all immaculate. Nothing to suggest anyone was aboard. From her pre-swim surveillance with her binoculars, she knew the flybridge was equally deserted. That meant Kit and his hostages, alive or dead, were below.

As she crept toward the stairs leading down into the lower deck, a splash in the vicinity of *Bellatrix* made her jump.

It's just Rhys, she told herself, refusing to look back. *He swims even faster than I do. He'll be here any minute.*

As she placed a bare foot on the top stair, her body seized up for a moment, refusing all commands. She'd heard a single gunshot. That meant Kit Verran, aka Derrick Christensen, a cold-blooded murderer, had probably taken another life. Not only was she unarmed, but she was also poised to navigate the most dangerous territory the yacht had to offer—approaching an armed man via narrow stairs. If he was somehow aware of her presence, either by hidden CCTV cameras or some other means, he might be standing at the bottom, pistol in hand. She'd be the proverbial fish in a barrel.

I can do this, she told herself. *How many times did I untie a runabout and nick it right under a fisherman's nose? How many times did I slip out of Gran's cottage without her hearing, even when she was in the next room? Kit's not James Bond.*

On silent feet, she moved down the stairs in increments, listening carefully. Eight steps descended in a tight spiral. On the sixth step, she heard someone sobbing quietly.

"But he was *old,*" a boy gasped. It was Marv, his voice ragged with fear.

"You should've thought about that before you went rambling up into the pilothouse," Kit Verran said. He sounded infuriatingly calm and reasonable, like an accountant explaining a column in the red. "Now, who did you raise on channel sixteen?"

"No one."

"Not Sergeant Hackman?"

"No."

"Not Bart the FUBARed Ferryman?" He laughed.

"No. I called mayday, but no one answered. Then I heard you coming and tried to get back down here before you saw..."

"Which was stupid. I told you I'd shoot you if you tried anything. Didn't I?"

Marv didn't answer.

"Didn't I?"

Marv began to sob. "Granddad saved me."

"I reckon he did. Not a bad end for an old duffer. Useless otherwise, if you think of it. Still, it was stupid. Trying to rush me in his condition. Geezer was two steps from dead already."

Marv sobbed harder.

"Listen. Truth is, I wasn't ready," Kit said, still in that tone of offensively sweet reason. "I haven't run through all the possibilities yet. Didn't I say you two were okay until I hear from my mate in Luxembourg? That's still true for you now. *If* you behave. Who knows, maybe I'll take you along to Lucilinburhuc. *Sprechen sie Deutsch*?" There was nothing particularly human or believable in those words; he sounded like he was speaking only to amuse himself.

Marv gave a little groan. He recognized the cruel toying note in Kit's voice, too. Jem felt a stab of pure rage.

Controlling herself by sheer force, she placed a bare foot on the seventh step, peeking around the corner. If Kit was looking toward the stairs, he would see her legs and the side of her face.

He wasn't looking. He was dragging Terry O'Dell's lifeless body across the floor toward an open Stow n' Go deck box. The old man's hands were bound in front of him with zip ties. His shirt was stained red. As Kit dragged him toward what would surely be his makeshift coffin, he left a thin smear of red on the pale floorboards.

Next stop: burial at sea, Jem thought.

Her mind seemed to take in the living quarters all at once. Marv knelt on the floor with his back to her, staring at the smear of his grandfather's blood. From the way his hands were positioned awkwardly in front of him, she assumed he was confined with zip ties, just as Terry had been.

The open floor plan flowed from sitting area to kitchenette to bedroom and presumably bathroom. A duffel bag and a cardboard box overflowing with small items sat on the built-in sofa. Kit hadn't tried to take the taxidermized shark, it seemed, but his business award peeked out of the box. Displayed around the room were various trophies. A framed front-page newspaper story about the John R. Derry "Annunaki" mastermind who got away. A photo of Kit, younger and with curly brown hair, shaking hands with a man who looked like Julian Assange. A deed of property. A shadowbox filled with multicolored passports from a variety of nations. And the spectacular mounted swordfish that had once hung inside Bond House.

Groaning slightly, Kit hefted Terry's body toward the deck box. The old man's arms flopped horribly, eliciting a cry from Marv.

"He's a person. Treat him like a person!"

Kit glared at Marv. He was dressed much as he had been the night Roger spied him through the louvered closet door—tan chinos, red windcheater. The black butt of his semiautomatic was visible just above his waistband.

"Shut it, kid. Or you're going in on top of him." With a grunt, Kit managed to maneuver Terry's head and torso into the white plastic box. That left his legs hanging out, like prawn tails on a cocktail glass.

"He's a person!" Marv gained his feet in a blur. One second, he was facing down Kit, whose eyes widened in surprise. The next, he'd launched himself at his captor, hands bound, helpless but maddened by desperation. Kit's hand went for his gun.

"Rhys!" Jem screamed, hoping he was on deck by now. She didn't think, she just moved, leaping over the eighth step and landing with a *thump*.

Even as his finger squeezed the trigger, Kit's head jerked

toward Jem. The gun went off with an earsplitting bang, but the shot missed Marv, who leapt aside. Jem surged toward Kit. Instinct told her that her best chance was to rush the man while his brain still struggled to process her appearance. But something hard and heavy knocked her to her knees.

Kit swore at the sight of Rhys, dripping wet and shoeless, bearing down on him. As Marv hovered protectively over his grandfather's body, Jem struggled to rise.

Damn the man, he really bowled me over.

Shaking her head, she got to her feet just in time to see Kit point his handgun in Rhys's face. She screamed.

The gun went off with another boom. This time Jem felt a sizzle of air as something whipped past her. Rhys, who'd slapped the gun aside, was grappling on the floor with Kit, who was struggling to fire again. In the taxidermized swordfish, a small round hole gaped. The ricocheted bullet had found a home.

Xiphias gladius, Jem's dazed brain supplied. *Their bills can be over three feet long. With a sharp, pointed end.*

The trophy came off the wall with a crack. It was surprisingly light—the living fish could weigh fourteen hundred pounds—and incredibly slippery, making it awkward to hold. With the thing in her arms, Jem whirled toward Kit, who was on top of Rhys, bringing his gun around. Not stopping to think or even aim, she drove the swordfish bill into Kit's body with everything she had.

While they waited for Hack, DS Conrad, and various Fire & Rescue entities to arrive, Rhys took charge. Jem was grateful. From the moment she dove off *Bellatrix*'s deck into the cold Celtic Sea, she'd been operating on sheer determination. Now that Marv was safe and the authorities were en route, everything she should've physically experienced in the moment was unfolding thirty minutes late and all at once. She was shivering; her teeth were chattering; her head hurt; her palm hurt where she'd sliced it on a taxidermized fin; she felt sad for Terry O'Dell, though he'd died heroically; and last but not least, every time she closed her eyes, she saw Kit pointing the gun at Rhys's face, even though the fatal shot had never come.

"Right," Rhys said, draping a duvet off Kit's bed around her. "That should help. Marv, I found scissors. Come here. Let me get those zip ties off."

"Thanks, Mr. Tremayne," Marv mumbled. "I wish... I wish I hadn't followed Granddad. Maybe he'd still be alive if I hadn't got myself caught."

"Were you treasure hunting?" Jem asked.

Marv nodded.

"I saw a light bobbing around Neptune Cottage on Bryher. Was that you?"

He nodded again. "I've been all over, looking for treasure. I know the islands like the back of my hand. That's why I went out searching for Granddad. I figured I had as good a chance of finding him as the cops."

"How'd you end up as Kit's hostage?" Rhys asked.

"I told him what I was doing. Looking for the Sunseeker. Paid him to take me out on the water to find it," the young man said sheepishly. "He took me, all right. Tied me up in the ferry's hold, took me here, and stowed me with Granddad. At one point, I heard a helicopter and thought for sure I'd be rescued. But they went away, I reckon, and I ended up here." Shooting a dark look in Kit's direction, he added, "He hit Granddad over the head. Didn't give him any food or water. That's why I risked the mayday call. Figured it was his only chance."

"I hit him," Kit said weakly from his position in the middle of the floor, "because I caught him creeping about my yacht like a sneak thief."

"Shut it," Rhys and Marv said in unison.

"Anyway. I wish he hadn't died. He didn't even like me."

"He loved you," Rhys said.

"He called me a barnacle."

"Well. Still. Actions speak louder than words, don't they? Sit yourself down by Jem. I'm putting the kettle on. This one's biscuits are rubbish, but his tea seems all right."

"You know," Kit said, "I can't possibly hurt you. There's no reason to leave me like this."

"You're a double murderer," Jem said incredulously.

"I've been stabbed."

"You killed an old man. And you clubbed McArthur to death."

"Only because he threatened me," Kit said in a horrible tone that was probably meant to be ingratiating, but only succeeded in sounding false. "I was never a killer before he threatened me. I found a file on me in his cottage. I warned him. He wouldn't let up. I had to do something. It was temporary insanity, hitting him with the loaf. I didn't even know he was dead. After he hit the floor, I just took the file and ran away."

"You should've checked around," Jem said. "We found a wicker basket full of John R. Derry letters. Did he take them from here or Bond House?" she asked, eyes flicking to the trophies.

"None of that matters now. I'm hurt. Get me up," Kit said.

Rhys seemed to study the double murderer, still lying prone in the middle of the floor. The fiberglass fish-body had broken off, leaving only the three-foot bill where Jem had put it: driven smack into the muscle of Kit's right buttock. The man looked pale and frightened, but in Jem's non-medical opinion, he was stable. Stable enough for her conscience, anyway.

"If I pull that bill out, you'll start bleeding," Rhys said.

"I don't care. Please. Get it out."

Rhys put his head to one side. "No. I don't think so. You tried to shoot me, remember? Better wait till the police turn up."

"You can't leave me like this!" Kit roared.

"If it makes you feel any better," Jem said, clasping her shaking hands under the duvet as she forced herself to meet the killer's eyes, "I wasn't aiming there. I was trying to run you through. But things have a way of working out. You'll be all healed up before you know it. Then Scotland Yard and the FBI and OLAF can work their magic and who knows? Might be a fate worse than death for an arrogant tosser like you."

28

A BRAND-NEW DAY

By the time it was all sorted, the sun had climbed past noon and a television crew had set up on Bryher to interview the principal players. Kit Verran/Derrick Christensen had received medical care and been assured he would live to face every legal penalty coming to him. This included two counts of murder, two counts of kidnapping, and two counts of attempted murder. Those were just the preliminaries; DS Conrad had assured the pretty blonde reporter from the Beeb that additional crimes might be added. Judging from the gleam in his stony eyes, she believed him.

Marv Bennett acquitted himself well in front of the cameras, describing his grandfather's rush at the gunman, which had saved his life. If Terry O'Dell was looking down from cat burglar's heaven, he probably felt good about his grandson's televised tribute.

Rhys did his strong and silent routine, answering direct questions in as few words as possible, which probably seemed normal to anyone who didn't know him. Jem, who'd pulled herself together after drying off, warming up, and drinking two cups of tea, noted his trembling hands and the way he kept folding and refolding his arms across his chest. Of the two of them, he'd been in greater danger, yet steadfastly held it together even after the crisis, while she and Marv hovered on the edge of breakdown. Now the delayed reaction was hitting him. But Jem fully intended to help him through it. Maybe she'd drag him to Lyonesse House for some Shipwreck flavor ice cream. A pedicure might help, too.

She did five full interviews before she and Rhys were allowed to depart. The first one, with Hack and DS Conrad hovering on the sidelines, was the hardest, because it required some cheerful lies and some tough truths. While sitting on the Sunseeker awaiting the authorities, Jem had had plenty of time to imagine what she'd be asked, and to formulate answers. When the Beeb's reporter positioned a microphone in front of her face, she was ready.

"So, Ms. Jago, some people call you the Scilly Sleuth. How did you determine that A.J. McArthur's killer was actually Derrick Christensen, international fugitive?"

"It was a team effort," Jem said, smiling into the camera. "My dear friend Pauley Gwyn helped a lot. So did Clarence Latham, who runs an amazing B&B on St. Morwenna, and his cousin Micki Latham, who's also one of my best friends. Then there's Rhys Tremayne. He's an artist. You probably know his work. You might even have one of his paintings hanging on your wall at home. He risked his life to save Marv Bennett. I only wish we could've saved Terry O'Dell, too."

"My goodness," said the reporter, goggling at Jem's smooth recitation. "Do you mean you and your friends just went about gathering clues and solved the case all by yourselves?"

Nearby, Conrad let out an aggrieved rumble.

"Yes, but not intentionally," Jem said. "It's really quite foolish to muck about with anything approaching an open police investigation. I always say, trust the authorities. But the fact is, the lead investigations at Devon & Cornwall haven't been terribly receptive to anything I have to offer. And I'm afraid the Isles of Scilly police weren't interested in my theories, either. Since I couldn't get anyone to listen, I set out myself this morning to see if Kit—I mean, Derrick Christensen—was trying to flee the islands. When I heard the gunshot, I had to act. But if the police had listened to me…" She shrugged.

"Oh, my." The reporter turned to Conrad, who'd turned his back. "Excuse me, DS Conrad. Would you care to respond?"

With another rumble, he began walking away.

"What about you, Sergeant Hackman?" the reporter called in that friendly "gotcha" voice familiar to anyone who's watched five minutes of cable news. "Is it true that your unit was uninterested in Ms. Jago's theories?"

Stone-faced, Hack approached the microphone, cleared his throat, and said in a low voice, "I called them mental. And embarrassing. Obviously, I was wrong. Thank you." Then he, too, turn away, following the lumbering brown overcoat that was DS Conrad.

Jem took a deep breath. She suffered a brief temptation to take it all back but resisted it. Maybe she'd feel differently after she'd had time to process the morning's events. But the fact remained. If Hack had listened to her, there was a small chance Terry O'Dell would still be alive—and a one hundred percent chance that Kit would never have shoved his semiautomatic in Rhys's face.

"Well, my goodness. I seem to keep saying that," said the reporter, now in a mortified, extra cheery tone. "What's next for you, Jem Jago? My producer tells me you work for the Courtney Library in Penzance."

"I did," Jem agreed. "But we recently parted ways. I am so grateful to the Courtney for our time together. However, it's time to move on. I have several exciting offers coming in, and I can't wait to see what the future holds. It's a brand-new day."

A LETTER FROM EMMA

Thank you so much for reading *A Death at Neptune Cove.* If you would like to be informed of my future releases, please sign up at the following link. I love hearing from my readers and sharing writing news with them.

www.bookouture.com/emma-jameson

I always enjoy dreaming up adventures for Jem Jago and her friends, but this novel was especially fun to write. Especially the scene where Rhys dances the Lindy Hop with Clarence. Having Jem fall *on* the birthday cake gave me a giggle, too.

I also like to change things up, so for this mystery, I introduced Pauley and Rhys as point-of-view narrators, and even let them do some hands-on sleuthing. I also decided to force Jem into a tough choice: placate her boss, Mr. Atherton, or stick with her amateur investigations? So often in life, we find ourselves facing that sort of dilemma—trapped between the seemingly rational answer that makes our hearts sink and the slightly riskier option that we really, truly want.

As I wrote Jem's reaction to the loss of her job, I realized how much she's grown since returning to Cornwall and the Isles of Scilly. The Jem Jago we met on page one of *A Death at Seascape House* was rather closed-off, diffident, and lacking in a certain confidence. But by the conclusion of this mystery, she's making bold decisions and trusting herself to handle whatever happens next. That confident, adventurous spirit will come in handy the next time she trips over a dead body!

One last thing. If you enjoyed *A Death at Neptune Cove*, please consider posting a review online. Honest reviews are literally priceless and make all the difference in the life of a book. Thank you.

Until next time,

Emma Jameson

2022

www.emmajamesonbooks.com

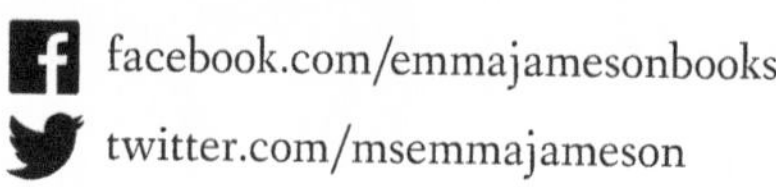

ACKNOWLEDGMENTS

Working with Bookouture has been a wonderful experience, and I have so many people to thank. First, my helpful and encouraging editor, Kelsie Marsden. She is always lovely to talk with and unfailingly kind. Second, my copyeditor, Jane Eastgate, who patiently corrects a multitude of sins, many having to do with hyphens.

I'd also like to mention Lisa Brewster, the talented artist who designed this book's beautiful cover, as well as the others in the Jem Jago mystery series. And I can't forget Tamsin Kennard, the voice of Jem and everyone else in my imaginary community, who performs the audiobook editions so vibrantly.

There are many others to thank, including—but not limited to!—Alexandra Holmes, Shirley Khan, Sarah Hardy, Noelle Holten, Kim Nash, Jenny Geras, Iulia Teodorescu, Rhianna Louise, Jess Readett, and Alex Crow. I'm so grateful for your support and assistance.

CPSIA information can be obtained
at www.ICGtesting.com
Printed in the USA
BVHW071015200922
647494BV00007B/581

9 781803 147277

A birthday beach party gone wrong, buried treasure and
This might be Jemima Jago's most baffling cas

When **Jem** knocks on the door of an isolated cottage overl Neptune Cove, she's hoping for help fixing a birthday cake She's not expecting to find the tenant dead on the tiled floor, specks of blood on the collar of his navy-and-red satin pajamas...

The victim is **Arthur Ajax**, a handsome and wealthy American businessma who arrived in the Isles of Scilly as a tourist ten months ago and never left There have been rumors about him in town, as he was known for his extravagant lifestyle. Perhaps he'd gone overboard, or could his death be connected to an unpaid debt?

Later that same evening, Jem stumbles across a hoard of buried jewelry dug up from the dunes by little dog Buck, and she immediately wonders if they could be connected to the rich man's murder. It's not every day you find expensive—and very real-looking—sapphire earrings stashed away in an antique biscuit tin!

Jem seeks help from a local jewelry expert to identify the gems. But whe he suddenly goes missing, Jem knows someone is trying to cover their tracks. Can she catch the killer before he makes her walk the plank too?

A completely gripping cozy page-turner set in the beautiful Isles of Scilly, from the *New York Times* and *USA Today* bestselling author Emma Jameson. Fans of M.C. Beaton, Faith Martin and Agatha Christi will be hooked by *A Death at Neptune Cove*.

www.bookouture.com
ISBN 978-1-80314-727-7
90000
9 781803 147277

Design © The Brewster Project
Photos © Depositphotos